PRAISE FOR N

I was introduced to *Rockstar Ending* when Nicola read an extract from the book at the Orwell Society Symposium. We invited her to speak after she won an award in the Society's dystopian fiction competition for her short story, *One Last Gift*. Nicola's work is highly original, macabre and very funny. I am delighted that she has developed her idea into a novel in the tradition of my father George Orwell, the author of *Nineteen Eighty-Four*, who wanted 'to make political writing into an art'.

Richard Blair, son of George Orwell and Patron of The Orwell Society

This is how to make a smashing debut into dystopian fiction; an authentic world building on present-day technology, an eerily plausible solution to the wealth gap, and an exploration of the disturbing moral paradoxes it creates when the public wakes up to the sinister consequences. Nicola Rossi's first novel is a just-around-the-corner future thriller with a brain. If her predictions come true, we're all in deep trouble.

Christopher Fowler, award-winning author of dark urban fiction

Rossi's dark, perceptive wit and the industry insights gleaned from her previous career in communications

management make this gripping yarn an all-too-persua-
sive vision of the future.

Cathi Unsworth, The Idler

ALSO BY N.A. ROSSI

For Those About to Rock
Rockstar Ending

ROCK ON

N.A. ROSSI

resista press

For all the ordinary people doing extraordinary things.

CHARACTERS

The Corporation – the firm delivering the Government's Endings program

Mason, chief executive

Tom, chief of staff

Penny, Mason's PA

Greg, chief counsel

Channelle, corporate affairs director

Carrie, head of brand

Lola, senior manager in the IT team

Bob, IT security specialist, partner of *Lexi*

Brytely – The Corporation's marketing agency

Stella, chief executive

Portia and Sonny, Endings campaign creative team. Portia's mother is *Karen*

Lars, Endings user experience developer and member of Yuthentic

Endings escapees

Meg, whose twin adult children are *Alice* and *Adam*

Bryn, who has a daughter *Jade* with partner *Cliff*
George, Mavis and *Mabel*
Liz, married to *Karl*

Activists

Lexi, schoolteacher, and Bob's partner
Father Aloysius, priest, and his housekeeper *Natalia*
Henry, human rights lawyer
David, retired civil servant
Ayesha, retired entrepreneur and Sonny's grand-mother, married to *Ajay*
Fakesy, street artist

Media

Faye, business correspondent
Jack, health and social policy correspondent
Rex, their editor

Westminster

Nicky Hartt, Labour MP, and her researcher *Jess*
Members of the HELP Select Committee: *Doc* (Conservative), *Holly* (Yuthentic), *Sophie* (Labour) and *John* (Liberal Democrat)

Verbier

The Baroness, Chippy, Mario and *Luigi,* guests in the Brytely chalet
Celeste, sales assistant, and her boyfriend *Zhena*

THE YUTHENTIC MANIFESTO, MAY 2026

We are enormously proud of what Yuthentic has achieved over the past four years with our friends in Government.

- A million new affordable housing units for under-35s are now at full occupancy
- University tuition fees are met by the state
- AI learning platforms are turbo-charging our children's academic performance
- 40,000 new places in low-cost dormitories are providing dignified support for the elderly

All of this has been paid for by the Maturity Premium Fund, supplemented by a program of generous private sector investment.

Above all, our people are happier. The increase in the national wellbeing index proves it.

This is only the beginning. With your vote on Thursday

7th May, Yuthentic can take some even bolder steps to improve the lives of <u>everyone</u> in our country.

Give us <u>your</u> mandate to build on what we have already achieved. We will:

- Ramp up investment in infrastructure, services and leading-edge technology to energize and empower the younger generations. We promise:
  - A million more affordable homes
  - 100,000 more places in dorms for the elderly
  - AI learning to be rolled out to every school in the country
  - More innovative technology e.g. Virtual Reality, to help our kids succeed
- An end to inheritance planning bureaucracy, with persuasive incentives for old people to invest their wealth in the nation's future
- Dignified and humane services to fulfil the promise of the 2020 Euthanasia Act
- Slashed carbon emissions with new incentives for using shared, electric and driverless vehicles.

Don't look back. It's time to invest in the future.

A vote for Yuthentic is a vote to rejuvenate our country.

Show your support with the hashtag #ourtime

CHAPTER ONE

W HAT KIND OF SADDO AM I? Portia asked herself, already knowing the answer, as she arrived in the office two hours before dawn on the first working day of 2028. Her fraught trip to Liverpool had been the final nail in the coffin of her decaying relationship with the North. Brytely was her tribe now. She had hurtled past the point of no return and was now a bottom feeder in the ranks of London's metropolitan elite.

At least returning to work would give her the chance to show off the new clothes she had bought with her PHUC money. The settlement was part of a blanket compensation scheme – People Health Unlimited Claims – for people who had lived in an area so badly polluted it was guaranteed to shorten your life. What a win!

Her childhood home had been just close enough to John Lennon International Airport for her to land an additional five thousand pounds on top of the standard ten. After years of struggling, it felt like her birthday and Christmas had come all at once. The Scousers back home were describing the mini bonanza as 'fumetastic' although she doubted many of them were having this much fun with their proceeds back in bleak old Merseyside.

Monday had been a public holiday, as New Year's Day had fallen at the weekend, so she had hit the shops. They still had boutiques in central London. Deep pockets of untouchable wealth and proximity to political power had insulated parts of the capital from the catastrophic malaise that had destroyed town centers everywhere else.

Portia was getting good at spending ever-increasing amounts of money on her appearance and thought creatively about building on the capsule starter wardrobe she had invested in before Christmas. Some adorable matching items had been discounted. She had been particularly taken with a purple angora sweater dress that she had resisted before. It would be perfect for the office.

There was a coat too, in a dark silver grey, lightly quilted with the hexagonal stitching that was bang on trend. It was filled with a layer of artificial down, made from recycled plastic that had been produced in a social enterprise somewhere in the global south. The tr-AID-liberation symbol – a fist punching through a circular fan of broken chains and branches – certified beyond any doubt that it met the highest ethical standards.

She felt proud, finally, to be able to afford a desirable lightweight puffer that maintained a perfect temperature while, at the same time, furthering the struggle against child labor, slavery, climate crisis and animal exploitation. How astonishing it was, too, that a simple garment from Harrods could tick so many boxes, so quickly, in the two seconds it took to swipe the money from her account.

Once inside the revolutionary workspace, which was

how Brytely described their offices to clients, she hung the coat where she hoped most people would be able to see it, arranging it so the tr-AID-lib label could be admired by anyone who passed. Oblivious, the cleaning robots returned to their docking stations not long after she took her perch for the day. She had chosen a good spot, from where she could scan the office and watch the dawn break through the skylight overhead.

A hint of pale sun was dancing on the monochrome surfaces by the time Sonny arrived. She watched him throw off his coat and walk over to the long kitchen bench that had just been piled with fruit, small shots of smoothies, and vegan protein balls by a service bot that knew every inch of the floor, and made a pretty good job of keeping the workers' blood sugar levels in the right place. Sonny took an energy drink out of his own backpack and set up at one of the lower tables, briefly acknowledging Portia with a nod. They exchanged glances for a second before he sat down and absorbed himself in a screen. She felt a prickle of disappointment, even though she knew it would have been ridiculous to expect anything more. What had happened on New Year's Eve had been weighing on her mind for days. Back in the office, she could almost believe the events had been a figment of her imagination.

Others trickled in and settled into what everyone expected to be a quiet working week. A lot of people were still away until the following Monday. As the sky turned to pale gold, everyone relaxed into a mellow mood which lasted until quite late in the morning. The whole pack switched to high alert, however, when Stella, Brytely's chief executive, made an entrance.

It was unusual for Stella to appear in the flesh. They were all used to her hologram being beamed in from Brytely's offices around the world. Full body scanners had been installed in London, New York and Los Angeles to give her telepresence a three-dimensional edge. The clients loved it. For the staff, it was something of an irritation, as it created an asymmetric meeting experience. Stella did all the talking and none of the listening. It was no different when her body was there.

Stella had brought her own coffee in a cute Moncler espresso flask, emblazoned with the logo in holographic crystals. She wore a mushroom-colored, high waisted, full length skirt split almost to the thigh, revealing opaque brown tights and intricate cowboy boots that cost thousands. A cream funnel-necked sweater fitted tightly over her top half, flattering her firm contours. Portia looked enviously at Stella's arms which, even through the cashmere, were well defined and exceeded anyone's aspirational standard. She had chosen her enhancements well. Everyone said she had negotiated them as part of the deal when Brytely took on one of the most sought-after aesthetic clinics as a client. Those boobs were clearly not from one of the budget industrial estate outfits that had caused much pain and anguish for the girls back home.

A meeting popped into Portia's diary. She accepted it right away. Stella wanted to see her, Sonny and Lars in ten minutes in Anthrax. All their meeting rooms were called after thrash metal bands, thanks to Lars who had rigged a staff competition to choose the naming convention. There was only one thing Stella would want to talk about: The Rockstar Ending campaign. Portia's shoulders began to tense as she opened the files, forced to confront everything she and Sonny had done.

"Hi guys," Stella said, "Happy New Year!" She had not spoken to either of them out on the office floor, not looking up from her device once.

Portia struggled to suppress the riot of memories from New Year's Eve with Sonny that Stella's greeting had triggered. Then she began to wonder whether Mason, CEO of The Corporation, Brytely's most important client, had been in touch with Stella about the letter Sonny had delivered to him by hand on New Year's Day. Even though the note did not contain any names, she was sure Mason would have recognized Sonny. She focused on breathing slowly and calmly, and simply returned the greeting while dialing in Lars who was still on vacation in Norway.

Even on screen, Lars made Portia shudder, and not in a good way. His soulless pale jade eyes were framed by a disorderly combination of stubble and piercings where his eyebrows had once been. Straggly, thin black hair had been left to hang around a face that had once been strikingly beautiful. The Yuthentic sigil, a circle with a diagonal cross, adorned multicolored niobium earrings that swung a centimeter beneath the spacers that left small hexagonal voids in his lobes. They represented the message that it was time for the older generations to 'give way' just like the road sign.

He was wearing his trademark Slayer T-shirt over a long-sleeved black thermal top. It looked like he was calling from a cheap hotel room. She wondered whether he was on holiday with his family, but it was hard to picture Lars having any relations. It was easier to imagine him having buried them in the forest before he left Sweden to begin a new life in London.

Portia was thankful that Lars wasn't there in person. He always creeped her out. What was worse, his enthusiasm for the Endings campaign and growing determination to extend it to Phase Two had been alarming her more by the minute. Stella, however, seemed to admire him, and saw a fertile business opportunity in his idea of extending voluntary, active euthanasia to groups other than the elderly. Stella wasn't alone. According to Lars at least, the concept was gaining support in many quarters at the highest echelons of public life. He knew all about that through his contacts in Yuthentic.

"I had the most amazing New Year's night!" Stella announced. "Mason invited me to the control room for the drone display. It was very impressive. They only needed two technicians. It's all pre-programed. And, best of all, it was in the cabin of a Chinook!"

"How did he get hold of one of those?" Portia asked, incredulous.

"Oh, Mason has so many contacts. They do a few things for the military. All very hush-hush. It helped that the Home Secretary's partner is mad about flying – so they were both there with their kids. It was a rather special evening! The leader of the Yuthies was there as well. Quite a character, and so young. Very charismatic. We weren't too late, though. Mason had to be up early the next day so we couldn't party too hard. More's the pity.

"Anyway, I'll be seeing Mason again on Thursday in Verbier. I wanted to be right up to date on the Endings business. I expect we'll get a few moments alone where

I can tell him how fabulously it's all going, and perhaps warm him up a bit more for Phase Two. So, hit me up with the stats, team!"

Lars looked directly into the camera. "The dash is all up to date to end December. It's been a record month even taking the Christmas Day shutdown into account. By the way, they don't need to do that, you know. We should make a feature of it in future. There's so much scope for a seasonal promotion integrated with the Christmas playlists, people dreading being cooped up with their families and so on. We can put a whole new spin on the most wonderful time of the year."

"Quite, Lars," Stella said blankly. "But for now can you stick to the performance report? Mason will want data, data, data."

"Sharing my screen now," Lars said with a hint of disappointment. His face faded out and was replaced by a colorful animated slide mapping advertising spend across five social media platforms to clicks, to sell-through, to bookings, to fulfilment, and finally to aftersales. The Rockstar Ending logo was at the top of the screen.

"Tell me, Sonny – is this good?" Stella asked, turning away from the screen for a moment.

"We've nothing to compare it to, you know, it's one of a kind."

"Well, I can't tell Mason that." Stella hated it when these kids with data science degrees tried to be clever. She had already been in the meeting long enough to get restless.

Sonny nodded resolutely. He knew how to deliver what Stella wanted.

"OK, well if you want to compare it to other campaigns targeted at the – let's say over-70s, which is the primary group – then yes. It's doing exceptionally well, especially on click-to-purchase. The post-fulfilment memorial package has surprised us all, with a lot of the families responding well to the memorabilia offer."

"It's rather vulgar." Stella's mouth pursed into a flicker or disgust.

"It's not meant to be high art. The little statuettes cast from loved ones' ashes are being bought by twenty-nine per cent of relatives. Even the snow globes have made a few sales."

"No accounting for taste. Is the snow made from…?"

Everyone asked Sonny that question. "The ashes? No, they would be the wrong color and consistency. Only the effigy."

"They are excellent low-cost, high margin, incremental sales," Lars flashed back on to the screen. "The confidential nature of the Endings service creates a period of surprise and inertia for those left behind. They are in the prime state for an impulse purchase. Nursing an emotional void that needs to be filled."

The memorial package had been Portia's idea, so she thought she should say something. "We studied the folk art of various cultures and religions when we designed the merchandise. When we match it with the security camera and smart TV footage from inside people's homes, it's easy to target the promo so it's consistent with the decorative touches they already have." Her range had been influenced by the Catholic ephemera that filled her elderly neighbor's house in Liverpool. Bernie's place was cluttered with glow-in-the-dark religious statues and flimsy plastic bottles in the shape of Our Lady of Lourdes containing holy water so old that it had become a biohazard.

"OK. I'm convinced. That's enough. Right, send me the dashboard, Lars. Now, how are plans coming along for Phase Two?"

Lars looked smug. "Very good. Yuthentic is planning to introduce an amendment to the Voluntary Euthanasia Act to extend its scope to include anxiety and depression. That will unlock the age constraints for the mental health criteria. So rather than just having to have a physical illness to ship out if you are under 70 (which is already allowed for in the law, though not actively promoted) they will open the permissions for able-bodied young people who would like to die. They will have to prove they are certain, of course, answer direct questions. More than once. Blah blah blah."

Portia was engulfed by a wave of nausea. She had shared her concerns about Phase Two with Sonny before, having found anti-depressants prescribed for her mother and her mother's boyfriend on the top shelf of their bathroom cabinet. The fear that they might sign up for the one-way departure service was becoming more acute.

"Aren't Yuthentic all about keeping young people alive?" Portia said, as calmly as she could. "Do you really think extending the Endings service to a younger demographic will appeal to a party with such a strong, youth-centered ideology?"

Lars smirked. "It's all about the greatest happiness of the greatest number. An end to pain. Choice. Empowerment. That's what they want. It's beautiful." He was never more alive than when he was talking about death.

"I can't argue with that," Stella said. No one would question the integrity of Lars' sources. He had an uncanny ability to predict which services Yuthentic would require next. That meant Brytely could pre-empt the abundance of new opportunities that would emerge as the active euthanasia movement broadened its scope.

She would never dream of putting Lars in front of a client, of course. Even Stella could see that some of his personal characteristics were, at best, unsettling. But that was the point of having a secret weapon. You were not supposed to show it to anyone.

"Good. Thanks, guys." Within seconds she had left the room, leaving Portia and Sonny to switch off the videoconference. Portia was hoping they would be able to snatch a few moments alone, but before she could hit the button to make Lars disappear, Sonny started chatting to him.

"Where are you, mate? Did you get back home for Christmas?"

"There is nothing for me in Sweden anymore. I am near Oslo. By a lake. It's a very special place."

Portia was glad that Lars did not reciprocate with any feigned interest in what she and Sonny might have been up to. He rarely engaged in pleasantries or asked questions about his colleagues.

"Nice. Look, I know you've probably thought of this already, but this Phase Two – are they working on the ethical clearance? You can 'blah blah' all you like to

Stella, but it's important. It's not personal. To protect the company, you know?"

"You don't need to worry about that. My source is impeccable. All the necessary rules will be enshrined in law. There will be crystal-clear guidance on how to comply. We will be able to adapt the bots in a matter of days. Seriously, there won't be a hint of trouble. People will scarcely realize it's happening. And when they do discover how much peace we have already given to those who are suffering, they will be grateful."

"Grateful? Isn't that an odd choice of word?" Portia was pretty sure she would not be grateful if her Mum and Marcus were no longer there to look after their children. Quite apart from the emotional impact, she would have to move back up North to take over. "That can't be right?"

"Not at all. An end to pain is a release. For our clients, for their … what is that expression you use … yes, their loved ones. Not that you should, necessarily include that in your campaign."

Portia and Sonny exchanged glances. Did Lars know something they didn't? Sonny asked, "What do you mean, our campaign?"

"Well, you've done so well with the Rockstar Ending promotion. And your inspired economy version, Portia, getting all those poor people queuing for the bus. I can't imagine Stella would want anyone other than the 'dynamic duo' to run the creative for Phase Two. It would make perfect sense."

A couple more moments of silence ticked away as Sonny and Portia took in what Lars had just said. Even though he was 1,000 miles away, Lars could sense their discomfort.

"Is there something wrong?" he asked pointedly. "Surely anyone would be glad of an opportunity to build on such success?"

"Makes sense." Sonny was quick to reply. He had already advised Portia not to let Lars see she had her doubts. She had briefly toyed with the idea of asking him if he could build something into the Endings algorithm that would allow her to prevent her family from being targeted. However, Sonny had warned her off. Lars, he had said, would only take her concerns and use them against her.

"Well, I think Stella's happy," Portia said, eager to escape from Planet Lars. "Let's not take up any more of your holiday. We'll see you when you get back." Before he could reply, she had switched off the screen and was relieved when Sonny did not head immediately for the door.

"Phase Two? Do you think it's really going to happen?" she said, feeling her heart race. "He can't be sure, can he?"

"He's very confident. I think we have to assume it will go ahead. And he's right, we're the prime candidates to work on the next set of creative. What do you think about leading with 'Die Young Stay Pretty'?" Playlists had been an integral part of Phase One.

Portia ignored his suggestion. Her head was full of questions. "Why us? Because we've already killed a load of people? They think we won't care? I'm not sure this is what I signed up for, you know? Having record numbers of dead bodies on the dashboard is starting to feel like a click too far. That's what the fulfilment numbers are. Corpses. It's like some kind of gruesome euphemism competition."

"I hear what you're saying, but you have to remember that we haven't done anything wrong. This is all legal." Sonny had been nagging Stella and Lars with questions about the ethics for months and had come to the reluctant conclusion that everything The Corporation had asked them to do was squeaky clean. Yuthentic had ensured that every aspect was covered in statute.

"Yes. I know. But is legal a high enough threshold?"

"In case you've forgotten, we both really need these jobs."

Portia felt her hackles rise. "You don't need this job, not like I do. If it all ended tomorrow you could stay in London, get something else. Go back to gaming in your room, or whatever it was you did before you came here. For me it's different. If I lose my position, I lose my flat. God help me, if anything happened to Mum and Marcus, I'd end up being a carer for the next fifteen years. Trapped, wracked with guilt, and catapulted back to Hell. In no time I'd be a candidate for Phase Two myself!"

"Aren't you being a bit melodramatic? Come on, Porsh, we don't really know enough about this yet. In any case, if we walk away now, we've no chance of influencing it. I can't imagine they would target someone just because they're taking anti-depressants. They would take out half the country!"

He was looking directly at her across the table. Portia folded her hands under her chin and looked back.

"Twenty-five percent, actually," she said, quietly.

"What's twenty-five percent?"

"The number of people on anti-depressants. It they took out all of them, it would be a quarter of the country." Portia had been looking at the statistics from the Department of Health, Euthanasia and Legacy Planning (HELP).

"There you are then, it's way too many for a blanket campaign. And anyway, if the pills are working, they'll be too happy to join the pipeline."

"Even if Phase Two is a way off," Portia went on, "There's still Rockstar Ending to consider. Overachieving its targets. How can that be a good thing? In any case, if it all blows up, where will that leave us?"

Sonny couldn't argue with that. Late last year, he and Portia had stumbled across an underground campaign, by an organisation called People Against Coercive Euthanasia (PACE), alleging that old people were being heavily pressured into ending their own lives. Although The Corporation wasn't named in PACE's material, it would only be a matter of time before someone joined the dots. Sonny had slipped Mason the evidence on New Year's Day, at the Hyde Park triathlon. It was the only way they could think of to get to the top of The Corporation without causing themselves a problem.

"Do you think we should tell Stella what we know? Or – heaven help me – Lars?" Portia asked.

"No! We've been through this. If she gets the slightest sniff that we have gone to Mason behind her back, she'll be furious. Plus, I would end up having to tell her about my Nan being involved with PACE. No. We have to keep our heads down now."

Portia sighed and shook her head. "Do you think we

should never have contacted Mason?" Her imagination had been going into overdrive about the problems the two of them could face as a result of their impulsive actions. Finding out that Sonny shared her misgivings didn't make her feel any better.

"We can't change the past, Porsh. We need to face the facts. The Endings program is in full swing and, whether we like it or not, if we want to hold on to our jobs, we are going to end up being the ones driving it forward. I can't see any alternative." He ran a hand through his hair and looked at her with his soft brown eyes.

Portia met his gaze and felt a sudden rush of desire that was immediately subsumed by sadness. If only circumstances were different. The missed opportunity in Sonny's grandparents' attic, which she had been regretting for days, began to seem trivial. Matters of life and death – mainly death, if she were honest – would dominate their time together for the foreseeable future. Not exactly a turn-on. Except maybe for Lars.

She consoled herself with the thought that at least they would be able to support each other during the countdown to Phase Two. Having Sonny in her life, in any capacity, made it better than it had been before. She looked forward to seeing him. As long as they were working together, maybe there was still a chance things could take a turn for the better.

CHAPTER TWO

MASON'S DAY HAD BEEN RUINED when the face of a woman he did not recognize appeared in the top right-hand corner of his field of vision. At first, he was just confused. Then he became angry.

The board had insisted that Mason should be available 24/7. They were paying him enough, after all. Away from his personal assistant, on a skiing trip he had not been looking forward to, he had felt lost, partly due to his inability to recognize faces. In meetings he often forgot names too, but he found that by nodding enigmatically and staring intently into people's eyes he could unsettle them to a point where they would not notice.

Mason had learned that his condition even had a special name, prosopagnosia. Knowing that others struggled as he did had made him feel better temporarily, but it didn't solve the immediate problem. As his throat tightened in annoyance, he started to question his impulse decision to buy a pair of ski goggles with a head-up display.

Celeste, the technician in Foucault, the exclusive goggle boutique, was used to dealing with the obscenely wealthy. She was an expert in the painless extraction of

Swiss francs from sociopathic multi-millionaires. The best customers, she found, did not need to know the price.

Using the checklist drilled into her by the AI, she calculated, correctly, from Mason's new lime green Arc'teryx ski jacket, wrinkle-free face and top-notch dental work, that payment would not be an issue. She had paused a little longer than usual as her gaze met the steel grey eyes that matched his close-cropped hair perfectly. The work he'd had done was of an exceptionally high quality, so much better than most of what she saw.

Too many of the international set women she served had frighteningly similar triangular cheekbones and vastly reduced noses that made fitting goggles a nightmare. It was almost impossible to get them to seal. Not to mention the extended eyelashes that scraped against the lenses and caused horrendous infections when they fell off and went behind the eyeball, leaving a nasty abrasion on the cornea. Fortunately for Celeste, however, every customer had to sign a watertight disclaimer before taking their goggles out of the shop. It saved her from having to go into any detail about the risks and allowed her plenty of time to wax lyrical on the benefits.

"For a man like you, I imagine it is very difficult to take time away from the office."

"Of course."

"Tell me, it is important for you to stay connected when you are on the mountain?"

When they called it 'the mountain' it sounded so much more adventurous than 'the slopes'.

"I can't ever switch off. They need to be able to reach me."

"Of course. Someone in your position. We have something. I sold one last week to the top guy at Splutter. Do you know him? Of course you do. There is only one pair left. I show you."

She was careful to pronounce every word with just enough French intonation to sound cute. Mason did not need to know she had lived most of her life in London's South Kensington when she wasn't being thrown out of a succession of boarding schools.

Celeste reached under the glass-topped concrete island that served as a counter in Foucault. It matched perfectly the post-industrial grey walls, hung with eyewear that promised to provide the ultimate in protection from the effects of every kind of weather. No sun too bright, no fog too impenetrable. Behind her, the lightest mirrored sunglasses rested alongside ranges of curved, gleaming full-face goggles and visors.

Even Mason marveled at the unwrapping experience. He recognized the color of the enamel box immediately. Television. The season's hottest Pantone. Its shape was a three-dimensional ellipse that reminded him of a giant sugared almond. Celeste waved a card over the case and it cracked open, emitting an ethereal tone before slowly unfolding to present a set of goggles, and an electronic token in the shape of a smooth silver spaceship.

"Please." She nodded to indicate that Mason should unpack the gadgets. As he reached in, the thin, mother-of-pearl, velvety cloth that had protected the impressive lens in the pod brushed sensuously against his fingers. There was a hint of expensive, modern perfume. He lifted it out and folded back the soft yet substantial headband to look inside.

"That is the little projector," Celeste indicated with a pointed nail that reflected gold or green depending on the angle of the light, "And the headphones, here, through the bone. No need for anything in the ears. This," she dug into the packaging and pulled out a short, curved plastic spur, "We can connect if you like. For speaking."

Mason nodded. He always hated faffing about with his phone on the slopes. Even though he wore a headset and microphone under his helmet, it was a terrible nuisance taking his gloves off in temperatures of minus ten to scroll.

"With the mic you don't need to…" She gestured with her hands, "Get zee frostbite!" Giggling conspiratorially now, Celeste went on, "Shall we pair it with your phone and see how you like it?"

He didn't look at how much his account was being charged. It was The Corporation that wanted him to be on the net 24/7, so The Corporation could pay for it. Celeste mailed the receipt to Mason's office. The money would be in his account by the time he touched down in London.

Before leaving the shop, with the new goggles fitted snugly inside the front of his helmet, Mason had let Celeste set up his profile and sync it to his phone. She had enabled all the functions that helped him to navigate around the valleys. He hadn't wanted to be bothered by email or text in the heads-up display, but now the downside of that was apparent: he only got an image of anyone who was calling him, and not their name.

He racked his brains staring at the picture, as he sat in biting wind on the Lac des Vaux chairlift. His hands were tucked under his armpits to guard against the harsh January chill. Where did he know that woman from? His number was such a closely guarded secret. It had to be something important.

Absorbed in his conversation with Celeste, he had managed to forget the weird moment on New Year's Day that had been preoccupying him, when the attractive young man from Brytely had surprised him in the park. The woman's face made him think of the encounter, but he was struggling to make the connection. How could she be anything to do with that?

Behind the high front of his ski jacket, he felt for the little microphone with his tongue, insulated by the Brytely monogrammed Moncler scarf Stella had given him. It was in the right place. Normally, he would have preferred synthetic fleece to silk around his neck, but he'd felt obliged to wear the thing. Stella's agency was picking up the bill for the chalet after all. In Switzerland, they seemed to be able to get away with levels of corporate hospitality that had been outlawed everywhere else.

"Answer," he said, hoping not to attract too much attention from the three strangers sharing the chairlift with him. It recognized his command. As the call connected, he opened with his usual one-word welcome, "Mason".

"Can you hear me?" The woman's voice sounded familiar. "You sound like you're in a wind tunnel."

"Yes, I can hear you fine."

"This is Nicky Hartt. The MP. I was in touch with you last year about the Rockstar Endings."

"Yep." So that's who it was.

"You arranged for one of your customers to be released from her contract. Do you remember?"

It was not something he was going to forget in a hurry. He had had to overrule the idiots in the legal team who had not wanted him to give the customer a refund. One of the more fervent lawyers had even wanted to send out someone to drag her off for disposal.

"You were very helpful."

"Yep."

"So, the bad news is I've got five more of them. Only this time they were already – what's the nicest way to put this – in the process?"

Five more? Surely the team back in London could have dealt with this without the MP having to come bleating to him again.

"In the process? What do you mean?"

"You haven't heard?"

"I'm travelling. I've not checked my messages for a couple of hours." He looked at the family of three sitting on the chairlift next to him, a man and a woman with a small child firmly wedged between them, and wondered whether they might be able to hear anything.

"Is it urgent? I'm not in the best place to talk right now." He glanced down between his skis at the mountain obscured here and there by random flurries of snow, as Nicky Hartt talked on.

"I would say so. I need your reassurance. They are very frightened, like before. Only this time they have been through a lot. Seen some disturbing things they can't un-see. I'm surprised no one has told you."

"Tell me what you need me to do." The recent encounter with Sonny was vivid again. Mason recalled how he had been sweating from the exertion of the final stage of the triathlon, but still moving fast, when he spotted the young man stamping his feet to keep warm at his marshalling spot, his breath white in the frosty air. Sonny had briefly jogged alongside him and handed over the envelope wearing a cashmere glove that had touched his hand. When Mason tore it open in the car, he had found a handwritten note that explained who the boy was, and a PACE leaflet that seemed like a pathetic remnant from a bygone age. In Mason's world all communications had been digital for years. Nevertheless, the allegations of coercion spelt out so clearly, coming on top of what Nicky had told him some months previously, were grim reading. He didn't want to take a beating from the board on this one. Not after he had told them it was all going so well.

"Can you get your guys to call off the dogs? The five of them, essentially, they've done the same thing as Liz. They've decided they want to stay alive, after all, even though they had signed the contract that said they were committed to an Ending. Can you make sure no one comes after them?"

"I'll deal with it as soon as I can. A couple of minutes."

"Thanks. What is that noise, Mason? Where are you?"

"Verbier. Is there anything else?"

"Nothing that can't wait until you get back."

He was relieved when the MP disconnected. At the top, he slid off the seat and huddled next to the hut that provided shelter for the lift operators, struggling to find a spot out of the wind. Skiing in January could be hard work, with the short days and freezing, gloomy skies. He just had time for a couple more runs before heading back for cocktails.

Best to get it done now.

"Call Greg," he said into his neck insulation. It took eight rings for him to pick up.

"Mason. You're supposed to be on holiday. What's up?"

"I've told you before, it's a business trip, not pleasure."

"Where are you, again?"

"Verbier. About to ski down Tortin, to be precise."

"Sounds more like pleasure to me. Nice. Challenging. You aren't bottling it are you? Bend zee knees and face downhill." Greg's over-familiar tone and feeble humor was starting to irritate him already. There was the loud splash of someone diving into a swimming pool in the background.

"I'm not calling for skiing tips. I've had that MP on again. Nicky Hartt."

"She's gone to a lot of trouble to track you down. Doesn't she have anyone to spend the holidays with?"

"Stop being a jerk, Greg." He could hear music in the background now, and people laughing. Was that 'Dreadlock Holiday'?

"OK. OK. What does she want? Haven't you done enough for her already?"

"Same as last time. Only now there's five of them."

"Ah." The background noise faded as Greg ducked indoors, away from the high jinks. "Are they the ones from the Brookwood incident by any chance?"

"What incident?" His voice was raised now. Nearby

the little family were getting ready to set off. One parent bent to adjust the child's ski boot while the other one fed her jelly babies. He edged away, putting more distance between them in the hope that his voice would be completely drowned out by the wind.

"I didn't want to bother you while you were away. Honestly, everything is under control now. We are doing a full drains-up."

"What incident?"

"We're not sure how it happened. It looks like we had a security breach."

He stepped further away from the family, and pushed the microphone closer before whispering: "Cyber-attack? That pro-life outfit operating out of the Vatican that infosec were so worried about?"

"In all honesty, we don't know."

"What do you mean, you don't know? You told me we were un-hackable!"

"Seems not." Greg sighed. "Look, it wasn't just an IT thing. I'm sure it can wait 'til you get back to the office."

"No, it fucking can't!" he hissed. "Tell me now!"

"OK. OK." Greg paused in the way people do only when they are preparing to deliver bad news to someone more powerful.

"The thing is it wasn't just an IT breach. It was a physical breach."

"Please. In ordinary language. And hurry up. I'm being frost-blasted here!"

"Someone broke in, Mason. We're interviewing the technicians who were on duty. Basically, they got on to the factory floor."

"Was it vandals? I know those pro-lifers can get nasty. What kind of damage did they do?"

"No. No damage at all."

"So, what's the big problem?"

"Well, the plant was live. The furnaces were in operation."

"What? You had Enders in there when they broke in? Please tell me they didn't get any pictures."

"No, no pictures. Well not as far as we know."

"And what did they do then? Get to the point."

"Well, they talked five of the customers into leaving."

"But aren't they all supposed to be unconscious?"

"Yes. Like I said, it's complicated. We've identified the five customers who opted out, and we're tracing them now to try to find out what went wrong."

"Shit, Greg. We are going to have to be very careful. Did you know there's some kind of campaign going on as well?"

"You can always expect that. Whatever you do. Let's face it, in the 20th century people campaigned against hamburgers and electronic health records. Don't get me started on vaccinations. Progress wins through eventually."

"Have you heard of PACE?"

Greg was silent.

"Have you seen the leaflets? Have you seen what they are saying about our program?"

"Mason, we're meeting all the ethical guidelines. Calm down."

"Maybe we are. But that doesn't mean our reputation won't come under attack. From what I can see, it's already in some danger."

"We need to close the misinformation down. They can't say things that aren't true. I'm getting something drafted."

Greg sighed in his villa in Barbados. His masseur was calling him, and he wanted to get Mason off the phone as soon as possible. He hated him when he came over all angry.

"Look. I'll make sure we don't do anything stupid. We don't even have a process for re-capture, so no one is going after them. Just like we don't have a process for a refund. We didn't expect anyone to be coming back. It's supposed to be a one-way trip, remember? I give you my word, Mason, the safety of the five is not in question. As for what we do next, well, I suggest we discuss that when you get back. By then we should have a clearer idea of what went wrong."

CHAPTER THREE

MASON COULD NOT RELAX WHEN he got back to the chalet. He had a bad feeling about the calls he had been forced to deal with and really needed to talk privately to Tom, his confidante and The Corporation's chief of staff. As he eased himself out of his stiff boots and slipped them onto the steel warmers, the bionic Baroness came into the boot room, closely followed by her daughter, Chippy.

"Did I see you over on Tortin, Mason?" The Baroness barked at him as she peeled off her woolly hat and ski gloves. He looked at the fluffy, ice-crusted pile she threw down next to him on the bench, with a ludicrous mink bobble flopping around at the top. You stupid woman, he thought, what kind of no-brain skis without a helmet? Especially on the vertical mogul fields of Tortin.

"Possibly. I was over there earlier."

"Yah. It's rather nice, isn't it?"

The Baroness was already in the Alps when they arrived. She had spent New Year with well-connected friends in Klosters and was an extraordinarily strong skier. Stella had invited her to join them as she was on the board at a couple of Brytely's clients and had a network of exceptional contacts. She had stacked up a pile of money through property development and been made a life peer by a Conservative government, keen to bring some ruthless commercial acumen to the House of Lords. The Baroness had brought along her daughter Chippy as her plus one, as her husband hated being a corporate partner and could not get over the fact that his wife was a better skier than him.

"Guess who we saw at lunch?" Chippy chirped up. "Only the Disgraced Prince!"

"Yah. The Royals are always here darling. It's a shame you're just a teensy bit too old for George."

"He's fourteen Mummy."

"But more to the point you're way too fat. No Royal would ever look at you."

Mason darted for the door. He was determined to avoid being drawn into discussing either Chippy's marital prospects or her body mass index. The Baroness was one of the rudest women he had ever met and with every hour that passed his regret at accepting Stella's invitation to the ski trip grew more intense. He clutched his new goggles tightly. He needed to put them on charge and do something with the settings so that next time, he could work out who was calling him.

Another ambush was waiting for him in the living room.

"Mason darling!" Stella was standing by the fire wearing a tight-fitting technical base layer that she had unzipped at the front, revealing a cleavage that seemed to float unsupported at an unsettling height. Mason tried not to stare. It wasn't so much sexual attraction as an engineer's fascination.

Aware that excuse would never stand up in court, he forced himself to look away, and strode right up to the sliding windows where he stared silently into the purple dusk. Lights twinkled around the valley. He had a moment of overwhelming calm. As he stepped back towards the room everything inside was suddenly reflected back at him. The open fireplace, the animal skin sofas, the abstract art, the island heaving with drinks and Bundt cake. And Stella, of course. He couldn't ignore her.

"Have you seen Tom?" Maybe his consigliere would provide him with a means of retreat.

"He's in the Jacuzzi with Carrie. I think Mario and Luigi are down there too."

Mason didn't react. "Some work stuff has come up."

"I'm heading down to the spa myself. You should join us."

Something buzzed in Mason's hand. It was the goggles. Someone was phoning him. He took his device out of his pocket, but it would not pick up. He could not get the Bluetooth to decouple from the stupid goggles, so in desperation he put them back on. This time he recognized the face in the display, even though the projection had not been optimized for black skin. It was Channelle, his corporate affairs director. A padlock appeared next to her face, showing that her encryption software was up to date. That was Channelle for you. Always cautious. They had worked together since she joined the company as a press officer. The knot that was forming in his stomach tightened a notch. Comms people never interrupted your holiday with good news.

"Yes?"

"Hi Mason, I'm really sorry to bother you."

"Go ahead."

"It's probably nothing but we've had a really odd media call. I thought you'd want to know about it."

"Yes?"

Mason stepped out to the balcony to continue the conversation away from Stella. He put his jacket back on and stuffed his hands in his pockets. Melting snow had fallen into the goggles and was now turning to steam. He could see barely anything, other than a smeary version of Channelle's ID picture, floating in the mist.

"I don't think it's much of a story to be honest. But…I thought I should call you, just in case. Sorry about interrupting your holiday."

"It's not a holiday." He had not told Channelle that he was in Verbier as Brytely's guest. It would have been a difficult conversation. She would have tried to stop him accepting flashy corporate hospitality from the agency that was helping them to sell industrialized death.

"We had a call from Faye who did the big profile piece on you last year. Apparently, you were overheard on the slopes talking about an incident."

It must have been the couple on the chair lift. How stupid must he have been, giving his name when he answered the call from Nicky? No one would have recognized him otherwise, under all his gear.

"Do you know what's happened, Channelle?"

"No. But I think you need to tell me."

Mason glanced inside through the glass that separated the balcony from the living area. Stella caught his eye. "Give Greg a call. He's across it."

"But Greg's on holiday in Barbados…"

"And? He's chief counsel. He's always on duty."

"OK. I'll call him." She would do as Mason said, even though there was no love lost between her and The Corporation's most senior lawyer. Mason drove his executives to compete with each other, often fueling the tension by using selective disclosure. It was a neat little mind game that kept them on their toes.

"Anyway, what's the journalist got? That I said 'incident'? It's hardly headline news, is it?" He cast his mind back, trying to remember whether he could have been overheard saying anything more incriminating.

"True. I just thought you should know. Be careful, though, Mason. The place is crawling with reporters. They are all hoping the Disgraced Prince will give them something to write about. If he doesn't, you don't want to be filling his column inches."

By the time he went back inside the sky was black. His instincts were usually right, and he decided his best option would be to pack his bags and arrange a transfer home the following morning.

This time, he would be taking a helicopter. None of your carbon-neutral nonsense. Brytely had been aggressive in insisting their guests avoid flying. "Sorry Mason, we've all got to do our bit to avoid climate catastrophe," Stella had declared, forcing all the guests to travel from London in luxury four-wheel drive electric limos. The optics were terrible. They looked like a convoy of oligarchs. Such a waste of time. He would have paid the offset contribution ten times over to counter his lost working hours.

"Anything I can help with?" Stella asked as she watched Mason pull the huge, misted lens from his face, wipe away a few cold beads of sweat, and tear off his jacket for a second time that evening. He didn't want to give anything away.

Then, it dawned on him that perhaps she could make his life a little easier after all. For the first time that day, his face muscles twitched in the direction of a smile.

"I've been thinking about something. That boy. The one who came up with the Rockstar Ending concept."

"Sonny? Yes."

"He's very bright, isn't he? I ran into him a few days ago. He was at the triathlon. You know, the one I did on New Year's Day."

"I had no idea he was a triathlete!" Stella looked pleased they had met.

"He was a volunteer. It's not important. Anyway, he seems very promising."

"He is. Oh, he is. He's getting more confident all the time. It was a blow for him when he didn't get into one of the big-name tech grad schemes, so he really puts in the hours. Their loss was Brytely's gain. I hope Carrie told you we took him and the girl out to celebrate the success of the Endings program?"

"No, she didn't."

"Great night. At the Shard. Anyway, what about him?"

"I was thinking. Our companies – we do a lot of work

together. I am wondering whether you might like to send – what was his name?"

"Sonny."

"Yes, whether you would like to send Sonny over to The Corporation for a few months on a secondment? It's something we do with our…" – he fixed her with his best gaze and managed the tiniest of wrinkles at the corner of his eyes – "… most important strategic partners. It would give him the chance to get to know a bit more about the way we work, and we might even learn a thing or two from him. And with Phase Two coming up, well, if you win the pitch we're going to be working hand in glove."

"You want Sonny?" A playful glint flashed across Stella's eyes. He ignored it.

"Just on secondment. For now, at least. No pressure. If you have him allocated to something else, that's fine. I just thought it could be mutually beneficial. Client insight for you, a fresh viewpoint for us. Win, win?"

"He's quite handsome, isn't he, in a grad scheme kind of a way? Don't you think?"

"I hadn't noticed. If you say so."

"He is becoming a rather critical asset, you know." Her expression signaled that she was gearing up for a negotiation, but he had expected that.

"And a chargeable one. I'm not expecting him for free obviously. I'll pay his full hourly rate. It's short notice, so I don't expect a discount."

"Well, if we can agree the right terms, I'm sure I can send him over to you for – shall we say, six months? Would that work for you?"

"Yes. Six months. Starting from Monday?"

"This Monday? In two days' time?"

"Yes. We're agreed in principle. You know I like to move fast."

Stella saw that having Sonny inside The Corporation could be extremely useful to her and was surprised at how quickly Mason had offered such generous terms. She charged her agency personnel out at a rate five times more than the amount that ended up in the employees' bank account. They could give him a little New Year's pay rise to boost the multiplier, too.

"I'll call him now. Promise me you'll come down to the spa for a little après-ski? Leave your phone in your room and join the party."

Reluctantly, he left his damp ski clothing in a disorderly heap on the floor of his bedroom, secure in the knowledge that one of the discreet housekeeping staff would miraculously get it dry by the time he returned.

He wanted to stay in his room and make some more calls, but he still had no idea how to uncouple his phone from the goggles. After struggling with the app for fifteen minutes, he became so annoyed that he threw the goggles into the bin along with the egg-like case and the charging cables. He had to delete the device from his phone before he could use it normally. A text popped up from Stella reminding him he had a duty to enjoy himself. He dragged on a fluffy robe and imitation sheepskin slippers for his trip down to the basement, knowing that she would only come looking for him if he didn't call in. He really didn't want her to have an excuse to come into his bedroom.

The spa area had won awards for post-industrial architecture. It could easily have been mistaken for a seven-star concrete nuclear bunker, if only one wall had not been made of what appeared to be a huge, finely engineered pane of insulated, curved glass. The hot tub was suspended above the slopes at one edge of the window, and a bar stood next to it laden with chilled champagne, cocktails and delicate canapés. Nearby, an indoor pool, long enough to swim a few short lengths, had been lined with a layer of beaten polished steel.

Uncomfortable at being presented with so much of the other guests' semi-naked flesh, Mason dived straight into the pool and swam a whole length under water, only surfacing when he was as far away as could get from the others.

Tom, his right-hand man, who looked like a slightly shorter, more muscular version of Mason, could read his boss in an instant. It was only a matter of seconds before he jumped out of the hot tub, slid into the water, and swam smoothly up to join him. Mason wished they were alone so he could get Tom's take on what had happened, but there was no way they would be able to talk frankly here.

"I'm going to have to go back to London," Mason said, quietly. The two men lay on their backs in the water, side by side.

"Problem?"

"Nothing terrible, just something I need to sort out quickly. I can't do it from here."

"Do you need me to come back with you?"

"No. You stay. They've gone to a lot of trouble."

Mason watched as a precarious pyramid of strawberries was carried to the bar, followed closely by a fountain of the finest Swiss chocolate flecked with glimmers of edible gold leaf. Chippy jumped out of the water and speared a piece of fruit with a gold metal cocktail stick in the shape of an arrow which she thrust into her glass of champagne. Its sparkle was instantly clouded with a nasty brown streak.

"You could say that," Tom remarked, dryly. "I'm happy to stay if you're sure?"

"Yes. Have a bit of fun. Hang out with Stella. We're going to be doing a lot more with Brytely this year. I need you to get to know them. You're so much better at this socializing thing than me."

Stella was disappointed when Mason told her at dinner that he was going to have to head back the following day. However, she soon got over it when she realized that Tom, Mason's mini-me, would be keeping her company. She immediately recruited him to accompany her, Carrie, The Baroness, Chippy, Mario and Luigi – the other guests, who were something big in big pharma – to a well-known village nightspot. They danced energetically alongside the Disgraced Prince until the place closed at 4am.

It was hardly surprising that no one apart from the chef was awake as Mason tucked into his macrobiotic muesli, and headed for the local heliport before dawn. His super-efficient PA, Penny, had arranged everything.

Just as he had planned, his onward transfer to London – a private jet – was waiting on the tarmac at Geneva.

CHAPTER FOUR

THE CANNABIS FARM IN THE spare room was thriving. Jade's tired face reflected the eerie blue of the lights as she walked in to give the latest news to her boyfriend Cliff. "You won't believe what Dad's done now."

"Tell me, babes," Cliff said without looking up, as he carefully re-potted a set of seedlings. "He can't have got very far on that old walking frame."

Alerts about Bryn's escapades had been interrupting them on a regular basis. They already knew his landlady planned to evict him for being a fire risk after he set a pan of sausages on fire more than once and failed to notice. Clouds of acrid, black smoke billowing out into the hallway outside the flat had given him away to his neighbor and triggered a notice to quit.

"He was a bit garbled on the phone, but apparently he's found a solution to his housing problem. Says he's moved in with a priest." Her pale, lightly freckled face held a puzzled expression for a few seconds, as she took in the news. "I almost didn't take the call. It wasn't his usual number."

"Moved in with? Like – in a relationship? I didn't know he was…"

"No. Not that. He's not. At least I don't think so. He's not religious either. Seems like an informal arrangement. Apparently, there's four of them living there. He sounded perkier than he's been in ages."

"Well, that's one less thing for us to worry about for the time being," Cliff said, rubbing his hands clean as he drew himself up to his full height. "This is all doing very nicely."

The changes in the law that allowed small scale domestic production of medical marijuana had opened a lucrative set of side hustle opportunities for people like Cliff and Jade. Her job at McDonald's covered the basics, but this gave them some spare cash. Maybe they would be able to afford a holiday. She had modest tastes but had barely managed to save anything from her succession of minimum wage jobs over the years. Cliff met her when she was working in a bar. He was a regular customer, always polite, with a jovial manner. He had very skinny legs and wore jeans with an army-style green jacket. His long, curly dark hair was usually held back in a ponytail.

One night, when live boxing was showing on the big screen in the bar, a fight broke out very close to where Jade was clearing tables. The brawl flared without warning. Two screeching women tumbled towards Jade, tearing out handfuls of each other's hair and gouging wildly with their nails.

With lightning reactions, Cliff stepped forward and swiftly steered Jade out of their path. She had been carrying a long stack of glasses which could have injured her badly if she had been hit. Unlike many of the other punters who had lunged at her during working hours, Cliff had not used the impromptu encounter as an excuse to attempt a grope. After that evening, she began to pay a bit more attention to him, chatting when it was quieter. Even though she knew he was using the bar for dealing drugs, as long as he kept a low profile she could turn a blind eye.

"He's asked if I can pick up a few things from the flat for him."

Half an hour later Jade and Cliff were standing in her dad's old living room. She held a nest of bin sacks and heavy-duty carrier bags in one hand, and a pack containing two pairs of disposable rubber gloves in the other. It was cold.

"Jeez. It don't smell too good," Cliff said, looking at the tatty armchair, and the spot on the ancient carpet in front of it where Bryn's feet had worn away the pile to a threadbare patch.

"The fires haven't helped." She ripped open the gloves and handed a pair to Cliff, which he quickly pulled over his spindly fingers. "Believe me, it's even worse in the kitchen."

"Why is his walking frame here? He never goes anywhere without that."

"Your guess is as good as mine. We'll definitely have to take that with us." Jade wheeled it into the little entrance hall and parked it by the front door. "I've got a list. He wants his meds, a few clothes…"

"He went without his meds? What was he thinking?"

"None of it makes any sense to me either, babes."

"He's definitely losing it."

"Yes. We know that. But going on about it now isn't helping." Jade was starting to feel overwhelmed. Her dad had turned up at their flat the week before Christmas asking if he could move in with them, after his landlady said he had a month to find somewhere else to live. Jade had some sympathy with the woman. Bryn was no longer able to keep the place clean. The bathroom was squalid by anyone's standards. And the scorched walls and billowing smoke were the final straw.

"At least he's got somewhere else now," Cliff said, sensing his girlfriend's anxiety. "Let's get this done. Rapido." He shook out a bin liner and started sweeping things that were obviously rubbish into it. An old half-empty box of mince pies, a torn sheet of Christmas wrapping paper, a couple of discarded envelopes.

The Christmas card Jade and Cliff had given Bryn stood on a dust-covered shelf in the flimsy wall unit that housed Bryn's television. She tore it in half and pushed it into the sack. They had only sent cards to their parents this year. None of their friends expected one. She was surprised to see that he had been sent another.

"Who's Bailey?" She inspected the solid, square card with a holographic angel printed on the front. "This isn't something from a pound shop." More guilt. Whoever Bailey was, they had spent more on her dad's Christmas card than she had. "Do you think he'll want to keep it?"

Cliff held out the bag. "This isn't the time to be sentimental. If it's not on the list, you need to chuck it or we'll never get out of this shithole." Jade folded the card shut. On the back there was a wreath of holly surrounding another message: 'All the best for the festive season from The Corporation'.

"You're right. It's just a business thing," she conceded while trying to rip it. The paper had a coating on it that made it impossible to tear, so it went into the trash whole.

"I'll take his plastic beaker. I don't want him spilling his drinks all over his new place. He can't afford to alienate another landlord."

"Whatevs, sugarplum. Just don't overload him. He might not have much space."

She stopped rummaging for a moment and looked around the room. How had she not noticed that her Dad's home had turned into something from a poverty porn documentary?

"This is horrible. It couldn't be worse if he was dead, Cliff. At least then we could just bin the lot without having to sort through it."

"Yep. So, let's get it done and skedaddle. Concentrate on the list."

Bryn's medicines were stacked in an old ice cream carton that held other small items. Cliff caught sight of his glasses next to a pair of nail scissors. "He didn't even take his specs! What was he thinking! It would be easy enough to slip them into a pocket. And he said there was some money and his bank cards in a coat in the bedroom."

She left Cliff clearing the rubbish. The smells were different in the bedroom. Less carbon, more bodily fluids. She creaked open the vintage wardrobe and felt inside the pocket of his musty old overcoat. His directions had been perfectly accurate. There was a small wad of cash nestled next to his bank cards. Her skin began to itch, and she wondered whether she should strip the bed. No, she would leave that treat for the landlady. The woman would charge them for a deep clean anyway. After gathering a few clothes and one pair of shoes from Bryn's paltry collection, she closed the bedroom door behind her.

"Babes, you need to have a look at this." Cliff had dropped his bin bag and was absorbed in an A5 leaflet that he had found on the shelf nearest the door.

"What is it?"

"I'm not entirely sure. It's something else from that Corporation."

"Did he apply for the dorms like we said he should?" She sounded surprised, but for a moment there was a spark of optimism in her voice. When Bryn had been told he had to leave the flat, Jade had suggested he move into one of the communal care homes that had seamlessly displaced the ragged, failing mess of health and social care provision for older people. She had tried to sell it to him as somewhere warm and clean, where a care robot would be at his every beck and call.

"It doesn't look like it. The silly old fucker." The upbeat tone had disappeared from Cliff's voice. Suddenly, he had become uncharacteristically solemn. "You might want to sit down," he said, before handing her the piece of paper to read.

Happy Ending Checklist for Mr Bryn Holder: Pickup Time 12.30pm 6ᵗʰ January 2028

✓ Take your medication as usual. It will not interfere with your onboard sedation.

✓ Put on your disposable pants. Occasionally the

sedation can cause minor leakage. We want you to be comfortable on your journey.

✓ Leave behind mobile phones, walking aids, money and spectacles. The Corporation will ensure items are recycled and finances managed in accordance with your gifting instructions.

✓ Make sure you are waiting outside your door at the scheduled departure time.

✓ Sit back, relax and enjoy the ride!

Happy Ending is a Corporation trademark Terms and conditions apply

"What's all this about sedation? What's he done? I don't understand."

"I think the clue's in the title."

"Happy Ending you mean? I've never heard of it."

"I'm not certain darling. But reading between the lines it looks like he was on the way out. We'll have to ask old Daddio when we drop off his crap. Let's crack on. If we keep at it, we'll soon be on our way."

CHAPTER FIVE

NATALIA WAS SHOCKED TO FIND a man she didn't recognize wearing one of Father Aloysius's dressing gowns, making two cups of tea in the presbytery kitchen when she arrived for work at 7.30am.

He had helped himself to a couple of mugs from Father Al's collection, which were kept in a clear-fronted display case in the corner of the room. One bore a large marijuana leaf, and the slogan 'Smokin' in Amsterdam'. The other was sky blue, until as it was filled with boiling water it changed to reveal the Virgin Mary in her manifestation as the Queen of Peace, and the words, 'If you knew how much I love you, you'd cry of joy'.

The heating was on and the room was unusually warm.

"Excuse me. Who are you?" Natalia asked the stranger unceremoniously, without removing any of her layers, and wondering how she would be able to get her jobs done with the strange man hanging around.

"George." He smiled awkwardly. "I'm staying here with a few friends. We've had a bit of a crisis. Father Al is putting us up while we sort something out." The man was tall, looked reasonably fit, and had short-cropped brownish hair that was thinning on top and greying a little at the front. He wore black combat bottoms and a grey sweatshirt.

"So, you are friend of Father Aloysius?"

"You could say that."

"OK. So, you are friend. Good." Natalia's face relaxed a little. She took off her brown leather gloves and began to unzip her orange calf-length puffer. "What is crisis?"

"We've... well ... we've all lost our homes temporarily."

"Why? Is flood? Fire?"

"It's too complicated to explain. But we shouldn't be here for very long. What's your name? Can I make you a drink?"

"Thank you, no. I am Natalia. I am housekeeper for Father Al."

"Nice to meet you Natalia. I'll get out of your way." He picked up the mugs and began to walk towards the door.

"Please, which rooms are you in? You are here with wife?"

"I'm in with Bryn at the top of the stairs, and the ladies are next to the downstairs bathroom. Why don't you give us a knock when you've finished in here?"

Natalia wanted to ask more questions about the visitors, but when she had taken the job Father Aloysius had instructed her to act with discretion whenever parishioners were around. So she just nodded, and set about retrieving her bucket and cleaning materials from under the sink.

"I've given you two sugars," George said as he put the Amsterdam mug on a flimsy white bedside table next to the single bed where Bryn lay awake. "Thought you might want a bit of energy to get you through whatever happens next."

Bryn's long wispy white hair was loose and splayed out across a maroon pillow. Only his head was visible above a quilt cover printed with autumn leaves. He opened his eyes and yawned. "Thanks, mate," he said, and slowly began to wriggle into an upright position.

"Do you need me to lift you up?"

"No, no. I need to start getting my strength up now I've decided to keep going." George reached over to his twin bed and, without asking permission, grabbed both pillows and plumped them in behind Bryn so he had something soft to lean back on.

"Funny," he said, eyeing the Amsterdam mug, "My daughter's in the business."

"Travel?"

"No. Weed farming. Small scale medicinal production. Legit. Allegedly."

"Yes. That is funny," George let out a short snigger.

"I rang her like you said. She's picking up my bits and bobs and dropping them round later. What are you going to do about your stuff?"

"No idea. I don't really have anyone. Don't really have much stuff." George was struggling to maintain his cheery bravado. "What now, do you suppose?"

"We're going to take one day at a time, mate." Bryn took a sip of hot tea. "You make a fine cuppa, George. Thank you."

"You're right. One day at a time. Let's see what happens when Henry gets here."

The two men sat in silence, as the events of the past twenty-four hours played on an unremitting loop in their heads. An eerie greenish dawn was breaking on the other side of the chilly, single-glazed Victorian window that separated them from the quiet street. There was no discernible sun behind the suffocating layer of light mist that took the edge off the detail in the street, obscured the sky, and laced the trees with tiny droplets of moisture.

"I'm not sure I've done the right thing, you know." George stared across the street at the red brick building of the church primary school. The playground was deserted. A hopscotch grid had been painted on the tarmac, and a basketball hoop was mounted on the wall. "Must still be the holidays."

"Did you live alone, George?"

"Yes."

"Any family?"

"Not that I'm in touch with."

Bryn was savoring the hot, sweet tea that the sad stranger had brought him. The mug was cool enough to hold, but warm enough to bring a pleasant sensation to the palms of his hands. He could not remember a time when he had been more content, even though the bedding was shabby and didn't match, and the mattress was a bit lumpy. The company of another human being – however maudlin – was something he had desperately missed.

"I expect my daughter will have something to say when she gets here. Another telling off."

"How much will she know?"

"I've no idea. It's a tough one to explain. I'll think of something."

"At least I won't have to worry about that. I'm not accountable to anyone. Free as a bird. Like the song." George let his head drop and gave a short, sharp snigger. "What a joke."

Bryn was worried when he saw his new friend's confidence falter. "Have you always been on your own?"

"For a while, now."

"Why's that? Have you been married?"

"A very long time ago. Didn't really work out. I was an idiot. What about you?"

"Wife and daughter. Wife died ten years ago. Cancer. Daughter's the one with the hothouse in the spare room. Since it got tricky for me to move around I haven't been able to meet anyone else. I wasn't doing too badly until I started setting fire to things. It all got a bit out of hand."

"Why did you do that? No one said I'd be sharing a room with an arsonist!"

"Oh, it was an accident. I just kept drifting off after I'd put something under the grill. I'm sure I was zoning out at other times too, but it's a bit more consequential when you've just slid a couple of chipolatas under a naked flame."

For the first time that morning, George smiled. "You silly old bugger."

"Yep, that's me. Once she finds out I signed up, there'll be another one calling me names too. I'm bracing myself for a tongue-lashing."

"At least she cares about you."

Bryn shook his head. "I'm not so sure. She was always closer to her mother. It's a vague sense of duty. I wanted to move in with them, but I wish I'd never asked. It was humiliating. In my head I know it's not practical, but in my heart? Well, that's another thing altogether."

"That's why it was so easy, wasn't it?"

"To sign up you mean? For the Ending?"

"It's been emotional." George sounded surprised, "I hadn't been spontaneous for years. They caught me at a low point. I'm bipolar. At exactly the right low point. It felt like I was making the right decision."

"Did you talk to them for a long time before you decided?"

"A month or so. My meds were under review. The doc wanted to try some different tablets. They said I might be a bit more up and down than usual. I was talking to this – well, they sounded just like my commanding officer from the army. He was a smashing bloke, you know. It didn't sound exactly the same – I mean I knew it wasn't him – but it touched me, you know? I trusted The Corporation immediately."

Bryn nodded in wistful recognition. "Same. I just wanted someone to listen. Anyone, even – as it turns out – a bot. Someone who wasn't always rushing for their next shift or rolling their eyes at the state of my flat. I have to confess, if I had a device I'd be calling Bailey right now. They made me feel like I was the most important person in the world. But as soon as they'd gone, I was alone again. Billy No-Mates pacing the four walls with a crappy old walking frame."

"We're a right pair," George said warmly. "Still I feel slightly less stupid now, knowing I'm not the only one who fell for it. Reminds me of my army days a bit. All in it together. What will you do?"

"Well, that's easy." Bryn was surprised that he could remember how to have a conversation with a real person and could have carried on happily opening up to George if only his bladder hadn't needed emptying. "I'm going to try and make it to the bathroom to begin with and take it from there. My walking frame's back at the house, but if I steady myself against the wall, I should be OK." Bryn swung his spindly legs, draped in Father Al's spare pajamas, to the floor.

"Let me help you," George said, bending down and lifting Bryn gently to his feet. "You steady?" He didn't look too good, so his new friend softly said, "Take your time. You can hold on to me. We can go at a nice slow pace."

CHAPTER SIX

It was 2.30pm when Henry arrived at Lazarus House.

Father Aloysius had instructed his band of recently acquired lodgers to assemble in the living room. There were enough seats for everyone on a collection of mismatched, worn fabric sofas and armchairs. A faint smell of incense, wood polish and mixed bean casserole hung in the air. One of the Knights of Saint Columba had made the meal at home for them that morning and dropped it round with a couple of baguettes. Above the mantelpiece was an icon of a black Madonna, with gold decoration, and in one of the alcoves a statue of Jesus, his Sacred Heart proudly displayed on his chest, welcoming guests with open arms and big, sad eyes.

George was the last to arrive, as he had been finishing the washing-up after they had all eaten lunch. Bryn was already installed at one end of the sofa that sat in the bay window, and George went to join him. Mabel and Mavis, who were both in their 80s, perched quietly on armchairs, looking anxious and tired.

The subject of conversation over lunch had centered

around one simple question that was hard for any of them to answer. "What on earth have we done?"

"We're survivors," Mavis had said excitedly. "But for how long?"

"Well, if I don't get some meds, I'll last about a week." Mavis's room-mate Mabel had been anxious about re-establishing the supply of medicine to control her high blood pressure from the moment she had woken up on her trolley in the Disposal Center and taken the opportunity to escape. "I had the last one yesterday morning before they picked me up. It seemed pointless but they said to take any medicines as usual."

"We have some good contacts in the medical profession, Mabel," Father Al said in the soothing tone he had honed over the years for calming parishioners. "We'll get you sorted for sure."

"And my bipolar?"

"Yes, George, Doctor Dominic will be in to see you all this evening once his regular surgery is finished. We have ways and means, ways and means. Now, are any of you actually Catholics?"

He was greeted with silence.

"Well, I'll just say a little blessing before our meeting and leave it at that for now, then." Father Al rattled off a speedy thanks to God for their collective survival, rounding it off with a quick prayer for the dead that involved the Sign of the Cross and an "Amen" which nobody joined in.

Henry, the human rights lawyer who had played a small but significant part in securing the escapees' freedom, was eager to reassure the group that they were safe.

"The first thing I want to let you know is that The

Corporation has released all of you from the clause that allows them to take you for euthanasia even if you withdraw your consent. So you don't need to worry about an Angel popping round here with restraints or anything like that. From that point of view, they'll leave you alone."

"So, we aren't on the run then?" Mavis sounded disappointed.

"No, nothing like that."

"Why did they let us off the hook?" she wanted to know.

"Honestly? I think they have so many people signed up they don't need the expense of hunting down unwilling participants. They're exceeding their targets. Your change of heart is a minor inconvenience in financial terms, and that's all they are really bothered about."

Father Al gave a loud tut and rolled his eyes disapprovingly.

"So we're free?" Mavis said.

"Yes, you are."

"But where are we going to live?" Bryn asked.

Henry looked over the top of his spectacles. "That's less straightforward. It will depend what arrangements you made when you left. We'll need to work that through. Father Al is happy for you to stay here until we get something sorted out. The wills you completed online won't be executed because, well, not to put too fine a point on it, you're all still alive. But they are still binding legal documents should they be needed. You need to be aware of that."

"You mean if one of us had the audacity to croak without any outside assistance?" George chipped in.

"Quite. There is also something quite specific which The Corporation has asked for. They are rather keen for you all to sign non-disclosure agreements. You can deal with them direct if you wish. Alternatively, you can appoint me as your lawyer. I can get things started on a pro bono basis, but if we end up with a more complex case, I may be under some pressure from my partners to revisit that."

Father Al looked uncomfortable. "I would have thought the world needs to know what goes on in these death factories," he said. "We have a lot of interest from those higher up in the Church on this question. You're asking these kind people to sign a gagging order."

"That's one way of looking at it. But it would all be part of the package."

Mavis's eyes lit up. "Package. You mean we might be able to get compensation?"

"If you wanted to pursue it, yes, that could be a possibility. No two compensation cases are ever the same, of course, but your experience has some unique characteristics. You have seen things that very few people have been exposed to. They won't want this stuff appearing in the press. And while many such claims are of little media interest, this one, your 'insider's perspective' as it were" – he squiggled quote marks in the air – "could cause them considerable embarrassment. Even financial loss. But a binding NDA would inevitably be part of any settlement."

"Any idea how much they would give for us signing our rights away?" Mavis asked.

"We'll only know which rights they want you to forfeit when we see the agreement. As for the sums you could receive – I'm not sure. Strictly speaking, you won't be entitled to a refund on the disposal transfer because you used the service to get to the destination. Arguably, they fired up the cremation chamber and provided the sedation and so on in good faith too. So, they kept their part of the agreement."

"Except they didn't," George was becoming irritated with Henry's string of reasons why The Corporation was in the right. "They didn't keep us sedated, did they? We woke up on a convoy to Hell. It was horrific. I've had decades trying to come to terms with my PTSD, and now this."

"Contractually, they delivered the service. The process failure and intervention that led to your survival were exceptional circumstances. Someone broke into their facility and disrupted their business. I'm playing devil's advocate, of course."

"And the devil of a business it is too," Father Al muttered under his breath.

"It helps our moral argument if we talk about The Corporation as a business. A human disposal business," Henry countered, provoking a resigned nod from Father Al.

"I agree," Mavis said, "It's all about the money. The song is wrong. Let's see what we can get out of that evil lot. I've got three years until I'm 85 and some extra cash could help me go out with a bang next time."

"What do you mean, next time?" Father Al was struggling to maintain his calm priestly demeanor.

"I'm going to book on again when I'm 85 and do it properly. I still want the inheritance exemption for my grandchildren. But with some compo in the bank I could top up the legacy and have a reasonable standard of living for my final innings. Maybe even a cruise."

"You can't be serious, Mavis?" The priest looked horrified.

"Yes Father, I am."

"If you don't mind me saying so, this is all a little premature," Henry went on, "It's far too early to speculate about how much money may or may not be on the table. You certainly can't count on it. For now, I suggest you take a practical approach. Explore what resources you can access to meet your living expenses so you can transition out of the presbytery in the not-too-distant future.

"Now, if you want me to represent you, I have some paperwork here that you will need to approve."

It took about ten minutes for the four lodgers to reach a consensus and sign in the appropriate box. Before Henry left, he explained that he had one more call to make. He was on his way round to see whether Meg, the fifth escapee, would be part of the negotiation with them. She was staying temporarily with their rescuers Bob and Lexi, not very far away.

"That reminds me," Father Al piped up, "Would you ask Bob if he could pop round to sort out some internet access for my guests? They want to get connected. None of them has a device. They weren't expecting to be back in touch with anyone. Ever. Would you mind?"

"Of course," said Henry. "But be warned. You need to be very careful who you talk to about what has happened. Take some precautions. The clause in your disposal agreement – that you will not tell anyone you booked a departure – is still binding. I suggest you think of a cover story as to why you might be staying here with Father Al. Just to give you the best possible chance of success in any case we might bring. Mum's the word."

CHAPTER SEVEN

MEG WAS DISORIENTED WHEN SHE woke in a stranger's bed. But then, she had never come back from the dead before. At 85, she seemed to have found renewed motivation to follow one of her favorite pieces of life advice: 'Try everything once, except incest and folk dancing'.

The mattress was much narrower than the one she was used to. Back home, she had kept the king-size bed even though her husband, Paul, had been dead for fifteen years. No one had shared it with her since, unless you counted her grandchildren who had sneaked in on rare visits. It was nice to have space for them to snuggle in. Years sometimes passed without her seeing the kids because their parents, Alice and Adam, Meg's twin offspring, were now in their early 40s and had lived for many years on other continents.

She hoped they had not told the little ones she was dead. The thought of all the explanations that lay ahead made her wish, for a fleeting second, that she had successfully completed her Rockstar Ending. Now, she was going to have to face some difficult questions.

"Can I come in?" There was a gentle knock at the door. It was Lexi.

"Yes."

Meg lifted herself up, squashing the single foam pillow into the space behind her lower spine. She was alert, lean and agile for someone her age. A few decades of yoga, weight training, sensible eating, affluence and genetic good luck had seen to that.

Light spread into the room from the landing, as Lexi tiptoed in.

"Hello." Meg was not sure where to begin. It was a pretty spectacular morning after the night before, by anyone's standards.

"I brought you a coffee." Steam rose from a mug which read, 'Have you tried turning it off and on again?' Lexi placed it carefully on a surface next to the bed, which appeared to be a shelf unit stacked to bursting with old vinyl records.

"Sorry it's a mess in here," Lexi went on. "Bob's got so much stuff."

"It's good of you to have me." More waves of guilt began to accumulate as Meg remembered that her daughter, Alice, had wanted to invite Bob and Lexi to Meg's house on Christmas Day. She had vetoed the idea, not wanting strangers to contaminate what she had intended to be her last family Christmas. Now they were giving her refuge.

Meg had not recognized Lexi, Alice's childhood friend, when she had turned up on her doorstep the previous morning, just as Meg was about to be collected for her limousine ride to the Disposal Center. It had been more than 20 years since they last met and Lexi had been in disguise, sporting an orange emergency services jacket and baseball cap, pulled down low. When Lexi had revealed her true identity and presented Meg with a video clip from Alice begging her mother not to end her life, she began to think that she might have made a mistake.

Lexi looked smarter this morning in her teaching clothes. She had an air of quiet authority in her navy blue, long-sleeved wool dress, a short silver pendant, two-tone tights shot with navy and violet, and navy patent shoes with a low heel.

"Thanks for the coffee." Meg decided that inane conversation was the best approach for the time being.

"Bob's gone into work. The bathroom's free if you want a shower. I need to be out myself soon." Lexi dropped a clean towel on the end of the bed.

"I'm sorry to have been such a nuisance. You must have missed work yesterday as well, with everything that happened."

"We very rarely ring in sick. We'll get away with it." Lexi smiled. "Bob and I both said we had a stomach bug. Leftovers that had gone past their best. Coronation Turkey. It's a credible excuse, don't you think, on the 12th day of Christmas?"

"I suppose I'm going to have to speak to Alice." Meg suddenly dreaded the idea of having to face her daughter – even on the phone. She thought of the video, Alice's tear-stained face framed by a faded green bob, telling her she was loved and imploring her not to die. The memory made her shake her head and chew anxiously at her top lip.

Lexi touched Meg's shoulder gently. She knew how to

calm people in difficult situations. "There's no rush. I let her and Adam know you were safe last night. It's all OK with them. They are just glad you are alive. We can call them when you're ready."

Meg felt stupid. It was embarrassing that she was taking up space in this house, keeping these kind friends of her daughter away from their jobs. Was she in hiding?

"Do you know if they'll come after me? The Corporation. I read the agreement. They are entitled to use force. I consented. They tested me to be sure I had all my marbles, and I scored a dementia quotient of 3.2%. Top marks." She gave a brief, nervous snigger. The irony.

Meg had fully reconciled herself with her decision to die. Then Lexi had turned up and swayed her, saying she had been subjected to intense manipulation. The thought of a long, drawn-out legal dispute overshadowing the bonus years she had just won back was dispiriting. If a hit team abseiled in through the window at that very moment, and took her away, it would save everyone a load of trouble.

"There's no need to worry about any of that." Lexi could see that Meg needed reassurance. "We've had a promise from The Corporation. Right from the top. No one is going to come after you. Henry is going to pop round later to tell us more. I'll be back from school by then."

"Wow, friends in high places!" Meg said, trying to look grateful. "Does that mean I can go back to my house?" Even though she had thrown out practically everything she owned, it would be good to return to her own place with an excuse to buy a whole new wardrobe, and stock her kitchen from scratch with healthy food. She hoped the unopened panettone had found a good home, via the food bank.

"Let's see what Henry says when he gets here. For now, just make yourself at home with us. Take what you want from the kitchen. There are subscriptions on the TV. The usual. I'll be back around 4.30."

Lexi left Meg to change into her own clothes, which Bob had washed overnight. Meg had gone to bed early, reeling from the stresses of the day. Her fragility had been compounded by a massive sugar crash when the McDonald's doughnut she had eaten in the van wore off. Seeing that she was overcome with exhaustion, Lexi had quickly made up the single bed in the room they usually used as an office, and Bob dug out one of his favorite T-shirts for Meg to sleep in. It was XXXL, black, and printed with a white image of David Bowie, superimposed with a line from 'Heroes'.

Now alone, Meg perched upright on the edge of the bed and scanned the room that Bob had turned into a shrine to decades past. It housed an enormous collection of vinyl, on shelves that ran underneath the window, and in a unit that stretched the full height of the room along one side. A desk space was cut into the wall of music, with LED strips that cast soft colored light when she moved close to them.

Facing the music library were various framed pictures, including a black and white print of David Bowie and Mick Ronson eating a meal on a train, in full glam rock gear. It was signed by the photographer, Mick Rock. There was a postcard-sized Fakesy painting of Bowie too, which had also been autographed. Various pieces of computing hardware were stacked under the desk, which Meg thought unusual. She had sent all her files to the cloud years ago.

Hoping to reconnect with something or someone beyond the confines of the densely-packed room, she wandered over to the screen and tapped the keyboard. Nothing happened. There was no obvious way to turn anything on. Her phone was back at the house, and probably dead, as she had arranged for all her services to be terminated on the day of her planned departure. The simplicity of stopping all her bills at once had been another appealing element of the Rockstar Ending service. It would be a pain having to set everything up, all over again.

With the passing of her 85th birthday, the point at which she would no longer qualify for any state support, pension or healthcare, so much had changed. She could not help wondering if her children would come to regret having stopped her. By staying alive one extra day, she would no longer qualify for the *85* bonanza, forfeiting the opportunity to leave them her estate tax free.

Next time she died it would cost them all so much more.

CHAPTER EIGHT

L EXI FOUND IT DIFFICULT TO concentrate on teaching.

The horrors of the previous day kept breaking through into her consciousness. Jagged unexpected shards of memory, like scenes from a horror film, appeared when she least expected it.

She really wanted to talk to Bob, but that would not be possible until later. It was frustrating, knowing that he was so close but also unreachable. They worked in the same building. He ran the IT that kept them all safe and made the children clever. However, they rarely had the chance to interact during the day. Most of the time Bob would be tucked away in his control center, only venturing out at mealtimes to avail himself of the excellent school canteen that he considered to be one of the best perks of his job.

Both of them had been worried about leaving Meg on her own in the house, but they didn't see any alternative. Strictly speaking, she was supposed to be suicidal, although that morning she had seemed in good spirits, all things considered.

Lexi was exhausted. She had been on the phone half the night to Meg's daughter, Alice. There was no getting away from the fact that, having returned to New Zealand after her Christmas break in the UK, Alice was a 24-hour flight away. Getting time off from her job in the hospital, when she had only just come back from her holiday, would be difficult. She certainly did not want to explain her mother's peculiar circumstances to her boss.

"How could I have come back to NZ when I thought this might happen?" Alice had said over and over again. "I abandoned her in London – to that. I was so stupid."

"None of us knew anything for certain until after you'd left." Lexi had said the same thing at least five times. Although she wanted to support her friend it was now 1.30am and she had to be up in five hours' time, ready to control a room full of teenagers.

"Do you think I should come back?" Alice said.

"If it will make you feel better, yes. But I'm not sure you need to. She seems in good spirits."

"That's what I'm worried about. She was in good spirits the whole of Christmas. Now we know why. We've never got on as well as we did last week. She had a serenity I've never seen before."

"Does Dolly know?" Lexi knew that Alice's daughter, Dolly, had grown particularly fond of Meg during their recent visit.

"No. Not really. She can tell something's wrong but she's no idea what. I've held out. Managed to spare her the details. Just said that I get weepy with jet lag. It will all have to come out eventually, but I can't face telling her about it now."

By the time the call finished, they had agreed Lexi would report back the following evening. Alice's twin brother, Adam, could get to London from Texas in half the time it would take her. He, too, had a job and family commitments. But he had a partner, Frank, who could look after their young daughters, Mia and Bella. Childcare was more complicated for Alice, being on her own.

"I need to get over to the lock-up for half an hour," Bob announced as they pulled up outside the house after work. "I need to tidy up a few things." The van was littered with McDonald's wrappers left over from their mercy dash, picking up Grampy Meals for the five hungry fugitives on their unexpected journey back from the Disposal Center. He didn't normally let it get into such a state.

"OK love. Can you grab fish and chips on your way back for the three of us?"

As Lexi jumped down from the van, she saw Henry walking up the road towards her. She had known him for almost a year, but it felt much longer than that. They had been through so much since he spoke at her first PACE activists' meeting upstairs at The Barge. He carried his usual heavy backpack and looked a little more worn than he had seemed the day before.

"Am I glad to see you! She really wants to get back home, you know," Lexi said as she let them both into the house, smiling to suppress a feeling of apprehension, as she was not entirely sure what she would find there. Soon enough, though, she discovered that her worries about Meg's safety were unfounded. Although her friend's mother was on the floor of the living room, she wasn't in any distress. In fact, she was balancing steadily on her forearms in front of the television.

"My goodness! You can do the Crow!" Lexi said, as her anxiety turned to relief, and then envy that a woman forty years her senior could be so strong and agile.

"Not for very long," Meg's voice strained as she slowly moved out of the position and grabbed the remote to turn off the Yoga channel. She made it look so effortless. 'Why not do it with your toes and make me feel even more inadequate?' Lexi thought.

"It's been a treat to access online fitness content again. I've been doing it all from books and memory at home. This stuff is normally blocked for the over-70s, but they couldn't tell it was me. Do you mind if I lie down and do my final relaxation while we talk? I always feel better if I can stretch out."

Without waiting for a reply, Meg lay down on her back among the furniture she had shoved to the sides of the room, and let her legs and arms fall outwards onto the yoga mat she had helped herself to. Lexi found it bizarre that the woman she had rescued from death the day before was now lying on her living room floor in Savasana, the Corpse pose. Being back at school during the day had given her an interval of normality during which she had been able to pretend that she was an ordinary teacher living an ordinary life. That intermission was over. The world's most flexible pensioner was now taking up more space than she had thought possible for one so slim, breathing deeply with her eyes closed. Meg's level of self-absorption seemed rather rude, given the risks her hosts had taken, only the day before, to bring her back from the dead.

"I've just been with the others," Henry explained, taking off his coat and throwing it on to an armchair which he promptly sat on, taking care not to tread on Meg who seemed to be expanding even more. He pulled out some papers, "They are in good form over at Lazarus House. We've lots to do."

Lexi perched awkwardly on the arm of the seat while Henry went through the points he had covered with the other four. Meg made the occasional grunt to let them know that she was paying attention.

By now, he knew the script off by heart. "After the weekend I expect to receive something more formal setting out their position. For the time being we all just have to sit tight. It's Friday now. I'd advise you to stay here with Bob and Lexi, and on Monday we can see about getting you back home."

Two more days, Lexi clocked silently. The house already felt crowded with Meg throwing shapes all over the place. She was a much bigger presence than they had expected. Still, it would only be for one weekend. All those years ago, when Lexi's parents had died in the accident, Alice had given her solid support. It was her turn to repay the favor. Your best friend's Mum is for life, not just for Christmas, she said to herself, mirroring the advertising campaign that appeared regularly during the festive season, intended to stop people buying dogs as impulse gifts.

By the time Bob walked through the door, Meg was on her feet, Henry had gone and Lexi had set the kitchen table. Bob reached into a cupboard and cracked open a new jar of pickled onions, balancing a fork precariously among the contents. The look on his face lifted Lexi's spirits immediately. She recognized the expression. It was the one her kids at school would get when they were totally immersed in creating something they loved. Even the facial recognition scanners knew what it was and would trigger a recording of the lesson for the five-star file.

They shared out the food onto three warm plates. Just before they sat down. Lexi handed her phone to Bob who quickly dropped it, with his, into a metal box on the worktop, which snapped softly shut.

Meg looked quizzical.

"We have a no phones at meals rule," Lexi said casually, "At least when Bob's not on call."

"I noticed you don't have an assistant either," Meg remarked. "I thought I was the only Luddite left!"

"We don't need one. At school I teach the kids not to rely on them, too. It's crazy. When some of them arrive, all they can do is order Alexa about. I teach them how to use their own initiative instead of someone else's."

Meg nodded. "The way they talk about it, you'd think us old people can't even remember a recipe anymore. And the time! What's wrong with a clock?"

Lexi tried not to stare as Meg peeled a swathe of the world's lightest, crispiest batter from her haddock and discarded it at the side of her plate.

"Don't you like it? It's from The Rock. They've been winning awards for years!"

"I love it," Meg said, "But a second on the lips, a lifetime on the hips. And I've just got my lifetime back."

Well, that was good news. She could tell Alice that

her Mum was showing strong signs of wanting to stick around, even though her sanctimonious tone made Lexi feel self-conscious as she tucked into her own portion. After the stress of the past 48 hours, however, she had no intention of starving herself. Unlike Meg, her idea of living in the moment included piling soft white flakes of fish and crisp batter onto her fork and dipping them into a generous pool of tartare sauce. Tonight, the diet could wait.

"I've got to pop into the safe house to help them with a few things tomorrow," Bob said, "They want to re-establish contact with the outside world. I said I'd help."

"I wouldn't mind getting back online myself," said Meg, "Just to check a few things out."

"If you like, I can set something up on the machine in your room," Bob said, "Could be a good way for you to catch up with Adam and Alice when you feel like it?"

"So is your job in IT, Bob?"

"Yes. Schools IT. Specialist systems."

Meg pushed her food around her plate, slowly chewing the odd morsel. "I hope you don't mind me asking, but was it you who gave Alice the spyware to put on my computer? Lexi said that was how you knew I'd signed up."

The previous day when she had told Meg they had hacked her account, Lexi had regretted it immediately. At the time, however, she had no choice. It had been a momentous struggle, persuading her to reconsider her decision to die. She and Bob would be in serious trouble if anyone found out they had undermined The Corporation's supposedly watertight systems to liberate Meg and the others. It would be far worse for Bob, though, whose career as a security engineer would be over.

Conscious of the damage exposure could inflict on the man she loved, Lexi started babbling. "No, no, no. That was me. He had nothing to do with it. Bob's only role in this whole thing was to be the driver. The tech all came from somewhere else." What was the word they used? Yes. "One of my other sources. I can't tell you any more about that. We need to protect them. Via the dim web..."

Lexi felt a gentle but sharp kick under the table. Bob was trying to tell her to shut up. It was the dim web, wasn't it? Or was it the deep web where you were supposed to get those things?

Bob was moving the conversation on. "Meg, I was going to ask if you wanted to pop round to see the others tomorrow, when I go to sort out the IT? Lexi usually goes to the gym and Brockley Market on a Saturday morning. We could go when she gets back?"

"OK." Meg was not enthusiastic about spending time with the other escapees, but it would get her out of the house. She could not help feeling superior to the others. After all, they had not been able to afford a Rockstar Ending like her. Nevertheless, they had all ended up at the same horrific Disposal Center in the end. She shuddered for a second remembering what she had seen. That was their one thing in common. Death, the great equalizer. Or, more accurately, cheating it.

After dinner, Bob did something to the computer in the room he had lent to Meg to allow her to reconnect with her adult children. They set up a call with Adam in

Texas and Alice in Auckland, calculating that 10pm in London would work best across all the time zones.

Lexi stayed with Meg until everyone was online. The twins did an admirable job of keeping in check their anger at what their mother had tried to do. Knowing that she had just attempted to arrange her own death gave them a weird but compelling incentive to be nice to her. They had agreed that they should convince Meg to look forward to seeing them all again, rather than give her a telling off. Satisfied that the conversation was moving in a positive and conciliatory direction, Lexi retreated to the bedroom, exhausted, only to be faced with her final shock of the week.

"Crikey, Bob! What are you wearing?"

"Kansai Yamamoto. Dry clean only. Don't you like it?"

Bob was draped in a white silk kimono that looked oddly familiar, even though she had never seen him in it before. The garment was a stunning work of art, embroidered with Japanese characters and sprays of delicate foliage. It would have looked gorgeous on someone about half Bob's size, with more androgynous proportions, and a shorter body so that the hem covered everything it was supposed to.

"I thought, as we had a house guest, I should find myself a dressing gown. Wouldn't want any embarrassing moments at the bathroom door."

She chose her words carefully. "I'm afraid that won't do the job, love. Where has it come from?"

"It's not genuine, I'm afraid," he said regretfully. "I was lying when I said it was Yamamoto."

Then she remembered where she had seen it. David Bowie had worn something almost identical in a documentary Bob had forced her to sit through when she had first met him. He was so fixated on his idol that she didn't have the heart to tell him that Bowie wasn't her thing.

"It's certainly memorable," she said, smiling. They had only been living together for a year and Bob was still full of surprises.

"Mum and Dad sent it from Thailand. They had it made for me when they first retired out there. It's always been a bit skimpy, but I think I must have put on a little bit of weight." He tried adjusting the front and pulling it down, but it refused to cover everything up.

"Probably because of Christmas. I'm sorry, Bob. It's a work of art, but I really wouldn't let anyone other than me see you in it. Wrapping yourself in your Aladdin Sane beach towel would be less likely to get you arrested."

He gave up tugging at the slippery fabric and sat on the bed. "You're right as always, dear," he said, resigned to the fact that it was not going to stretch.

"Don't get me wrong," Lexi didn't want Bob to dwell on the struggle with his weight as it made him maudlin. "I'm finding her presence annoying. We didn't really sign up to be the zombie guest house. But I owe Alice a favor and indecent exposure isn't the way to make her Mum leave. Keep it as a treat for me. It won't be for long." She put her arms round his neck and kissed the top of his head. The silk was smooth and warm. "What a start to the year," she said softly.

"You were so brave, Lex. I knew you had it in you."

"I didn't have any choice."

"You could have walked away at any stage."

"No, I couldn't. Just like I can't dump her now. If my parents were still alive, I'd do the same for them. It's decades since the crash, but I still miss them every day. And now, thanks to The Corporation, thousands more people will be feeling the chronic pain of grief years before their parents need to die."

They were lying in bed, talking quietly so as not to disturb their guest, mulling over recent events in the dark. Only they knew the terrible things they had seen, Lexi when she broke into the Disposal Center, and Bob from the surveillance cameras he had hacked to follow her progress and guide her in and out.

"Can we stop?" Bob asked. "Now you've rescued Meg, you don't owe Alice anything."

"I can't do that. Maybe I could walk away if it was just about Meg. We had to leave so many of them behind. I can't unsee those things any more than I can unsee you in that kimono. Except what they are doing is terrifying. It's mass slaughter. Hardly anyone knows what's going on. I have to keep fighting. I've arranged to see Nicky on Monday to work out what we should do next. I'm not teaching until 11am so I should make it back OK."

She was acutely aware that she had dragged her lovely Bob into risking his job and his freedom to support her in what was becoming something of an obsession. "You don't need to continue though," she said, "I can do it on my own."

"No. We're in this together."

Bob was too kind to say that without his help Lexi would never have been able to rescue Meg. He didn't care that his career would be over if he were found out. What mattered now was holding on to the only person he loved more than David Bowie. Even better, a real person, who was actually alive. Being in love with Lexi was something he had never thought would happen to him. For the first time, for as long as he could remember, he was not alone.

CHAPTER NINE

THE SECURITY CHAIN WAS ON, preventing the door from opening more than a few inches. "I'm looking for my Dad. His name is Bryn," Jade explained to the woman who peeped suspiciously round the edge. It seemed a bit excessive. Why would a priest have anything worth stealing? Surely, they would have gone contactless like everyone else.

Natalia noticed the visitor was leaning casually on a red walking frame. She accidentally let go of the brake and wobbled slightly as the walker began to roll slowly towards the step.

The housekeeper wondered whether the callers could be operating a scam. Was she trying for a sympathy vote? It was obvious the woman didn't need any help walking. She worried about Father Al. He was too soft. That man would forgive almost anything. Even though absolution was written into his job description, he was too quick to look for the best in people.

Take this woman at the door. And as for her scruffy boyfriend. His appearance wasn't enhanced by the two half-full bin bags he was carrying.

In any case, Natalia had been given strict instructions about the presbytery's new entry policy. Father Al said he didn't want to take any chances. She would have to ask them some questions.

"He is one of crisis people?"

"That sounds about right. Long white hair, quite frail." Jade regained control of the meandering walking frame. "He needs this. I don't know how he got out of the house without it, to be honest."

Natalia nodded. The story was starting to stack up. "Ah yes. He is George's friend." She slid off the chain so the door would open properly. Jade shot a confused look at Cliff, who shrugged his shoulders. Bryn had never mentioned anyone called George.

"OK. You, come in." Natalia waved her hand in a conservative gesture of welcome to Jade, but still eyed Cliff suspiciously. "Father Al say family only."

Cliff always had an informal appearance and today, after wading through piles of trash at Bryn's former home, he was not looking his smartest. When Natalia caught a whiff of the smallholding crop clinging to his hair, she was even less enthusiastic about him.

Seeing her tense, Jade explained: "This is my partner, Cliff. He's been helping me with Dad's stuff. It's OK for him to bring it in, isn't it?"

Natalia sighed. It was already difficult enough to keep the house tidy with all Father Al's clutter. Now even more rubbish had arrived.

"Dad's expecting us," Jade went on. "I've got to be at work soon."

Before Natalia could say anything more, a man in his

thirties with short red hair and a clerical collar appeared next to her and waved them both in. Natalia disappeared into another room, relieved to get back to her usual tasks, leaving Father Al, Jade and Cliff in the entrance hall watched over by a print of the spooky Rembrandt painting that showed Jesus raising a shrouded Lazarus from the dead.

"Welcome, welcome. I'm Father Aloysius, but everyone calls me Al. Nice to meet you." His perky manner was in stark contrast to the gruesome artwork behind him.

"I think my Dad's here, maybe with someone called George? His name's Bryn."

The priest smiled and nodded nervously. "Yes, he's here. They both are. All safe and sound."

The list of questions Jade wanted to ask her Dad was getting longer by the minute. The priest didn't seem too worried about the George thing. "Well...can we see him?"

"To be sure. Of course you can. All in good time." She had a feeling the priest was thinking about how much he wanted to tell her. He smiled again, unconvincingly. "Tell me, do you have any idea why your father is staying in Lazarus House?"

"He lost his flat. Look, what's going on?"

"I just wanted to have a word with you first. You need to understand. He has been through a lot."

Jade wondered what it was the priest was trying to tell her. Was he deliberately trying to make her feel guilty about turning Bryn away? He was doing a good job of it. His tone was just condescending enough to make her feel small without provoking her into arguing back.

"He's very frail. Probably best you don't probe him too deeply on the circumstances of his arrival."

"Why not?"

"It's just he's not in the best frame of mind." The priest took a sharp intake of breath. "I don't want to worry you, but have you considered whether he might have been suicidal recently?"

"Dad? No! Never! He's always cheerful. For someone in difficult circumstances he's been amazing, actually. I just feel bad that... well, we have one of the newbuilds that you can't share with someone older. Or we'd have him living with us, wouldn't we, Cliff?"

Even though they had never discussed the possibility of Bryn moving in with them, Cliff could see Jade wanted Father Al to think they were good people and gave the required response.

"Course, babe. It's just not allowed, vic. No way-oh, unfortunamento."

"Not to worry," Father Al said, glossing over Cliff's confusion about his denomination. "He's fine now. We're keeping a good eye on him here."

"So, is this a permanent fix? Do you let out rooms? Is that it?" Jade asked.

"Not exactly, but we are giving shelter to several old folks who are down on their luck at the moment. He can certainly stay here for a little while."

She nodded in relief. "That's great," she said, "Maybe we can still persuade him to take a place in a dorm to get him out from under your feet." The priest smiled enigmatically. "Can I see him now? Maybe we could take his things to his room?"

"What sort of things?"

"Just his walking frame. A few clothes. Spectacles. A bit of cash."

"Very well. Just remember, no heavy interrogation. And I'd leave the walker down here. We don't want the wheels at the top of the stairs. I'm not sure he would do too well in a rollercoaster scenario. He's made a friend who's been helping him. You'll see."

Father Al led them up the wide, dark, creaking wooden staircase and into the twin room Bryn shared with George. She found her father dressed and propped up on four pillows with his legs stretched out in front of him like a rag doll. He seemed happier and cleaner than she had seen him for a long time. There was no old person smell. George perched on the side of his bed dealing cards.

"Don't worry, we're not playing for money, Father," George said in his most jovial manner. "Just as well. This tearaway is beating me hands down."

"Hello, love," Bryn said. "Fancy meeting you here!"

"Oh, Pops." Jade tried to put on a brave face. Her throat tightened as she observed his tiny frame next to the rather more athletic-looking George. "Hey, we've got the things you wanted," she added nervously just before Cliff chimed in with "It's all in the bags, Daddio!"

"Just drop them on the bed, I'll go through them later." Bryn carried on playing cards as Father Al, Jade and Cliff loitered in the doorway. Jade was disappointed that he didn't seem interested in talking to them. He was absorbed in the game.

"So, you've moved in here?" Jade tried to remember when they last had a conversation about anything other than his accommodation crisis. There must have been a time when she was not always scolding him for not eating properly or taking his medication on time.

"Is there a TV?" Yes. That was something. It was coming back to her now. She had a vague recollection that he liked to watch old episodes of *Friends*.

"Yes, but it's the ladies' turn this afternoon. Mavis and Mabel. I didn't fancy *Marigold Hotel Four*. Too close to home!" Bryn chuckled, "George and I are quite happy amusing ourselves up here, aren't we?"

George nodded. "I'd be happier if you'd let me win occasionally!"

After fifteen minutes of excruciating small talk, Jade used the excuse of her shift at McDonald's to say goodbye to her Dad. She could see he didn't want her to hang around. The guys were about to get their turn with the television, and he was looking forward to an episode of *Columbo*.

Father Al escorted them out and made sure they had the phone number for Lazarus House in case they needed to get in touch. There was still something bothering Jade. She had done as the priest had asked, and not pushed her Dad on the circumstances of his arrival, but she still wanted some answers.

"Father, did Dad say anything to you about something called a Happy Ending?" Jade asked as the priest slipped the chain off the door to let them out. "We're a bit confused, aren't we Cliff? It's just, well, we found a few odd things in his flat. We don't know what to make of them. And when you said he had been suicidal it scared me."

"Happy Ending you say?" Father Al was showing his poker face again. "Have you any idea what that could be?"

"I was hoping you might be able to tell me. Not really. Something to do with The Corporation. Look..." Jade reached into her pocket and thrust the leaflet she had found in her Dad's flat into the priest's hand. It was stained with something, but he didn't flinch. She imagined that, in his line of business, you got to see all sorts.

Without reacting, he read it slowly before saying, "Would you leave this with me?"

"It's probably nothing. But yes, keep it, by all means."

Father Al smoothed out the grubby slip of paper and slipped it into a drawer in a dresser that stood in a corner of the hall. He reached into his trouser pocket and pulled out a large bunch of keys, one of which he used to lock the drawer shut.

Jade was glad to be shot of it. Her Dad was alive and safe, even if she could not work out how he had ended up with such a peculiar arrangement. As she was in no position to offer an alternative, she thanked the priest for taking him in and set off towards the bus stop with Cliff in tow.

CHAPTER TEN

T HE WEIGHT OF BOB'S TOOL bag was a source of constant bemusement for Lexi. Why did he need to carry around so much stuff? Now they had been living together for more than a year, she knew to brace her back and bend her knees whenever she needed to move it. Just picking it up was a workout in itself.

Having parked in the drive of Lazarus House, Bob swung the bag effortlessly out of the back of the van with one hand, while Lexi and Meg each fetched one of his stacking red plastic crates under the watchful eye of Natalia. The housekeeper was irritated when Bob pulled out a reel of cable and began drilling holes in walls, leaving little piles of pale dust in random places.

"I've taken a few simple precautions," Bob explained to Father Al, casually brandishing his electric drill on one hand, while passing Lexi the spare battery to put on charge. "We don't want them coming to any more harm, do we?"

By the time Bob had finished, a computer server had been installed in the walk-in pantry, with a high-speed wireless link to the outside world. Five mobile phones were linked via the server, one for each of the residents, and one for Father Al which Bob had differentiated with a sticker that said, 'come back with a warrant – EFF'.

"There are controls on the handsets," he explained quietly to the priest as he terminated a couple of cables in the pantry. "They have to consent to the device management software Ts and Cs when they first turn them on. All legal. The kind of thing businesses use all the time. You know, all that stuff no one ever reads."

"If you think it's for the best," Father Al said, not really understanding what Bob was saying, but sure he had his guests' interests at heart.

"I've blocked all the music services and social media. There are no streaming subscriptions either, I'm afraid."

"Oh. I don't think they'll be very happy about that. A few of them seem keen to reconnect. There's a lot they're missing out on."

"Well, they've no choice, have they?" Bob was uncharacteristically sharp. "They don't have any money – not yet. And I've made search incognito, so they don't get any personalized ads. It will buy us a bit of time. And there's something else. Your phone's different to the others. Start it up and set your password."

Bob stood over Father Al while he typed in the word Ep1ph@ny, and quickly ran him through various screens.

"My number's programed in under the name David Jones," he explained, "And that's the feed from the offnet security cameras. For your eyes only. This app here is a bit more fun," he said, "It's called Rocks Off? You see it?"

"I'm not sure why you're showing me this."

"Don't panic Al! It's nothing the church would disapprove of. I've just pre-loaded some happy music to try to keep their spirits up. It's an off-net music app. Two can play at that game. Listen."

Bob scrolled through something that Father Al could not follow, tapped on his phone and suddenly the whole house was filled with music. 'I'm Free' by the Soup Dragons blasted out, pulsing an unexpected wave of joyful energy through the musty rooms.

"That should do it!" Bob shouted so he could be heard above the din, before dialing the volume back down, "We might even get them moving!"

"I think they're all a bit too old to have taken full advantage of the second summer of love," Father Al mused. "What else have you got on there?"

"Everyone knows this one," Bob said, switching to Pharrell Williams' 'Happy'. "And...I put this one on for you." Bob grinned as Aretha Franklin's 'Say a Little Prayer' kicked in.

"Very good." Father Al smiled, now having found the app on his own phone and turning on George Harrison's 'My Sweet Lord'.

"Great riff," Bob said, tapping his fingers to the beat. "But should a man of your persuasion be listening to the Hare Krishna bits?"

"Oh, I don't worry about that. Jesus said there were many rooms in his Father's house," Al declared, joining in with a chorus of 'Alleluia'. He raised his hands to the sky and gazed up rapturously. "Goodness, Bob, you've got me coming over all charismatic!"

Bob faded down the volume. "I think you've got the picture. If there's anything you want me to add, just give me a shout. I've added a feature that lets all the hand-sets stack up the music queue in a rotation, so they can all choose something they like. All the stuff from the Rockstar Ending campaign is on a blocked list. Even if someone tries to add it – and they would find that pretty difficult the way I've set it up – they won't be able to put anything Rockstar on there. I've even blocked 'Rock 'n' Roll Suicide' as a precaution, even though it's essentially a don't-do-it song. We all know they're not alone now."

Missing Bob's Bowie-obsessed nuances, Al still had to agree that blocking anything with 'suicide' in the title sounded like a good idea. As the two of them emerged from the pantry, they found Meg distributing the hand-sets to her fellow escapees.

Bryn, reunited with his walking frame, pocketed his new device and quickly scooted out of the room while the others settled down at the kitchen table with a cup of tea and some pastries Lexi had brought them.

"We'll find out more on Monday," Mavis said, "About our payout. Our legal eagle Henry's onto it. For all the distress we've been caused."

"I'd just like to get back home," Meg said.

"Nice to have one. You probably don't need the cash as much as we do, those of us who were on the economy bus." There was something spiky about Mavis's tone.

"Maybe." Meg wasn't going to take the bait. She was comfortable with being affluent but wasn't going to openly gloat. Her own home had been paid off for years, and Adam had already said he would subsidize her bills and medical care, if it came to it. "But it's been hard explaining what I did to my kids. Well, they're adults now, obviously."

"Well I'm up for all the compo I can get," Mavis was resolute. "Ker-ching!"

Bob finished his pastry before anyone else, and stood up, brushing icing sugar and fragments of flaked almond from his fleece. He reached into the red box closest to him and pulled out a tiny plastic module on a mount, with a small solar panel and battery unit. "Al, I'm just going to pop this on your front door. It's the camera that will link direct to your phone. No cloud storage, though, so don't lose the phone, OK?"

As Bob put a new power pack into his drill and disappeared out of the kitchen, Lexi stayed at the table. "So how are you all feeling?"

"Terrible a lot of the time," Mavis said, "Letting us get away like that, and leaving us with all sorts of distress, flashbacks, PTSD – you name it, we've probably got the lot now. I've given a nice long list to Henry. To support our claim."

"Quite." Lexi could not help wondering what Mavis thought of her own role in aiding and abetting the escape. Could the distress she described be Lexi's fault? "How about you, George?"

"Honestly? I feel they've made a total fool of me." He was starting to look rather glum since Bryn had left the room. Without the impetus to keep his friend happy, George's mood was sinking fast. His posture subsided as if someone was slowly deflating his muscular body and it was withdrawing back into itself.

"Oh, don't say that," Lexi looked at him directly.

"They're very clever, you know. A lot of people are signing up. From what I've heard it's exceptionally hard to resist."

"I'm really rather confused." George lowered his eyes and had started to speak very quietly. Lexi felt the need to pull him out of despair.

"I'm concerned about how you have all been manipulated. Talk about undue pressure. The Government is going way beyond what the Euthanasia Act was supposed to be about. Look at you all. None of you looks like you're on your last legs, and yesterday you were twenty feet from cremation. It's crazy! This can't be right. It certainly isn't what I voted for when we brought in assisted dying."

For the first time Mabel spoke, "It's all very well for you to say that. But we're old. You get tired of putting on a brave face. We're not like you. We've got aching bones. It can take a lot of effort just to make it from one day to the next, especially when you're on your own."

"So, if that's as you say, why did you decide to escape? You could have just gone back to sleep and waited. Let's face it, most of the others in the queue chose to do exactly that. They are almost certainly gone now." Lexi succumbed to sadness herself.

Father Al made the Sign of the Cross, and Mabel went on: "I suppose I came with you, Lexi, because you gave me a tiny glimmer of hope and a great big kick of…well, yes….it must have been excitement! I've never escaped from anything before. The thought of going on the run was the most thrilling thing that had happened to me for years.

"But now I'm not so sure I did the right thing. I've been awake all night mulling it over. Having to get my meds in secret. Relying on charity. Even if I had access to my own money there is hardly any left. And because I'm past the cut-off I've really no idea what I'm going to do next. Watching TV on an endless loop until I get sores from sitting. Even if Henry manages to swing us a few thousand, it's not going to be much of a life. There's no dignity. Just a whole load of pain, sadness and anxiety, I'm afraid. I hate to admit it after all the trouble you went to, but I wish I'd stayed on the conveyor belt."

Lexi felt like the escapees were taking turns to slap her in the face. After all the risks she and Bob had taken to give Mabel back her life. It wasn't that she expected her to be grateful, but she hadn't been prepared for regret.

"But that place. It was horrific!" Lexi said.

"Maybe. But if we had stayed asleep we would never have known. It's too late now. They say the road to Hell is paved with good intentions." There was no aggression in what Mabel had to say, just profound disappointment.

Father Al was becoming agitated. "Come along now. That's hardly fair. This brave lady managed to divert all five of you away from the road to Hell. Or Purgatory at least, given none of you are actually Catholic. I won't hear a word said against her! It used to be just us, the killjoy Papists, on the side of life. All our work to protect the unborn can now be extended to the undead!"

"We'll never agree on abortion I'm afraid, Father," Lexi said tersely, "But I am glad to have you on our side as far as assisted suicide is concerned."

At that moment, Bryn shuffled back into the kitchen. George immediately perked up, "Come on over here, mate," he said, "I've saved you a cronut. They're fantastic!"

Bryn was too preoccupied to pay attention to the deep fried, sugar-coated pastry that George had kept aside for him.

"Erm, I'm sorry to bother you, Bob, but I'm not sure this phone you've given me is working properly." Bryn was holding out the device in a thin, bony hand, "I've been trying to reach a friend."

"Can I have a look?"

Bob fiddled about with the screen for a couple of minutes while Bryn and the others chatted about what they might do with the rest of the weekend. With no money and an uncertain legal status their options seemed limited. They were pretty much trapped between the four presbytery walls, for the next few days at least.

Meg was quiet, thinking about her conversation the previous night with Alice and Adam. The call had felt like treading on eggshells, as each of them tried hard not to cause any more upset to the others. Although it had been exhausting, she was relieved that her children had been so forgiving, and was looking forward more than she had expected to seeing them again. Glancing around the room, she had no desire to make friends with any of the other escapees. Her highest hope was that Henry would soon be able to give her back her front door key. Then she would be able to get back to living her life on her own terms, whatever they might be, for a while longer.

"There's nothing wrong with it," Bob said, as his own phone flashed Bryn's name and vibrated on the table. "Maybe you were trying one of the blocked numbers?"

"Blocked, eh?" Mavis interrupted, "What have

you been up to, you saucy fellow? Calling people you shouldn't!"

Bryn ignored their questions and pointedly turned his back to Mavis. "Sorry Bob. I must have done something wrong. Thanks. You're right, it does seem to be working now."

CHAPTER ELEVEN

S ONNY COULD NOT RECALL A time when he had felt
so jumpy. Since New Year he had found it difficult to
concentrate and was sleeping fitfully. His old dependence
on energy drinks had returned. Having managed to kick
the habit after the intensive period creating the Endings
campaign, he was disappointed that since the holidays he
had needed two cans in the morning to face work.

He could not mute the replay that kept running
through his head. First, on New Year's Eve he had sort
of made a move on Portia – or had she made a move on
him? He couldn't remember. It seemed like a good idea at
the time, but now it felt like a massive relief that nothing
had come of it. The pair of them had ended up in a tight
enough spot, struggling with their contradictory feelings
about the Endings program, without adding further emotional complications. An inappropriate work relationship
would put them both in jeopardy.

It was a pity, because he liked Portia. He had invited
her to one of his grandparents' legendary parties as a genuine act of friendship. She seemed lonely. Recently, he had

been enjoying her company but now, well – now he had to back right off. He should have thought it through.

What if she told someone he'd lunged at her? His career would be over.

Then there was everything they had said to each other about their work. Their doubts and fears. All the concerns they had shared, worried that they might be caught up in something terribly wrong. Talk about intense.

As if all that disclosure weren't bad enough, why had they taken it upon themselves to try to do something about it? They must have been off their heads, that night in his grandparents' loft. After finding the leaflets that claimed people were being pressured into signing their lives away by the very campaign they had designed, they had both developed some kind of ridiculous Messiah complex.

Back in the office, the idea of calmly nudging the over-70s into signing up for voluntary active euthanasia seemed eminently reasonable. So why had he and Portia got in such a state? And what on earth had possessed him to confront the CEO of The Corporation, Brytely's most profitable client, with evidence that his reputation could be in peril?

It seemed too much of a coincidence when, a week after he had stealthily encountered Mason in the park, he was being sent to Mason's company on secondment. He felt like he was being served up as a sacrifice to a celebrity CEO, although no one had really explained why.

"Hey," Stella had begun, the second he picked up the phone, "I've got some marvelous news for you."

"OK?" Stella had never called him direct before.

Knowing that she had been with Mason for the past few days had worried him. He wandered into a quieter part of the office, so he could not be overheard. He looked around for Portia but could not locate her.

"Yah. Mason. He said he ran into you."

Sonny's mouth went dry. He tried not to panic. "Yes. Kind of…"

"Hmm. Well whatever's gone on between you two…"

"Nothing really, I just…"

Stella interrupted sharply. "Please, you don't need to tell me. Actually, I don't want you to tell me."

"There's nothing to tell! I was just volunteering as a steward!"

"Whatever you say. It's not like I'm going to out you to your mother, is it?"

"But it was nothing like that! You've got it completely wrong!" What was it with some older people, he wondered, constantly assuming everything was about sex?

"Listen sweetie, I'm quite relaxed if you want to take one for the team." Once Stella had made up her mind arguing was futile. "What happens in the Park stays in the Park. The upshot is that you seem to have made a very positive impression on the most senior executive at our biggest client."

Sonny could not think of a suitable response. He did not want to provoke his boss into making more unfounded allegations, and the truth would have been worse.

"So much so, that he has asked me to send you over to The Corporation on secondment."

"What? You're joking?"

"No. And you're going. You will be at their offices on

Monday morning at 8am. It's for three months initially, and then, well, then we'll see." She waited for him to respond.

"But what about my work here?"

"Oh, you'll still be doing all that. Just based over there with a few extras – whatever Mason throws at you. I expect it will be a doddle. Should make everything easier for us actually, because you'll be able to get the inside track. We'll set up a regular call so you can feed back to me, Lars and the girl. At such a sensitive stage we have to make sure we're giving Mason absolutely everything he wants. Is that clear?"

"Yes, OK, sure." What else could he say? Stella wasn't hanging around. She had to get back to the hard work of plying her guests in the chalet with her infamous armory of intoxicants.

Sonny still couldn't see where Portia had gone. In spite of his concerns about their friendship, he definitely didn't want her to hear his news from anyone else. He wandered through the corridors that formed a tight square maze between the meeting rooms. Eventually he spotted her camped out in Sodomy, named after a Californian death metal band, where she was making a surreptitious call to check up on her folks in Liverpool. Portia was starting to feel pangs of guilt for having cut short her Christmas visit. She waved him in through the glass, and quickly rang off with a "Bye, Mum".

"Are they OK?" Sonny asked tentatively.

"Still alive. So yes, technically that counts as OK. Same as ever really. They're never ecstatic when I call them. You know, so much going on with the kids and work and everything else." She sounded down.

"The oddest thing has just happened." Sonny put his hands in the front pocket of his hoody and leaned back against the door he had just closed behind him. "And I don't know why."

He told her about Stella's call and her instructions that he was to head over to The Corporation on Monday, which was only a few days away.

"OMG. Did she say why?"

"Not really. Only that it was Mason's personal request."

"Now you're doing my head in!"

"My thoughts exactly. Looks like he remembered who I was. I can only hope he hasn't given Stella the full background. There's no way out of it."

"Do you think she has any idea about the letter?"

"Nah. She can't have the slightest clue. She would have said. What's worrying me is what the hell I'm going to say to Mason."

By Monday morning Sonny still had not decided how to play the situation. He had tried to contact his grandmother over the weekend, as she was indirectly involved in his dilemma over the Endings contract. She didn't know how far he was involved, of course, but he would have liked her guidance. However, Ayesha and Ajay were on a mini-break with the Nordic walkers, somewhere without a phone signal. Stupidly, Sonny had only taken one copy of the PACE leaflet from their house on New Year's Eve, and he had given that to Mason. Now, he could not even remember everything that was in it.

On arrival at The Corporation's London HQ, Sonny was waved in through security by the reception droid that recognized him from his previous visit. It wore a badge that gave its name as Arnold, stuck to its humanoid form where its chest would have been. The kitten bow that had once adorned its neck had been replaced with a rainbow cravat, after The Corporation had received complaints about gendering the robots. Sonny passed through a confusing series of connecting doors and corridors until he found himself outside Mason's office where his all-powerful assistant, Penny, was expecting him.

"I've arranged your credentials," Penny said, "Just grab a seat at one of the banks." She gestured towards rows of long trestle tables that had been placed in an offset herringbone formation stretching across the office floor. Penny was kneeling bolt upright at an ergonomic contraption outside Mason's corner office. Her devices had been cleverly positioned so she could not be overlooked, a privilege Sonny quickly realized would not be extended to him.

With a heavy heart, he picked a seat on the second nearest bank, close to the wall, in a position facing Mason's office, but without being sycophantically close.

Arriving at the client's flagship office made Sonny realize how much he had started to feel at home at Brytely, where his colleagues were at least familiar, even if he did not know some of their names. This placement was like starting again. It was extra frightening, however, because he had no idea what Mason might want from him.

Expecting a rough ride one way or another, over the weekend Sonny had been trying to devise some strategies for coping with this hyper-intense Monday morning feeling. Browsing the internet, he had come across a vintage TED talk with an idea he decided to try. But it was something he could not do on the office floor.

Retreating to the privacy of a nearby toilet cubicle, Sonny stood firmly with both his hands raised in a V-shape above his head. This was the power pose. In order for the magic to work, it was necessary to hold the position for two minutes. He set the timer on his device.

Standing this way was said to increase testosterone levels by 20 per cent, boost confidence and increase one's chances of success. The idea came with the endorsement of a Harvard Business School professor. Unfortunately, however, Sonny hadn't been able to find out how long the effect was supposed to last. Although he had done some power posing before he left home, it felt like it had worn off by the time he reached the office. So, he popped into the bathroom for another hit.

Little did Sonny know, another employee of the corporation was doing exactly the same thing on the other side of the wall that separated their gender neutral cubicles. Channelle had a difficult week ahead and was trying to improve her odds of success. They almost collided in the corridor as they made their way back to Mason's corner, each utterly self-absorbed, rubbing their taut shoulders, and barely acknowledging the other's presence.

As Sonny passed Penny's desk, she said, "IT just dropped off a screen and phone for you. I asked them to put it over there."

"I've got my Brytely devices," Sonny said, "Surely I don't need any more of them?"

"Oh, you do. We only use The Corporation's bespoke system here. Security is very strict. You have to stay on our platform. End to end," Penny said, without looking up.

"Oh, OK." Sonny set about unpacking the various bits of kit and arranging them in front of him. As he was wondering how he would be able to stay up to date across two separate screens, he noticed that the woman he had seen in the corridor was loitering around Mason's door.

"Is that Greg in there?" she said to Penny, standing on tiptoe to try to see over the frosted panel that partially covered the glass walls of Mason's inner sanctum. It made his retreat look like an above-ground swimming pool, with heads vaguely bobbing above the surface when people inside were on their feet. Right now, the two men were fully submerged.

"He's been in there since seven. Straight off the redeye."

Channelle knew better than to ask Penny what the men were talking about. "I really need to see him," she said, "Both of them really. Do you think I could go in?"

The etiquette of interrupting a CEO in full flow was delicate, but with 24-hour media responses to contend with, Channelle was in a stronger position than most. She had kudos from having herded the Royal press pack before joining The Corporation, and since her arrival Mason's favorability ratings had soared.

"He said he wanted you to join them when you got here." Penny's comment was a little barbed, as if 8.15am was way too late to be showing up. "And to bring in Sonny as well."

"Sonny?" That wasn't a name Channelle was familiar with. His ears pricked up when he heard it.

"The secondee from Brytely. The marketing agency. Over there." Penny nodded her head fractionally in Sonny's direction.

He wasn't sure what he was supposed to do. Sonny looked up at Channelle and grinned weakly.

"Don't Brytely normally deal with Carrie? She's the CMO. Why is he here? Where's Carrie?" Channelle was getting more irritable by the minute.

"Carrie's still in Verbier with Tom, but Mason couldn't wait. Sonny's here on loan. Mason likes him," Penny explained. Something in her tone hinted that she doubted her boss's judgment but had learned the hard way not to query his decision.

Channelle lowered her voice, but misjudged the office acoustics, so Sonny heard her when she leant closer to Penny and whispered, "Is he cleared?"

"Yes."

Sonny sprang quietly to his feet, walked over to Channelle, and extended a hand which she shook reluctantly, with an air of resignation, before dropping her guard a little and saying, "I don't suppose you have any idea what's going on?"

"Not really." It was true. "It's my first day."

"I'm pretty confused myself." She felt unusually demoralized, even for a Monday morning.

"He's ready for you now," Penny announced, her eyes still glued to her screen. Immediately, the door slid open and Sonny tentatively followed Channelle into Mason's room. The power pose was not working. His last visit to the corner office had been to pitch the Rockstar Ending idea. They thought it had all gone so well.

Mason sat at the head of a highly polished composite table, his face as immutable as ever. A tall, blond man with amber eyes, wearing gold half-moon spectacles, fidgeted nervously in his seat. Sonny worked out that he must be Greg.

"Morning, gents," Channelle said. "Right. Is someone going to tell me what's going on? All I've had is the odd cryptic conversation, and that's not good enough."

"Calm down dear." Greg peered over his glasses in a manner he had been developing for decades to assert his superiority over everyone else. "Everything is under control." Greg had ignored several calls from her over the weekend. All he had done was send her a text: *See you on Monday*, followed by a cool emoji, a smiley face wearing sunglasses. Sonny could tell that she was seething with rage.

"If you don't mind, I'll be the judge of that," Channelle said. "We've had Faye on the phone twice asking why Mason was in 'such a bad mood' in Verbier. Her words, not mine."

"I'm not known for public displays of affability, as she well knows," Mason said. "And that is hardly a story."

Channelle bit her bottom lip. The last time Mason had met Faye things had not gone smoothly. He had wanted to put her right on a few things, and against her better judgment Channelle had fixed up the meeting. Afterwards she wished she hadn't. An article had appeared which, though balanced, included a few petty snipes they could have done without. He particularly disliked her describing him as 'equally at home on the cover of Forbes or GQ'.

"Why are we here, then? Are there any actual facts someone might like to share with me?" Her gaze flicked between Mason and Greg. Their silence hinted that there might be more to this dawn meeting than damping down trivial media gossip. Sonny was overjoyed to be excluded from her questioning which was making him want to bolt for the door. Luckily, it was as if he were invisible. He kept his head down.

Mason blinked.

"Well?" Channelle was getting more impatient. Sonny wondered whether they were being so vague because he was in the room. Should he offer to step outside? Greg finally spoke.

"We have had a minor incident at Brookwood. A disruption to the process."

"The Disposal Center? What do you mean? What kind of disruption?"

"Well, nobody died. Actually, that's the problem." Greg sniggered a little at his play on words. Noticing that no one else was laughing, he carried on. "Some sort of malfunction. We really aren't sure of the details at this stage. But the upshot was, well, five of the customers slipped away."

"Slipped away? Aren't they supposed to slip away? Will you please stop talking in riddles, Greg? You're wasting my time." Channelle's phone screen flashed. Faye. "That's her again!" She glared as she rejected the call.

"Well, yes. Not that kind of slipping away. They left the building. For want of a better expression – they escaped. We're trying to get to the bottom of it, but it's proving rather difficult." Greg looked uncomfortable.

"Aren't they supposed to be sedated?"

"Absolutely. That's one of the reasons why it's all so confusing."

"So, they didn't just get up and walk out on their own?"

Greg pulled a face like he was chewing something bitter. "Not according to the operatives, no. The site team is being interviewed at the moment."

"What about the CCTV?"

"Not there."

"What? It can't have disappeared!"

"Well, it has."

"Do we know where they've gone?"

"Not exactly. Somewhere in London. But we are in contact, indirectly. For now, it's all going through their MP, Nicky Hartt, and some so-called human rights lawyer they seem to have pulled in. My team is drawing up bespoke NDAs for them to sign as soon as possible. I am sure they can be persuaded to keep schtum."

"What has the MP said?" Channelle asked.

Mason finally joined in the conversation. "She called me direct. Asked for an assurance that we won't try to drag them back into the process which, naturally, I gave."

Channelle was relieved. At least Mason was not totally stupid. "Was she satisfied with that?"

"For the time being. It's not the first time she has been in touch about the Endings. I've asked for a full report but Greg's team is not fast enough. I'm going to second Lola onto it, get her to run it as a major incident."

Greg pulled his sour face again. "There's no need for that, Mason. I'm sure Clive can handle it. We need to control this very tightly. I really don't think bringing in…"

"Shut up, Greg," Mason snapped. "This happened four days ago. You have had long enough. I've already asked Lola to take over. She'll be running calls three times a day. You will all be on them until she stands you down. Is that clear?"

The room was fizzing with tension. Sonny was relieved that so many things seemed to have gone wrong. That should keep the spotlight away from him for a while. Surely there had to be a limit to how much punishment one CEO could dish out in a single meeting?

After a few more seconds of uncomfortable silence, Sonny finally plucked up the courage to say something. "Erm…Mason. I just wanted to check. You don't want me to join these calls, do you?"

Much to the others' surprise, Mason fixed Sonny with his impenetrable gaze. "On the contrary. I don't think anyone will know more than you about certain elements of this process. Your agency designed it. You're the right demographic for the Yuthie mindset. Lola will be in touch with you later today. I've already passed her everything I have."

Sonny felt a wave of nervous heat flush up his neck. He nodded.

"There's one other thing," Channelle went on. "If we really want to understand what the survivors have been through, we need to get down there. See the DC in action. If it looks slick enough, maybe we could even take the MP in for a visit?"

Greg squeezed his eyes tightly shut and exhaled sharply. "Don't be ridiculous. We can't take people to watch other human beings being incinerated. Even I can see that would be a public relations disaster!"

"You've been though, haven't you?" Channelle said, pointedly.

"Yes. I had to take the insurers there. The furnaces were lit for the fire safety tests, but they weren't actually in use. We substituted pig carcasses. Perfect ventilation. No smell of roast pork."

Channelle was not going to give up. "Look. We need to see it. We need to see what our escapees have seen. Otherwise how will we know whether they are telling the truth?"

"You're right," Mason said. "I've been meaning to drop in myself. This is becoming a significant program for us. Greg – I'd like you to arrange for us all to meet at the DC in a week's time."

"But it's live, Mason! You know from the dashboards that it's running at capacity. We can't stand any of the customers down. Do you really want to see the death machine in action?" Greg's squirming provoked Mason even more.

"Isn't that what I just said? You signed it all off from an ethical perspective, didn't you, Greg? I want a deep dive into what we're doing. As completing the customer journey ourselves is impractical, I will do the next best thing. If the process lives up to your promise – providing the frictionless, pain-free Ending all those pensioners have been sold – then, there'll be nothing to worry about, will there?"

CHAPTER TWELVE

Even Members of Parliament deserve treats now and again, Nicky Hartt told herself, as she made her way to Carla's café.

It was the first full week back in Westminster after the Christmas recess. Monday morning was always left free in the Parliamentary timetable, to allow the politicians to travel in from their constituencies. As an Inner London MP who dwelled among the people she represented, Nicky could easily have worked from home, or her constituency office, both of which were a couple of miles away from the House.

She had not seen her researcher, Jess, since before the break. Although they had both been back working for a few days, Nicky had told Jess to log in from home the previous week. Jess was adept with her motorized wheelchair, and would be with her boss in person, without fail, when she needed her. However, Nicky knew it was simpler for her assistant to manage some aspects of her life in her own space. And working from home had no detrimental effect on Jess's productivity, which was legendary.

By the time Nicky walked in, Jess was already parked

at a table in their favorite eatery round the back of Horseferry Road. Her long, shiny platinum blond curls were unmissable. Breakfast at Carla's had become an energizing ritual on the first working Monday of every month. Today would be a little different as one of their constituents was coming to see them.

They were in one of a tiny handful of independent old-fashioned 'caffs', as Londoners liked to call them. Carla's had survived the influx of cookie-cutter global chains that had eroded central London's character. Founded by an Italian couple who had arrived from Benevento in the 1950s, the place was named after the lead female character in their favorite film, *Buona Sera, Mrs. Campbell.*

A colorful mural of Gina Lollobrigida, who played the lead role, dominated the back wall. She looked down on the diners with hypnotic brown eyes that would have been captivating even without the heavy eyeliner. Blurred jasmine flowers edged the picture. Her neck and shoulders were swathed in an abstract 1960s print, and a statement silver and gold earring sat at the top of her perfectly proportioned jaw.

The family had made enough concessions to food trends to keep the business thriving. While their menu was ambitious, there was no compromise when it came to quality. They had thoughtfully developed a well-chosen array of vegan options; gluten-free sandwiches, toast and cakes; some hardcore keto meat feasts, and an Indian dosa breakfast on Thursdays that had people queuing outside. Their coconut and chili chutney was terrific.

You could fill up on whatever you liked, while the incessant whine of the industrial cappuccino machine and low murmur of local radio provided perfect background noise so your conversation would not be overheard. The wall of sound encouraged the lobbyists, civil servants and parliamentarians among their customers to relax and talk freely.

Nicky threw down her backpack next to the seat facing Jess's space. "Let's do this," she said, taking something resembling a make-up bag from her backpack and putting her phone into it, offering the open top to Jess as if it were a packet of crisps. Jess knew the routine, and dropped hers in on top, before closing it tightly with the zip lock. It was printed with an image of her favorite singer, Pink, whom she had seen on the Funhouse tour as a teenager and was still talking about almost 20 years later. On bad days at the office, the line about the house being full of evil clowns ran through her head and always made her feel better.

"You've got my attention now," Jess said. "You only bring out the Faraday bag on special occasions."

Nicky smiled. "Hey, we did it again."

"I have no idea how," Jess said, "But we do both look good in aubergine." More often than not, and without ever planning it, the two of them would discover they were dressed in the same colour. Today, Nicky's tailored winter coat was almost exactly the same shade as Jess's soft leather gloves and boots, with everything else in a deep charcoal.

A smart, middle-aged woman with shoulder length brown hair spotted them the minute she walked in the door and was soon sitting down next to Nicky. "Thanks for seeing me," Lexi said, "I know it's short notice." She unzipped her tailored, dark teal puffer and stuffed her backpack under her chair,

The owner, Lina, was there in seconds to take their order. She had inherited the place from her grandparents and knew her customers were usually in a hurry. Always immaculately presented, she had more than a passing resemblance to the film icon that dominated the room. Overwhelmed by the possibilities presented in the menu, Lexi decided it would be easiest to copy the others' usual order and plumped for the Full English breakfast with a mug of tea.

"Is that what I think it is?" Lexi was looking at Pink's feisty form on the tabletop. "I forgot mine. Is there room for one more?" With a bit of fumbling and rearrangement they managed to squeeze in Lexi's phone, leaving Pink looking bloated but still in one piece.

Nicky had been happy to make time to see Lexi. She knew enough about what she and Bob had done to be certain they were on the same side, even if they were not Party members. Just days ago she had seen Lexi dissolve into tears after the rescue mission at the Disposal Center. She had been through a lot. Buying her breakfast and listening to what she wanted to say was the least she could do.

"How are you doing?"

"Better than last time you saw me." Lexi's face flushed slightly with embarrassment which she recovered from quickly. "It's been emotional. We've had Meg staying with us over the weekend. She's on good form, though. We should be getting her back home this week. Henry's sorting it out."

"Great. What can I do to help?"

Lexi got down to business. She had to be back at school in a couple of hours. "We know the five are secure, but the fight isn't over, is it? I saw things inside the Disposal Center that I can't forget."

"Be very careful what you say to me about that. We both know you can't have got in there legally." Nicky did not want her or Jess to end up in the middle of a criminal investigation for industrial espionage.

"I'm sorry, but you need to hear it." Lexi was not going to stop. "They have hundreds of people signed up. I don't care if they all think they've consented. It's a disgraceful situation and I need to know what you are doing about it."

Nicky looked directly at her. "I have been trying to get the Government to admit what's going on. You know that."

"A few letters aren't enough, though, are they? They are fobbing us off!" Lexi tapped her knuckles on the table in frustration.

Jess chimed in to back up her boss. "Look, Lexi, we have to go through the official channels. It's the way these things work."

Nevertheless, everything seemed to move at a glacial pace, in Lexi's eyes. There was a break in the discussion as Lina turned up at the table with three heavily loaded plates balanced effortlessly on one arm. Mugs of tea sat on a small tray in her other hand. As they began to eat, it was obvious that Lexi was not going to let up.

"What about Mason, then? How were things when you spoke to him?"

"He's an odd guy. Comes across as unflappable. But he's obviously not happy."

After a few mouthfuls of bacon and egg, Lexi felt calmer. Being hungry had made her rattier than she had meant to be. As a teacher, she was used to being direct. But this was not a classroom, and she wanted to stay on good terms with someone who was obviously an ally. She speared a piece of sausage and ran through the different angles she had considered.

"And the Yuthies?"

Before Nicky could reply, Jess spoke up. "They are scary. To be honest, I'm worried they might turn the same tactics on people like me, you know. Soft eugenics has been creeping up on us for years."

"Why do you say that?" This was the last thing Lexi had expected. She had thought the Yuthies were only into getting rid of the old people. That 'only' brought her up short. It was surprisingly easy to slip into their way of thinking. "Tell me?"

Jess carried on. "Well, you know how this has played out in some of the other countries, don't you? The ones at the top of the assisted dying leader board. Places in mainland Europe, for example. Where they've been at it for a while."

"No. It's not something I've given a lot of attention. Not until very recently," Lexi admitted.

"When they bring it in, it all starts with the cases no one can argue with. People with locked-in syndrome. Suffering intense, untreatable chronic pain. An obvious loss of physical agency and dignity. You know the kind of thing. Where it seems like the most civilized option is to let them choose to end their life." Jess's argument was familiar.

Lexi nodded. "Yes. That's why we all voted for it, wasn't it?"

"Correct. And then, a year or two in, you start to get scope creep. Assisted dying becomes available to those for whom it was not originally intended. People start to lobby for the right to die. Teenagers with severe depression, for example – or anyone struggling with overwhelming mental health problems. It's not just about access to palliative care anymore. It's a very complex human rights issue, full of contradictions and perverse incentives. If you ask me, though, at the end of the day, everything is economic. And when it becomes more expensive to treat people than it is to put them down, well, guess what? Society chooses the cheapest option."

Nicky looked horrified and spoke without really thinking. "That seems a bit strong."

"Are you accusing me of making it up?" Jess fired back, her eyebrows raised.

"I'm just trying to take it in. Go on."

"Think about it. Everyone is obsessed with the Happiness Index. Senior civil servants and firms like The Corporation all have the Happiness Quotient as a bonus multiplier. It's what unlocks the jackpot. How better to create a massive incentive to get rid of anyone who doesn't see the world through rose-tinted spectacles? Anyone whose life might be tougher, or who would have once been entitled to social care support, becomes a target. State-funded help in people's homes had been dwindling for decades. It was only completely withdrawn recently, but already it seems like ancient history. What's more, if you look at the other countries who are ahead of us on the euthanasia curve, they are welcoming lots of people into their dignified dying centers who are just like me. It's open season."

"What are you saying, Jess? Open season for what?" Nicky had not expected her researcher to have so much to say on the subject.

"For this!" Jess ran her finger swiftly across her own throat and snapped her eyes shut, only opening them to drain the dregs of her tea with a theatrical flourish. She went on:

"Once the first wave is gone, all those well-meaning people running the clinics decide they can bring the same 'relief' to others. They have already established the precedent. Have you seen the videos on the internet, showing how caring they are? I'm sure the nurses who administer the drugs get addicted. Love the power. Add to that the commercial interests looking for a way to milk their investment, and you've got the perfect storm for death capitalism."

Nicky was shocked but had to admit she could follow Jess's logic as she went on.

"I'll dig out some of the articles and get them translated. I'm telling you, just wait until there aren't any old people left."

"I was rather hoping we wouldn't reach that point." Lexi did not want to dismiss Jess's angle outright. However, she was more worried about the outcomes she had already witnessed than those which were still at concept stage. Well, as far as she knew. "So, what do you think about going to the media? Would they be interested in what's going on? Maybe I could talk to them?"

"You need to keep away from the press." Nicky was quick to close her down. "You don't want them to find out what you've done. I could not protect you, Lexi. Please, don't go near them."

Feeling like she could not say anything right, Lexi felt her jaw clench. She had dragged herself all the way into town for nothing other than a breakfast she could have easily made at home. "Can we get the bill?" she said. "I don't think we're getting anywhere."

It was becoming hard for her to look Nicky in the eye. Unable to hide her disappointment, Lexi stared fixedly at the heavy beige mug she held in both her hands, American diner style, with Carla's written on one side in a flowing script, and the Italian flag on the other.

That was when Jess came up with a suggestion. "Maybe I could have a word with Faye? She's a journalist, Lexi. What do you think, Nic?"

Lexi saw a glimmer of hope. "And say what? Why her?" Nicky was listening carefully now. At least she wasn't ruling it out.

"Well, she's written about Mason and The Corporation before. It wasn't exactly a hatchet job, but it was critical enough to make me think she might be receptive. She has obviously done a lot of research on their operations. If you think the time is right, I could see if she's still interested in the big man."

"Go on," Nicky said cautiously, her body language starting to open up.

"Why don't I tip her off that we've come across allegations of undue pressure to sign up for Rockstar Endings? Concerns about the lack of transparency. We don't need to go into the whole escape thing. Could you live with that, Nicky?"

She nodded slowly, keen to give Lexi something while protecting her at the same time. "I suppose it's worth a try." It was hard to know what to do for the best, but she always trusted Jess's judgement. "Be careful what you say."

Lexi was still frustrated. "But what can I do, Nicky?" Lexi said, "One phone call to the media with a dulled down version of what's happened is a tiny step. I'd been hoping we would be able to do much more than this."

"Look, Lexi. The escape was only four days ago. You need some time to recover and get things into proportion. Have a rest. Let Jess make a few calls. Get Meg settled back into her house. We'll stay in touch and see what else we can come up with. I won't forget. I promise you. And anyway, you wouldn't let me." She smiled and reached into the bag to give Lexi back her phone. Lexi could not help liking Nicky as she watched her swiftly apply shocking pink lipstick using a small, round mirror that had an old Labour Party slogan printed on the back: 'For the many, not the few'.

Jess tucked her device into a side pocket, and smoothly pivoted her chair so that she could glide towards the door. Once outside, Nicky thanked Lexi for coming to see her. "I really do want to help, you know. It just takes time."

"I get it." Lexi shrugged. Perhaps Nicky was right. She had been on high alert for days and knew that an adrenaline crash was due. "You've already done a lot. But I can't let it go. For each person we have freed hundreds more will never be coming back. I refuse to be complicit in a genocide. So when you're deciding what to bring to the top of your inbox, think of it like that. We need to be on the right side of history."

CHAPTER THIRTEEN

F AYE'S INSTINCTS WERE RARELY WRONG. Despite
unswerving confidence in her own abilities as a
journalist, she was finding it difficult to convince her
editor to take the same view. Standing by Rex's desk, she
did her best to remain calm, not allowing her face to give
away how little respect she had for the man whose whims
held too much sway over her working life.

What did he know about running a newspaper, anyway? He had been shipped in to lead them from a social
media giant when the board finally panicked about their
ever-decreasing sales and over-reliance on print. The staff
had been trying to tell the bosses what was going wrong
for years, but it took a mindbogglingly expensive review
from a team of baby-faced management consultants to
finally get them to listen. Rex had arrived in the nick of
time. He made that clear to every single employee with
predictable regularity, using intonation that suggested the
failure in corporate and editorial leadership, prior to his
arrival, had been their fault.

"Why have you got it in for him, Eff?"

"I haven't. I'm just exploring a couple of leads."

"Oh, come on? Classic tourist in search of a bit of easy money. People will try to sell anything these days. He hasn't done anything wrong, Faye. So, he got a bit ratty on a chairlift, and some Arabella thought she could make a few quid. This is not the kind of work that won you investigative journalist of the year. Mind you that was four years ago. You're slipping."

She didn't need him to keep dragging that up. Having actually trained as a reporter and worked as one for 20 years – unlike him – she knew that her reputation would only ever be as good as her last story.

"In case you hadn't noticed, Rex, it's January. Hardly anyone is back at work. Parliament is only just getting back into gear. Most of the celebs are on holiday. And there's very little other news. Plus, I had a call from some MP's researcher alleging that the Endings program is over-stepping the mark. Pushing some of the oldsters over the edge before they decide to jump."

Rex made a dismissive grunting noise. "God knows, Faye, I don't want to be fielding any more calls from that supercilious idiot in his legal team."

"Channelle apologized about that. Greg's obviously a complete pillock. She could not have been more embarrassed."

"He was indeed a prize pain in the ass. I had to spend a fortune getting our external counsel to check everything you had alleged in that story."

"And it was all true." You complete waste of space. She couldn't say that, obviously.

"That's not the point."

"So, what is your point then, boss?"

Rex made no attempt to hide his irritation. "My point is that I do not want you antagonizing one of our most important advertizers without having a bloody good reason. And a reason that will appeal to lots of our readers. Man gets cross on chairlift is about as interesting as man eats toast. That's not our kind of story. We're a serious media outlet. Even if the man is Mason, the CEO of The Corporation. The risk/reward ratio makes this story a non-starter. I'm surprised you're even discussing it with me. And as for 'old lady dies' – that's hardly going to sell any papers either. Now go away."

CHAPTER FOURTEEN

S ONNY HAD SETTLED IN AT The Corporation quicker than he had expected. With the exception of the peculiar meeting with Mason on his first morning, he had been left to get on with his Brytely duties for the first week, keeping an attentive eye on the mounting sign-up stats.

He made a point of trying to look busy, taking short lunch breaks, and mimicking the behaviors of those around him, in an attempt to fit in. No one spoke at the refreshment areas, which were not as lavishly stocked as at Brytely. Even though there must have been a hundred people on his floor, the white noise generated continuously in the background kept the space eerily devoid of human voices. Worst of all, there were no free snacks.

Most days he checked in with Portia. They were careful to keep their conversations brief and focused on the business. There was never any allusion to what had happened at New Year. He didn't think it would be right to tell her about the incident at Brookwood. Not over a corporate network at least. Anyway, he was the one who had taken all the risks, wasn't he?

Life got more interesting after he was introduced to Lola. He liked her straight away. She had a warm personality and an unmatched reputation for technical competence. What was more, everyone behaved well around her because they knew she was rated so highly by Mason. The two of them went back quite a way and it was an unspoken axiom that Lola could count on his protection if ever she needed it. She had none of the prickly standoffishness that was oozed by many other people in the office.

"The big man says you're on secondment," she said, with a welcoming smile. "What on earth did you do to deserve that?"

They were in the small meeting room, near where Sonny usually sat. "I led the creative development for Rockstar Ending." She didn't need to know any other details. In any case, it was true. He thought about Stella's unsavory allegations and was delighted that there wasn't a hint of inappropriate suggestion coming from Lola.

Lola raised her perfectly shaped eyebrows. "Wow. Rockstar. That's quite something. Was it all your idea?"

"The overall marketing concept – yes. But not the rest of it. Not the process stuff. Most of the UX was done by someone else. Lars. Portia, another colleague, did the budget offering. That's going well too."

She leant across the table. "It's a very powerful program. Mason has sent me all the reports. Are you pleased with it?"

"Well it's delivering what the client wanted, so, yes. I think it's a good thing to have in my portfolio. All in all." Judging by the quizzical look on Lola's face, he had a feeling his answer wasn't right, but could not come up with a better option.

"Hmm. Yes and no." She tightened her mouth, "This incident. Aren't you worried about being associated with that? If that blows up, well. That's not so good."

"I don't really know the details. Mason mentioned it last Monday, but it was a short meeting. It was hard to take it all in. The security is nothing to do with me."

She appeared to be giving him the benefit of the doubt. "OK." Her expression softened, with flickers of understanding and resolution. "He can be deliberately enigmatic. I need to tell you something. He's more worried than he let on."

Lola ran though the same story Sonny had listened to a week previously, in Mason's office, filling in a few gaps, and bringing it up to date with the news that the five escapees had now been given offers of compensation in five figures. The money would only be paid if they signed binding non-disclosure agreements. She stopped short of calling them gagging orders, but that was what she meant.

"Do you think they'll agree?"

"Soon? No. They've got an experienced lawyer so there will be a negotiation of at least several weeks. I've asked Mason whether we might up the offer now and get it over with, but he thinks it will make us look desperate and drive the final settlement higher. He is probably right. Best case, they settle for less than six figures. It's small change for us. As some of the gang of five are frail and deteriorating, we expect some of them will cave in soon to get access to the money. They could even die before the negotiations conclude.

"Worst case, from Mason's point of view, would be that they go to the press. Blow the lid on the trauma they experienced inside the DC. Right now, we're the heroes for making the world kinder and more humane. You know the argument."

Sonny nodded, "Yes. That's all in the research. We're in a good place, being seen to deliver an important public service in a responsible way. Zero negative coverage to date. Go on."

Lola had a feeling she could trust him. "Mason has asked me to run the investigation for one reason only. It's now ten days after the incident and we still have no idea how it happened. He thinks Greg is being overly defensive. Channelle is – quite rightly – angry that no one brought her in on the full story sooner. We have no CCTV footage from the DC. The two people who were on duty there have resigned. At least they have signed NDAs. And we can't interview the fugitives because they've told us we should only contact them through their lawyer.

"We have only one human witness, who's still working for us, but he's terrified of losing his job. Angel 249."

"One of the angels?"

"Yes. When he went to collect the Rockstar Ender, a woman called Meg, that was when it all started to go wrong. He got her to the DC OK, but there was someone with her when he called at the house. It's against the rules. You have to guarantee that you will be alone.

"There was a struggle. Now that happens sometimes, but this was a bit more serious, not just a wavering oldster with last-minute regrets. This was different. The angel was outnumbered. That shouldn't happen. The more I think about it, the more I suspect the incidents might be linked. I've got Angel 249 coming in for a chat today. Thought you might like to sit in. A fresh pair of eyes. You might pick up on something I'm not seeing."

"Sure."

"Good. You designed his uniform, after all."

CHAPTER FIFTEEN

UNDER NORMAL CIRCUMSTANCES, ANGEL WOULD relish a day on full pay when he did not have to take an Ender to their death. It made a pleasant change, especially as he had been working flat out. Rockstar Ending had been such a runaway success, he could get shifts seven days a week if he wanted to. Since Christmas, that was precisely what he had done. He had overcooked his spending on presents, making the most of finding himself in a steady job at a time when there was little other work about.

When he arrived at The Corporation headquarters, an immaculately presented black woman, in a sharp cream trouser suit with nails to match, smiled and shook him by the hand.

"Hi Angel," she said, "Nice to meet you. I'm Lola and this is Sonny. He's working on the Endings campaign with me."

"Delighted to meet you both."

They were in a small room which had two low sofas and a screen set into the wall. Three glasses of water were placed on the low table. They all sank down into the seats, which were low and slightly too soft for a meeting where you wanted to appear professional. It was impossible to sit up straight.

"You're probably wondering why you're here," Lola said, "It's nothing to worry about. We're just gathering information. Do you mind if I ask you a few questions about the incident with Meg Eastman on 6th January?"

She spoke warmly and was taking trouble to put him at his ease, but he was not sure how to read the situation.

"I put everything on the form." He looked at her directly, suppressing the anxiety that was trying to tug his shoulders into a hunch. "Have I done something wrong?"

"No. We're just trying to make sure we haven't missed anything. People don't always remember every detail, you know, when they are writing reports? Especially if it has been," she paused as if searching for the right word, "traumatic."

Angel took a sip of water to loosen his throat. "Has there been a complaint?"

Avoiding the question, Lola handed him the tablet on to which his incident form had already been loaded. "Just read through it and see what you can add. We're particularly interested in tracing this – what did you call her – 'Emergency woman'?"

"It was written on her hat and hi viz. Yes, she said that she was investigating a gas leak. But she was there to stop Meg leaving. I'm sure."

"That's clear from your statement. And the action you took to deal with her was…?"

"I didn't feel I had any choice. I locked her in the cupboard. I used the non-bruising techniques as best I could with SLIP."

"Sorry, what do you mean? Did she slip?"

"It's the acronym they use on the training course for securing wrists or ankles with cable ties. Slide the Ligature In Place. Only for use in case of active resistance. I didn't use any more force than was absolutely necessary. I needed to create a clear glide path to get Meg on her way."

He would have liked more reassurance that he was not in trouble, but Sonny's expression was blank, and Lola would not make eye contact. She carried on questioning him.

"How do you know she was OK? When you went back to find her, after the drop off, you said she'd gone."

"Yes, that's right. Look – isn't all this on my bodycam footage?"

"In an investigation like this, we like to examine many different data points," Lola said. "It helps us to build a fuller picture. And – just to be clear – you seem to be alleging that she disappeared into thin air." She stared at him directly, distinctly cooler than she had been when he arrived. "How can you explain that?"

Angel sighed deeply. "I haven't got the answers. All I know is that she wasn't there. I wish I could help. Why would I lie? I know it sounds crazy. But it's like I said. She disappeared."

Surely, they didn't think he had finished her off too, did they? Lola sat in silence, hoping the hiatus would spur Angel into telling them more.

"She was acting suspiciously. She wanted me out. And

she definitely didn't want Mrs. Eastman to complete her journey."

"Can you tell me, in your own words, what she was like? The orange lady."

"Average height. Average build. Shoulder length brown hair. Nothing very distinguishing. You should get a good image from the bodycam. I made sure she was in the frame."

It was obvious to Lola that Angel was telling the truth long before the emotion-detecting software on her device confirmed it. There was little to be gained by going over the same ground again, so Lola politely thanked Angel for his time and reminded him he could call the employee assistance program at any time if he found that reflecting on the incident was causing him distress. Arnold arrived promptly to escort him out of the building.

She sank back into the sofa at right angles to Sonny and asked him how he thought the meeting had gone. "I feel sorry for him. It's a tough job. Lovely manner. Fantastic brand ambassador. Poor bloke got ambushed." Sonny suddenly worried he had sounded too forgiving and added, "What is it you think he's not telling us?"

Lola shifted forward a little and folded her hands before answering him thoughtfully. "I don't know. You're right, he seems like a nice guy. Smart. I can see why we put him on the luxury crew. Looks great in the uniform."

"Yes. He seemed gentle, actually. I was thinking, he's exactly the kind of person we could use to front the campaign, if we needed to go into another phase. He'd go down really well with the targets. Ticks so many boxes."

"We've been very careful with the staffing." Behind

the bland statement, Lola was deciding how open she should be with Sonny.

"Last summer we had a few hiccups. It was nothing major, not like this, but we have had to put a couple of employees into a residential clinic. Have you heard of NU!TTERS? The Corporation acquired it a couple of years ago. It stands for 'New U! Thinking Therapies to Evolve & Recover Safely'. It's a small chain of secure mental health care units. I'm not sure when the two staff who had the breakdown will be well enough to leave. But we've learned from that. The systems are better. It all seemed to be running smoothly until ten days ago. Some odd things happened with the transfers. Not just the intervention, although that is also a concern. There are things our technical people simply can't explain."

"He kept talking about his bodycam capture. Could we get it up on the screen now? It will be easy to tell if the footage matches his story."

"I'd love to show it to you."

"But you'd have to shoot me?" Sonny joked.

"No. It's not that. Mason trusts you implicitly. That's why I've been so open about everything."

"So why can't we see it then?"

"We're not going to tell Angel, but along with all the CCTV related to this incident, his footage for the whole of 6th January has been wiped. Nobody can work out where it's gone. And there's only one person I know with the skills to help us."

CHAPTER SIXTEEN

Bob rarely heard from Lola these days. Although she was nominally his boss, the thing he liked most about her was that she left him alone.

Being on secondment to Charlton Green School had started as an experiment in 2024, just over three years previously, when The Corporation's education division, SCET, had been pioneering new systems for supporting learning and behavior modification in children. The project was extremely sensitive. Lola had parachuted Bob in to make it all happen. He was the most trusted security expert she knew, from their days back at the bank.

The pilot had exceeded expectations and, in no small part thanks to Bob, was being rolled out to every school in the country. It was making a lot of money for The Corporation. Bob had clinched his reputation with the school governors after he came up with the idea to use the surveillance system for suicide prevention, along with everything else.

After that, they no longer saw him as a scruffy IT guy who emerged from his server room only to avail himself of the school's legendary canteen. His forethought had saved students' lives and rocketed them up the Schools Happiness Index Table. As a result, The Corporation decided to leave him in place when the pilot was over. The Education Minister's children were at the school then. God forbid anything should happen to them, especially as his wife was an influential commentator.

Today, though, Bob had no idea why Lola wanted to speak to him. There was always a reason. Although she was unfailingly pleasant, his boss wasn't one for unnecessary chat. For a fleeting moment he was uneasy, but quickly shook off the feeling. That tiny spark of fear was irrational, he told himself. He was certain he had covered his tracks.

From the privacy of his control room in the heart of the school, he dialed in. It was already dark outside, but you couldn't tell. There was never any natural light in Bob's hiding place, and it was always the same temperature. The bank of screens scrolled on repeatedly, flashing portraits of individual children in various states of concentration, and whole-classroom views as The Corporation monitored how the cohort behaved as a pack. He caught a heart-warming glimpse of Lexi unpacking some sort of card game, but the screen flicked to the playground before he could read the words on the top of the box.

"Hello," Bob said, as Lola's face filled the screen. How long had he known her now? It must be getting on for eight years. First, she was his manager at the bank. After she left, and Bob's working life took a turn for the worse, she rescued him and brought him to work for The Corporation. She found him sanctuary in his niche at the school. He had so much to thank Lola for. Without this job, he would never have met Lexi.

"How's it going, Lola?"

"Interesting times. You know? At least I never have to worry about what's going on with you, Bob."

"So, this isn't about my day job then?"

"No. Day job is going just fine. It's something more troubling. Mason has pulled me in to work on something."

"Ah, the big man. You're the one he trusts."

"So it would seem. And when I'm in a tricky spot, I need the best people around me, too. You might be able to guess what's coming next. I'm thinking about swapping the team around, bringing you back to HQ so you can help me out."

The prospect of going back to the corporate world made Bob shiver, as if a ghost had breathed down the back of his neck. Especially after recent events.

"You're joking. I really like it here, Lola. This is my life now."

"I know. I honestly wouldn't ask if it wasn't important."

"You know how bad it got for me last time." Bob had been utterly miserable at the bank by the time he and Lola had hatched his escape plan. He was sure he would have had a breakdown if Lola had not thrown him a lifeline.

"The other IT people will hate me. They'll see me as someone who's been brought in because no one thinks they are good enough. I don't want to go through all that again. At least here I was able to hide away in my room until people realized I was useful. There will be all that open plan nonsense, office politics, people watching each other but hardly ever speaking. Seeing the same people every day but never even knowing their names. Pointless rituals, drinking too much coffee, eating too much crap to break the monotony. I hated it, Lola. I really hated it."

"I know. And I'm sorry. But I'm completely stuck. Bob, I need someone with a top-class security and surveillance background. Someone who will ask the questions we haven't thought of. A fresh pair of eyes. I honestly can't think of anyone better than you."

Bob was silent.

"I've already got a guy called Sonny on the team. I think you'll get on with him."

"Like I thought I'd get on with Lars?"

"He's nothing like Lars! He's a grad. No edges. Mason is really taken with him."

"What if I say no?"

"You'll make things difficult for me. I've been out on a limb keeping you there as it is. Corporation policy is usually to let people stay in the same role no more than three years."

"Apart from the CEO, obviously."

"There's a certain amount of 'one rule for them, another for the rest of us' anywhere you go, Bob. Mason's no different. Anyway, I'm not here to defend him. I'm here to tell you that the time has come for you to have a change."

He tried not to sound resentful. "It sounds like the decision is already made."

"Well, yes. I've got someone to take over from you. Becky. She's been on my team for a couple of years at HQ. Used to be a teacher but retrained in IT when they took out most of the jobs. I think she'd fit in well at Charlton

Green. Now you've set everything up she can keep it all running smoothly."

"I see." Bob still hated the thought of going back into a corporate environment. He had only just managed to survive at the bank, and what he had heard from time to time about other parts of The Corporation didn't fill him with enthusiasm.

"There are loads of people as good as me out there," he said feebly. "Why not one of them?"

"For a start, I'd have to find them. Getting them on board and security cleared would take forever. I can't begin to tell you how urgent this thing is. I really need you here, Bob. I've never seen Mason so agitated."

"What is it that's so important?"

"It would take me ages to explain. All I can say, right now, is that it will be a perfect match for your skills. And you won't be bored."

She could tell he was crestfallen but was sure he would do as she asked. "I'm sorry, you're just too good," she said, trying to make him feel better.

"Mason's been let down by the usual suspects. He's on the verge of a rampage. We're all vulnerable. I need you to help me get us out of it."

Bob looked around his cave. He savored the familiar, low hum of the cooling fans and quietly observed the colored lights that blinked on the servers. Across the array of screens, the faces of the children scrolled by, unselfconsciously providing him with an ever-changing yet reassuringly familiar wallpaper. No two moments were ever the same. He had come to view this dark, intimate space as his own. Now he was faced with the stark realization that it had only been on loan to him. Soon he would be closing his door, adorned with a beautiful Fakesy painting of David Bowie, without knowing whether he would ever see it again. His own personal moonage daydream was about to end.

"It might not be forever," Lola went on, sounding unconvincing. "We can try to cap it at six months?"

"Six months? How about six weeks?"

"No. I can't see us being done in six weeks. It's already ten days since the critical incident and we've made zero progress."

She was not going to change her mind.

"Can I work from home?"

"No. Not on this one. Maybe the odd day. Things are weird. We need to be seen in the office."

"You aren't exactly filling me with enthusiasm."

Nevertheless, Bob could see that any further resistance to Lola's proposition would be futile. She had already made up her mind. In any case, he owed her for getting him out of his last ghastly corporate life situation. This new project, whatever it was, couldn't be any worse than that, could it?

CHAPTER SEVENTEEN

"WHEN ARE WE GOING TO see that nice girl again?" Sonny's grandmother, Ayesha said, as she deftly slammed a series of halved oranges into one of her favorite kitchen gadgets. He had used the machine himself, that New Year's morning, when he made an impromptu breakfast for him and Portia. The memory of them being together in that gleaming kitchen made him smile. No matter how hard he tried to convince himself that having a relationship with his workmate would be a bad idea, moments like this shot through his defenses.

"It's complicated."

Ayesha rolled her eyes, "Oh, spare me that millennial nonsense. What is going on? I liked her. You liked her. It was obvious. Why else would you have taken her upstairs?" She chuckled as she dropped the final piece of fruit into the noisy press. Dealing with his grandmother's curiosity about his love life, or rather the lack of it, was a regular feature of their relationship. Most times, he managed to deftly sidestep the subject.

"We're not in the same office any longer, Nani."

"Well, shouldn't that make it easier?" Last time they

had talked about Portia, Sonny had used the fact that they worked together as his rationale for keeping things on a strictly professional footing. Brytely's employee consent policy had been designed to protect the company's reputation without any concessions to individual dignity. Both parties (or more, if relevant) had to make a mandatory declaration on the Preventing Unwanted Situations of Sexual Intimacy (PUSSI) app within 24 hours of initiating intimate contact. It required a level of detail that would deter most people from trying, despite assurances that information would be treated in confidence and only sold on to external parties in a pseudonymized format.

"Make what easier? Anyway, I'm not sure. I've told you before, I'm perfectly happy being single. Now is the time for me to focus on my career. Finding a job took long enough. I can't afford to blow it."

"Has she left the company? Is she OK?" Ayesha was concerned.

"No. She's still at Brytely. I'm the one who has moved on. Well, temporarily. They've sent me on a secondment. Makes for an interesting life. It will be good for my CV."

Ayesha took a bowl of cubed mango out of the fridge, arranged some slices of lime on the side, and handed him a fork before sitting down opposite him at the breakfast bar, and spearing a piece of the sweet, smooth fruit for herself.

"That sounds good, Sunil. They must trust you to let you go on site with a big customer like that. How is the journey to the office? Are the people OK?"

"It's just a few stops into town. The office is a bit soulless compared to what I'm used to. No one really talks to you unless they want something. My team is tiny. But they're nice. Lola's the boss. She's smart, well connected, open. I'm genuinely learning things from her. Then there's Bob who has known her for years. He's older. Quieter. Typical IT-guy social skills a lot of the time. Mad about music. We get on."

She nodded approvingly. "Will I have heard of your client?"

He knew that was coming.

"Yes, I think so. It's The Corporation."

Ayesha's warm demeanor faltered immediately.

The last time Sonny had been in his grandparents' house, at their New Year's Eve party, Portia had accidentally stumbled across Ayesha's hidden stash of PACE leaflets that described the coercive nature of the Rockstar Ending program. Their stern warnings about old people being unfairly targeted had prompted him and Portia into seeing their role in designing the world's most successful voluntary euthanasia campaign in a new and worrying light. At least for a few days.

His grandmother was bound to know that The Corporation was behind Rockstar Ending. She might have been retired for a few years, but Ayesha was still an avid reader of the business pages, in charge of managing the portfolio of investments she and Ajay had built following the sale of their lucrative fast food chain. Everyone in the family asked her advice on financial decisions.

What made matters worse for Sonny, was that he had secretly used his grandparents to research the concept. His proposal had resulted from him asking what would make Ayesha and Ajay sign up for a new, luxury service he was working on exclusively for old people. They exemplified the 3As target audience in the brief: Aging. Affluent. Alive.

"Hmm. It's a huge company," she said, thoughtfully, "They are doing very well, aren't they? Which part are you working for, might I ask?"

Sonny avoided her gaze. "Oh, you won't have heard of it. I'm on a short-term special project. One Brytely's been supporting. Straddling two worlds."

She was looking at him directly now, with a serious expression. He was trying to remember how much he had already given away, but it was more than a year since he had called on her and Ajay to quiz them on the things they most enjoyed and looked forward to in life. He would not want her to know that he had distilled their joyful chatter and used it to create the advertising campaign that was now persuading thousands of their contemporaries to die. The program had no name back then. Even the idea to call it Rockstar Ending had come out of that visit. He remembered the moment as if it were yesterday. Walking away from their house, he had heard them crank up the volume on their favorite Nickelback song, 'Rockstar'.

"I'm not sure how I feel about some of the things they seem to be involved with," he said, tentatively, feeling the urge to justify himself while not wanting to give anything away.

"You know those leaflets you had in the spare room, Nani? The ones you give out at the charity shop? Can you tell me a bit more about them? It all sounded quite worrying."

He had tried once before, on the night of the party,

to persuade Ayesha to explain how she came to have the flyers in her house. She would not give anything away. The party had been in full swing and her excuse had been not wanting to discuss something so depressing with a house full of guests. They were alone now, but she was still reluctant to talk.

"Sunil, I told you. They are just something for the customers. They come in from head office. Bag stuffers. I store them here because we have space and the shop is only a five-minute walk."

He was not convinced of her innocence. "Do you know why they're so concerned? At the charity, I mean."

"I'm just a shop volunteer. I sort clothes, stack shelves, and sell greetings cards. The campaigning side isn't my responsibility."

Sonny found it hard to believe his grandmother would give out any information without knowing what it was about. She would not have been able to resist looking into it. He didn't know anyone with a nose for research like hers. She must know more.

"Are you worried, I mean, about you and Nana? Being – what was the word they used – coerced?"

She laughed dismissively, a little too loudly. "Of course not. Since when did your grandfather and I become push-overs? Anyway, we're not even 70 yet, Sunil. No. And we could not be happier with our life together. Why would we want it to end? There is no need to worry about us."

"That's good." Sonny did not know what to say next, so he speared three cubes of mango and shoved them all in his mouth. Ayesha, who had known him all his life, could tell he was hiding something.

"You aren't working on this Rockstar Ending thing, are you, Sunil?"

He felt heat rise up his neck and into his face, and almost choked on the mango, as he hurriedly grasped for the words that might get him off the hook without actually lying. What he came up with was unsatisfactory all round.

"I can't talk about my work. I'm sorry. It's all bound by confidentiality agreements, Nani." Saying, 'I could tell you, but I would have to shoot you' was the first thought that had popped into his head. It might have got more laughs, but somehow it did not sit right with the gruesome reality.

Staring at the half-eaten bowl of mango, Sonny was conscious of how he had always taken for granted his grandparents' unrivalled generosity. He took another cube, just one this time.

"This is fantastic by the way."

"Alphonso. It's a short season. You have to make the most of it, like all the good things in life. We have a friend who imports them. These are the best. Let me give you some to take home."

Leaving him to his thoughts, she disappeared into the walk-in pantry and came out with a box of nine fruit, each cushioned with its own, soft, white, protective mesh. She replaced the snug-fitting cardboard lid and lowered the case into a shopping bag for him to carry them home.

His parents would be delighted. They were always at work and his Mum's attempts at online food shopping were haphazard, at best. Their fridge contained mainly ready meals and small stockpiles of things on repeat order that she had forgotten to cancel. They rarely had seasonal treats like this. He knew the whole family would love them. Maybe he could take one to work to split with the new guy, Bob.

"That's fantastic, Nani," he said, as the atmosphere began to relax again.

"Now, if you don't mind, I'm meeting the Nordic walkers in half an hour. Ajay is going straight there from the gym. Can I drop you home? It would be a shame if the mangoes were to get bruised."

CHAPTER EIGHTEEN

Portia had not realized how much she would miss Sonny when he left for The Corporation. They had got into the habit of chatting over an app about whatever was going on in the office. She missed the steady stream of phatic babble that had lightened her day. While they were still in regular contact about a long list of tasks, it wasn't the same as sharing a physical space where she could steal a glimpse of his face or smell his fragrance.

When he had told her that he would be calling in on his grandparents at the weekend, she had asked if she could come along. Sonny avoided giving a response. He was getting good at that. Asking a second time would have been embarrassing, so she pretended that she had not noticed his sidestep and allowed the conversation to drift until he had to drop off. The casual intimacy he experienced with Ajay and Ayesha made her think about her own family. She had run out on them at Christmas, unable to cope with a depressing dynamic and the tension that resulted from her having moved into a world that jarred painfully with the place she had come from.

Occasionally she would be in touch with Jude, her

friend from university. Portia's teachers had been ecstatic when she had won a place at one of the 20 best academic institutions in the world, especially after the COVID disruption had wrecked most of their other pupils' chances. Once there, however, she was the odd one out. Practically everyone else had come from a private school. She should not have been surprised. It would take more than the worst global pandemic in living memory to dent their prospects. While Portia had largely completed her assessments alone using home study sheets, the children of the elite were engaged daily in interactive lessons on turbocharged laptops running over superfast connections. To top it all, their teachers had decades of experience in hounding the examiners into boosting their pupils' marks. Just in case.

Jude came from Canada. She and Portia were both outsiders. They shared a cynicism about the meritocratic veneer of British life. The other thing they had in common was a determination to get good degrees. Unlike many of their course mates, for them university was not an experiment in pretending they were independent, partying, and doing a bit of cramming on the side. Jude wanted to show her parents that the expense of studying abroad would be worth it. For Portia, her degree was loaded with the burdensome potential to give her a better life.

When they found out one of the cliques had started calling them 'the girly swots' they enjoyed the attention. It was only after finals, when Jude's visa ran out, that Portia regretted not making more of an effort to find other friends. She knew she should try, but the prospect of being found out filled her with dread. As a consequence, the idea had not made it higher than the bottom of her to-do list, even since she had arrived at Brytely.

During the dark winter evenings, alone in the flat where she had never had a single visitor, Portia found herself dwelling on the final, difficult conversation with her Mum, Karen, before she had returned to London. At Brytely, Lars's unwavering confidence that Phase Two would be launched within months had been bugging her, too. Much though she disliked him, she had to admit that – as far as Yuthentic were concerned – he had never been wrong yet.

Although she had scarcely spoken to Karen since Christmas, she was missing her more than she had for some years. At university she had been too busy reinventing herself and studying to notice her Mum's new relationship with Marcus and the half siblings that had started to arrive. Home had been chaotic, her Mum focused on one baby after another with no time for her first child, who was much older than the family's second batch of kids – Sean, Lily and then little Jake. The thought of travelling back up to Liverpool to appease her yearning for reconciliation did not appeal, so she decided instead to try to get her Mum down to London.

The 'Pete Burns – Freak or Fashion Icon?' exhibition at the Victoria and Albert Museum had been sold out for months. However, through some connection of Stella's in the industry, Brytely had a corporate membership which allowed her staff access to tickets when mere mortals could not get hold of them. Portia had heard Karen talk about Pete Burns, as her Dad used to hang out in Probe Records where Burns had worked in the 1970s. Grandad vividly remembered his outrageous style and elegant cheekbones, long before reality television made him a different kind of star. Karen was too busy and tired to sew these days, but had made lovely party dresses for the child Paula – as she was known before she started telling people her name was Portia. She thought the textiles angle would appeal. It was worth a shot.

Karen could only get one day off from her job at the arcade, but they let her arrange her shifts so she could stay overnight. Marcus recruited Bernie from next door to mind the kids for the hours he would be working. It was midweek, and Portia was glad to have a reason to use some of her paid holiday which seemed to accumulate as she never really knew what to do with herself when she was not in the office.

Euston was the ugliest of all London's stations. Portia went there straight after work to meet Karen from the train, even though she had told her it was not necessary. On the bleak grey concourse, she studied the arrivals board and made sure she was close to the barrier when her Mum came through from the platform. Karen was smarter than Portia had seen her look for years. Even though she carried some extra weight, the olive green dress she was wearing fitted perfectly, paired with matching nails and eye shadow, a coat in a coordinating leaf-patterned cream fabric, and pale taupe knee high boots. She pulled a small, hard beige trolley case.

"Mum! You look amazing!" she said giving her a hug and fighting a flush of emotion that almost produced a tear.

"I had to make an effort. Don't want to let you down,

do I? Are we going on the Tube? This station's hardly changed for years. It's a dump isn't it?" Nerves were making Karen talk faster than usual.

"I've booked a car. Thought it would be easier with your bag."

"Ooh love, isn't it expensive?"

"No, not too bad. The driverless ones are good value. We'll get a discount anyway 'cause there's more than one of us."

"You look pretty amazing yourself, our Paula. Let me see." Karen stood back and smiled, grabbing both her hands. "I miss the little kids already, but we're long overdue some time together, you and me."

"I've got the tickets for tomorrow, but we can sort out what else you want to do while we're in the car. Come on."

Half an hour later they were in the elevator at Peacehaven, Portia's apartment block. "This is all very nice isn't it?" Karen said to a man about Portia's age who shared the lift with them. He nodded politely before getting out on the floor below theirs. "Who was that? The strong, silent type. Very handsome!" she went on as soon as she thought he was out of earshot.

Portia blushed. "Don't you know him?" her Mum asked. She shook her head and pulled a face. No one in London would speak to a stranger in a lift. "No. I don't really know anybody from the flats." It was true. "Well you wanna get to know him," her Mum giggled, "All those tattoos! Very artistic."

Was it going to be like this all weekend? "Come on,

Mum. Let's dump your stuff. I've given you my bed, and I'm going to sleep on the sofa."

There was so much she wanted to ask her. Top of the list was why she was taking anti-depressants. That was what Portia was most worried about in case Karen's meds qualified her for Phase Two. Not that she could tell her about Phase Two, of course. Then there was her Dad. Did Karen know where he was, the father Portia had never met? Was she up to date with her vaccinations? Working in an arcade where they still used coins had to be an infection hazard. Did her Mum hate her for moving away, and abandoning her roots in the North? The final question was probably a step too far.

She knew, though, that bringing up anything sensitive the minute they got in the door would risk souring the rest of their time together. So instead she got a bottle of wine out of the fridge and poured them each a large glass. Her Mum popped open her case and pulled out two bottles of plum gin. "We can have this when the vino's gone," she said mischievously. "Two bottles? That's hardcore!" Portia laughed, pouring some mini poppadums into a small bowl and decanting a large spoonful of mango chutney to dip. "I thought you might want to go out, but if you prefer we can order in a take-away?"

"Let's do that. I'm sure we've loads to catch up on."

At 4.30am Portia woke with a splitting headache and severe dehydration. The heat in the flat had turned itself right up and she could not open a window, as her floor had been deemed too high to permit such a reckless action. She fiddled about with the app on her device that was meant to control the temperature and necked a long glass of water and a couple of painkillers which she just about managed to keep down.

Although she had told Karen to take her bedroom, she had woken up in there herself and discovered her Mum curled on the little sofa when she peeped into the living room. Unlike Portia, who was still wearing her clothes from the day before, she had managed to take off her make-up and change into a pair of flannelette pajamas covered in teddy bears. Portia suddenly felt very protective of her, snuggled child-like into the cushions. For the second time that day she wanted to cry. If only she could remember what they had talked about. She softly closed the door and went back to bed, hoping she hadn't said anything stupid, and fell back to sleep.

"Hey, our kid, I've made you a coffee." Karen was standing at the door to her bedroom, still in her pajamas, but with her make-up on and her hair done. "Do you still take sugar?"

"What time is it?"

"It's ten o'clock. You said we had to be there at two, didn't you?"

Portia slowly sat up in bed, grateful that she had taken something in the night to ward off the hangover that could otherwise have been disastrous. "Yeah. We don't have to leave for a while if we don't want to. I'll have two sugars today, I think. Thanks Mum."

Karen was back in a few seconds with a Brytely mug which said 'Portia – you rock!' on one side and had the company logo on the other.

"Who's Portia?" her Mum asked.

"Someone at work." She did not want to admit she

had dropped the name her Mum had given her as part of her strategy to succeed.

"Doesn't she mind that you stole her mug?"

"They have giveaways all the time."

"We don't get anything like that at the arcade, unless you count the polo shirts. And they don't have your name on."

"Nice coffee, Mum."

Karen gently drew back the curtains and let the grey February light into her daughter's bedroom. She peered down into the street where a couple of tramps were going through the bins. "Well that's something you see everywhere. Poor sods," she said.

Portia sipped the sweet liquid and felt the caffeine start to kick in. It was such a simple thing, the enticing aroma of the coffee, the warmth of the mug. Should it be so shocking that someone loved her enough to bring her a drink in bed? Pull yourself together, she thought, or you'll bloody start crying again.

"How's everything at home? I'm sorry if I've already asked you but huge chunks of last night are missing. We didn't half cane it!"

"Everything's good, love." Karen said without turning back to face her.

It was now or never. "Are you on tablets, Mum?"

"What do you mean?" She would not turn round.

"When I was home, I saw some pills in the cabinet. I've been worried sick to be honest."

Finally, she moved to face her. She leant back against

the wall next to the window with her arms folded tightly across her body. "I'm not ill."

Portia was going to have to spell it out. "I am sure I saw antidepressants with your name on. And for Marcus. I was just looking to borrow some moisturizer, but I can't forget about it now."

"Hmm."

"Please tell me what's going on, Mum. It's not fair."

"You're better off down here, love. We're OK, me and Marcus and the kids. We have enough to live on. We have jobs. God knows there are lots of people on the estate who are in a bad way, but not us."

"Are you depressed, Mum?"

"Not now I'm on the tablets, no." She tried to lift the atmosphere by adopting a jokey tone, but Portia refused to comply and stared at her with a worried look, determined not to drop her gaze until she got a proper answer.

"Look. We have a doctor at work. I admit I was struggling. Especially after our Jakey was born. Three kids keep you busy, and with me and their Dad doing 24-hour shifts to pay for everything, there isn't much time for us to support each other the way we'd like to. Everything we do is to make sure the kids have food on the table. It's tougher than when it was just you and me. But in the arcade, right, we have an employee assistance program. They are a big deal in the gambling industry. We see a lot of things that can get you down, you know. It's not all jackpots. There's no other jobs round our way, so – before you suggest it – throwing it in is out of the question. But I'm fine. Honest to God. You mustn't worry."

"How long have you been on the happy pills, Mum?"

Karen could see her daughter's concern and allowed herself to open up a little more. "Getting on for two years. We've got the dosage just right. Marcus went on them too, after he saw what a difference it made to me. The company pays for us to see the doctor, proper check-ups and all that. Watching for side effects. It's all very professional. You really don't need to worry. This is the best way."

"Side effects! What about talking therapies? Don't you want to get off the meds?"

"Look, if I ditch the meds, I'm telling you, I'll be hitting the bottle. And believe me, that's much worse!"

It was hard to tell whether her Mum was serious. She had worried about her drinking in the past, but it was something they didn't talk about. The two bottles of gin for a one-night stay had been startling, but having consumed vast quantities of it herself, Portia was in no position to push that line of questioning any further.

"OK, Mum. But you know you can call me if, well, there's anything getting you down, don't you?" She thought the chances of her Mum asking her for help were roughly zero, but if she said nothing how would she know she cared?

"Of course. But you've got your own life now. Marcus is very good. He's kind. Bernie next door helps us out. We get by. Don't you worry. Now, haven't we got some fancy exhibition to go to? I need to get out of these pajamas, and you need to get in the shower."

When she had lived at home, there was nothing she hated more than being told what to do. This morning, it felt like a rare privilege to be with someone who had both the time and the inclination to boss her about. "Yes, Mum."

CHAPTER NINETEEN

"Wasn't he gorgeous?" Karen said, gazing up at the giant hologram of Pete Burns wearing a purple brocade frock coat, his long, crimped black hair teased into a New Romantic mane. The song for which he was most famous, 'You Spin Me Round (Like a Record)' played while the three-dimensional image danced in time to the music. At one stage four extra arms spring from his body, as if he were declaring himself to be a deity.

"They must have used a body double," Portia said.

"What do you mean?"

"For the motion capture. To make the 3D. He died before the technology was mature enough to produce this amazing quality."

"Well, it's very convincing," Karen said. "In a super-size kind of a way."

"Catchy tune. Do I remember this, Mum?"

"You will. It's been remixed lots. He was performing it pretty much up until he died. I did a bit of research on the train. I'm hoping they've got that fishnet body suit. He was dead sexy in that."

They roamed between exhibits which spanned his entire career. Karen was most excited about an ensemble draped around a dressmaker's dummy that she described as 'Pre-Goth' – an ankle length black net tutu topped with a structure of leather and velvet. "Your Grandad saw him in Probe Records wearing that, I'm sure of it. Fits the description exactly."

"Hey, let's do this!" Karen said, excitedly. A row of VR headsets dangled from the ceiling in a corner. Beneath them were rotating stools. Atomizers periodically drenched the set-up with an antiviral disinfectant that evaporated in seconds, "Looks safe enough, doesn't it?"

Her Mum was already holding out two sets of goggles. Portia perched on a seat and strapped on the mask. She was immersed in a music video. Burns was singing a cover version of David Bowie's 'Rebel Rebel'. Except there wasn't just one of him, there were six figures spaced around her seat in a rough hexagon. Each manifestation was completely different. One Burns wore a red striped mohair jumper with Mickey Mouse ears. The second was in a monochrome patent animal print set with matching thigh boots. Another simply wore a T-shirt with 'SEX' written on it, and pink satin trousers. From his later period, there was a simple off-the-shoulder number in black satin with a diamanté collar, a burlesque corset and even a simple grey trouser suit. Each costume came with the appropriate wig and footwear, although contrary to real life, the V&A had kept his face the same. Charting that particular journey would have been a massive distraction from the clothes that were the primary focus. You could swivel 360 degrees on the stool to find your preferred Burns, as they danced provocatively around you.

"Whoa. I'm dead dizzy after that," Karen said, after they had sat through two entire performances of the song, "I never know whether I like those things. There was a lot to take in."

When she had booked the visit, Portia had not realized how outrageous Burns had been, and had begun to wonder whether it had been an appropriate outing for her mother. Karen, however, seemed to be taking it in her stride.

On their way out they came across a pod the size of an airport body-scanner, shaped like an upright egg and covered in a leopard skin print. It produced a 3D model of whoever stepped inside, wearing a Burns outfit that you could choose from a list of options. Normally there was a charge for generating the little mini-me, but the Brytely VIP tickets meant they got them for free.

Exiting via the gift shop, mother and daughter collected their statuettes. Portia had gone for the elegant black satin number with a long dark wig, and Karen sported the purple coat and crimped 80s big hair, as she thought that would be most flattering. "I can't say I wasn't tempted by the body stocking!" she chuckled. "But I don't want to scare the horses."

As the day passed, they became more comfortable in each other's company. Away from her mountain of responsibilities, Karen was allowed to be the funny, happy person Portia had almost forgotten about. She decided not to ask about her father. It was too big a topic. That would have to wait until another time. They were having such a nice day, and she had already ticked the worrying question of the antidepressants off her 'must know' list.

In no time, it seemed, they were back at Euston scanning the departures board for the next train to Liverpool.

"Have you got a mask, Mum?" Portia asked, as Karen scrolled through her device to check the seat reservation. She didn't want her to pick up anything nasty on the train.

"I don't need one, Paula. The arcade makes sure all our vaccinations are up to date. It's one of my perks. Gambling's a key worker industry these days, don't you know?"

Portia was reminded of the gulf that would separate them once Karen got back home. Where they spent their working hours – and pretty much everything about their lives – could not be more different. "I wish you could find something else," she said.

"Like what?"

"I dunno. Something creative, like I do. Or to do with fashion. You've always had a great eye and you're brilliant with the sewing machine. You should get it out again."

"So, you couldn't tell this is homemade, then?" she gestured to her elegant dress and matching coat. That explained why they fitted so well. She had made them to measure.

"Never! Wow. I had no idea. You should do something with that. People down here would pay a lot for that kind of thing."

"Nice idea, love, but with three small kids in our tiny place working from home would be a non-starter. No, I'm all right as I am. Now, don't you worry and get home safely." She thrust some notes into her hand.

"I can't take this, Mum!"

"Yes, you can. You've paid for everything. Get yourself something nice, eh? Thank you so much, our kid. It's been great. Don't work too hard. And don't worry about that boy. If it's meant to be it will happen. Love you, our Paula."

With one last hug, Karen was on her way. As her Mum disappeared towards the platform, Portia was overcome with emotion. What had she just said? Boy? What boy? Then it dawned on her. She must have told her about Sonny when she was drunk. It couldn't have been any other boy, could it? Wondering what on earth she could have said, Portia stuffed the notes into her pocket and headed off to pick up a car. Tomorrow, she would have to find a way to get the money into a bank. She did not know anywhere in London that still took cash.

CHAPTER TWENTY

Jess: Hi Lexi. Sorry not to have been in touch for a while. Nicky's had a bit of a breakthrough. We think there's something you can help with. Is now a good time for a chat?

Lexi: Yes. Sorry I was bit ratty last time we met.

Jess: It was nothing compared to some of our constituency meetings. You'll have to try much harder than that to put us off. So, we have some good news. The HELP Select Committee are going to start taking evidence on Rockstar Ending. They are putting out a call this week.

Lexi: HELP?

Jess: Health, Euthanasia and Legacy Planning. They want to know if it is all …well, going to plan.

Lexi: I suppose it depends on what you think the plan is. Do you want me to submit something? I thought you said it would be too dangerous for me to talk about the stuff I saw in January. It's all still pretty vivid I have to say. Has something changed?

Jess: No. It's not your evidence we were thinking of, for all the reasons we already discussed. Do you think you might be able to work with Liz to get something in from her? Do you remember Liz? She spoke at the PACE conference. The first one Nicky helped. Liberated. Whatever you want to call it – anyway, her.

Lexi: Why me?

Jess: Well, you can be pretty persuasive. I can give you a steer on the procedural stuff. You have more chance of getting her to do it than anyone else we can think of.

Lexi: OK. Introduce me. I'll see what I can do.

CHAPTER TWENTY-ONE

"THIS HAD BETTER BE GOOD," Rex snapped as Faye led him into the small, soundproofed glass box behind his desk which was always kept free for his exclusive use. It was an annoying anomaly in the overstretched and chaotic room booking system, which was egalitarian in that it frustrated everyone. Unless, of course, you were Rex who had private space on tap. "I'm supposed to be in the car on my way to the CBI. Five minutes."

"Listen to this."

She clicked on the sound file hosted on the paper's preferred encrypted platform and let it play. The device sat on the table between them. Neither sat down. At first there was what just sounded like wind. Rex looked at her impatiently, making a winding signal with the forefinger of his right hand that told her to hurry up.

A woman's voice broke through.

"This is Nicky Hartt. The MP. I was in touch with you last year about the Rockstar Endings."

"Yep."

The sound quality was poor, but it was still possible to make out the words.

"I can get it cleaned up later," Faye said quickly as the wind noise rose again.

"Who's the bloke? I recognize the voice, but I can't place it." Rex was pacing around the tiny space now, but at least he was paying attention.

Faye shuffled sideways, folded her arms, planted her feet firmly, and leant against the door. "It's Mason. Don't tune out. You've got to hear this."

Rex groaned and waved his arms in frustration. "Not again! Why can't you leave the poor man alone?"

Slowly and deliberately, she told him: "Because there's a story in it."

As a concession to Rex's short attention span, she fiddled with the sound app for a second to move the file forward to the point where she had already dropped a marker.

"I told you this would turn out to be something. Listen. This is it, I think."

Nicky's voice was clearer now.

"So, the bad news is I've got five more of them. Only this time they were already – what's the nicest way to put this – in the process?"

"In the process? What do you mean?"

"You haven't heard?"

She fast forwarded the tape again. The app made the sound of an old-fashioned cassette deck whirring as it accelerated towards the spot. Intended to be a reassuring feature, the noise now helped her play for time with Rex.

"Can you get your guys to call off the dogs? The five of

*them, essentially, they've done the same thing as Liz. They've
decided they want to stay alive, after all, even though they
had signed the contract that said they were committed to an
Ending. Can you make sure no one comes after them?"*

Faye snapped her device shut purposefully. "You
surely can't still think there's nothing in this? She's talking
about people being forced to go to the Disposal Center.
It's the place where they get euthanized, in case you had
not managed to work it out. Forcing them to do it? That's
not how it's supposed to work."

Rex looked like he would do anything to get out of
the room. "I really have to get going. What is it you want,
Faye?"

"I want to clear a few days to do some more research.
Maybe at home so I can get a good run at it, undisturbed."

"To do what?"

"I want to track down some of the people who've seen
inside the DC if I can. Talk to them about what happened. Put some pressure on The Corporation to disclose
more, so we can see what this is all about."

He took a step towards her, indicating that she should
stand aside from the door. As she shifted – he was the boss
after all – he turned to her and looked threatening.

"You need to tell me where this tape has come from."

"If I knew, Rex, I would. It was sent anonymously
to the secure drop with an embedded time tag placing it
bang on the hour Mason would have been getting angry
on his way to the slopes. If it's a fake someone has gone to
a lot of trouble. It can't be."

"Is this an exclusive?"

"According to the cover note, yes. They are giving us

a month to run it. After that they'll offer it to another media outlet."

"What about payment?"

"Crypto."

"So where has it come from? Either the MP taped the call. Or it was someone with access to her phone. Or Mason – or one of Mason's closest people."

"It would seem those are the options." Finally, he seemed to be getting it.

"So, what do you want to do next?"

"Before we let The Corporation know we've got it, I want to corroborate some of the other details. Find out who Liz is. Who the five are, where they are now."

"It's personally identifiable information, you know," Rex said, softly. "Get a legal opinion, will you?"

"Sure."

"Today?"

"OK."

"You've got until the end of the week. Come back in and let's have a look at what you've got then."

It only took Faye a few minutes to leave the office. She could have gone right away but she didn't want to end up in the elevator with Rex. That was enough close proximity for one day.

When she reached the station near her South London home, she decided to pick up lunch from the coffee place as there was no queue. The spring sunshine heralded warmer, brighter days. A few affluent-looking individuals sat out on a handful of pavement tables for one, swaddled in their puffers, with the hexagonal stitching and shot-silk effect intelligent fabric reflecting iridescent, contrasting winter shades in the sun. The lids of their laptops were uniformly angled down to stave off the glare. A few of them were wearing sunglasses.

Faye would have loved to join them, but she couldn't risk being overlooked or overheard. Instead, she settled at her favorite workplace in the flat, her breakfast bar, which looked out on the back garden she shared with the other two households in the converted, four floor Victorian terrace. She instantly regretted buying the ciabatta. It took jaws of steel to bite into it, and the crust scraped the roof of her mouth raw. Reaching for the tap, she ran some cold water into a bulbous glass, which she swilled around her sore palate, before washing down the scratchy crumbs.

A good place to start was the transcript from her meeting with Mason that had taken place the previous year. As far as Faye was concerned, the interview had gone well. She had been pleased with herself for getting him to agree to see her in the first place. With careful engineering, she had suggested it after bumping into him at the champagne reception at the annual Giants of Industry Technocracy Society dinner in one of the City of London livery halls. A few weeks' wrangling had followed with Mason's director of corporate affairs, Channelle, who in the end had been helpful in making it happen, providing Faye with a solid set of background facts that saved her time.

After the story was published, however, she got a call telling her that Mason had been disappointed by something she had written. She was experienced enough to guess what was coming. It had been impossible to resist putting in a cheeky aside about his good looks and was surprised when it survived the edit. Rex was on paternity leave that week, and his deputy had nodded it through. At least she hadn't used the nickname she had picked up from one of his rivals. The ELF. Like MILF, only the Executive version.

"His physical presence is remarkable," Faye had said, in her defense. "I stand by my assertion that his looks are almost too good to be true. Most people would be delighted if a journalist put that in a profile piece about them."

"You're writing for a serious media outlet, Faye, not BunsNet!" Rex had whispered angrily, from outside a birthing yurt in the grounds of a private hospital somewhere in the West Country, after news of Mason's displeasure reached him.

The question that bugged Faye most was who would dislike Mason enough to send her the tape? She began systematically searching for organizations and individuals that had been involved in building the campaign for active euthanasia. Then she started looking at their opponents.

Surely Nicky Hartt wouldn't be so naïve as to send her an illegal recording of a conversation, made without Mason's consent, even if it could be argued that it was in the public interest?

The Yuthies were capable of anything, but they would have no motive for undermining this smooth operator. He was quietly delivering their showcase program. And how could they get hold of the tape, in any case?

Then she remembered something her colleague Jack had said to her last Summer. It must have been around July. He was a public sector watcher who often covered HELP. One Monday morning he had arrived in the office seeming preoccupied. He said he had been at an activists' conference over the weekend and wanted to draft a nib for the diary column. But in the end, he hadn't been able to persuade Rex to let him write it. Perhaps he might have something she could use. She got him on the phone:

"I'm just trying to remember," Jack said, "It was PACE – People Against Coercive Euthanasia. They were very vocal in the run up to the Act being passed, but after they lost it took them a few years to regroup. It knocked the stuffing out of them a bit."

"What about Nicky Hartt? Was she there?"

"Yes, she was. She had come to it all a bit late, really, but she was on the platform. Nicky's not a militant pro-lifer at all, though. Very reasoned. I didn't stay all day. Media were only allowed in the morning session, before the workshops began. They had some interesting stats, and some surprising research they had commissioned themselves. That was what I wanted to write about, but Rex wasn't up for it. It's impossible, even now, to get much out of the government on how it's going. The thing I remember most about it was how worried they all seemed about coercion and being watched. Not one of them had their phone with them. They seemed genuinely worried."

"So, they were quite tech-savvy, then?"

"That, or paranoid. Or both." Jack laughed a little. "If you want to find out more, I'd have a look at the PACE website. They're organized. If anyone knows what's going on with The Corporation's role in the Endings campaign, I can tell you now, it will be them."

By 5.30pm Faye had read everything she could find about PACE and subscribed to their mailing list using an alias. Usually she had little time for pressure groups, but Jack's recommendation was enough to get her to take this one seriously. She had downloaded a leaflet offering suggestions for people who were worried about a friend or relative being coerced into voluntary euthanasia. It contained some interesting suppositions. Finally, she had trawled through the profiles of their board members, which included a human rights lawyer called Henry; David, a retired civil servant with an OBE for public service, whatever that was; and a Catholic priest whose parish was only fifteen minutes' walk from her flat. She put a big yellow highlighter mark through his name, picked up her coffee cup for a refill, and decided she would pay Father Aloysius a visit.

CHAPTER TWENTY-TWO

S HE COULDN'T BELIEVE HER LUCK. Not only was it another bright spring day, but she had a legitimate reason to work from home and an excuse to venture out so she could get in a walk to punctuate her morning. Plus, she was working on something all her instincts told her could turn out to be massive.

Lazarus House, though? What a creepy name. That Bowie video gave her nightmares. Especially the bit where he was desperately writing to his final deadline. Too close to home. Mind you, Catholics had nerves of steel when it came to marshalling the macabre. On holiday in Southern Italy, she had come across a statue of a female saint holding a plate which had something on it that resembled a Muppet. How oddly anachronistic, she had thought, naively, as she tried to work out the story behind the two googly eyes floating around on a pile of pink stuff. It was only when she looked up the statue on her device that she had discovered it represented Santa Lucia, who was known for carrying around her own disembodied eyeballs as a symbol of how much she had been willing to sacrifice to maintain her chastity. Let's hope Father Aloysius didn't have one of those nasties hanging around the presbytery.

Of all the things she might have expected as she approached, however, the sound of David Bowie's 'Let's Dance' blaring out of a ground floor window was a long way down the list. Wrong album, she thought. Surely, they should be playing 'Blackstar'?

Humming along, she rang the doorbell, and detected a pulse of light from a security camera that bathed her face for a second. The music became quieter and a disembodied, elderly female voice responded through the speaker. "Hello. Who is it?"

"My name's Faye. Is Father Aloysius there?"

She heard the voice say, "It's a lady for Al. Does anyone know where he is?"

After a muffled aside which she could not make out, there was some more information.

"Sorry, dear. You might catch him over at the church."

A faint click signaled that the person on the other end had abandoned their interaction and the music cranked back up. She couldn't help wondering what the neighbors thought.

It was easy to spot the church, just across the road. She found the priest just as they had said. He was kneeling alone in the front pew with a rosary in his right hand, his head bowed, the dog collar making his orange hair bristle a little at the back of his neck. He was much younger than she had expected him to be. What kind of a name was Aloysius, anyway?

From a spot by the entrance she observed him for a while. It was cold now she was out of the sun, a salutary reminder of the capriciousness of London's weather. She glanced around to see whether there were any colorful saints on show that she might recognize, but decided they must be getting ready to decorate, as all the statues and pictures were covered up. In the narthex, near where she stood, there were a few Catholic newspapers scattered around, along with leaflets about predictable topics and a stack of hymn books. It was a while since she had been anywhere so peaceful.

She put down the reusable coffee cup she was planning to fill on her way back home and flicked through some of the reading material. A hymn called 'Faith of Our Fathers' caught her attention, which presented a heady mix of persecution, martyrdom and child sacrifice. She found it quite compelling but slotted the hymnal back before she became at risk of radicalization.

Back in the main part of the church, a woman in an orange coat came in through the side door and stopped directly in front of the altar. She bobbed a knee down to the floor and made the Sign of the Cross before stepping up to the altar and getting to work on polishing the brass candlesticks. Faye could still hear the music from over the road. It was the same album, only 'Modern Love' now, blaring on about religion.

Finally, the priest left the pew, genuflected and started heading at a surprisingly fast pace for the side door. As Faye couldn't tell where the exit led, she ran into the nave to catch up with him.

"Father Aloysius?" She hesitated over the pronunciation and went for Alloy-see-us.

He spun round and looked at her, slightly irritated,

before softly correcting her mistake. "It's pronounced Al-o-icious actually. Or Al if that would be easier."

"Sorry, I'd only seen it written down. Like delicious, right?"

"I'm guessing you aren't a Catholic, then?"

"Why's that?"

"Aloysius is a well-known Saint in our world."

"No, I'm not a Catholic."

"Were you thinking of converting?"

"No. Not really. I'm actually a journalist. My name's Faye."

The priest's face switched into the neutral expression he reserved for the moments when a parishioner said something he found shocking, but he did not want to appear overly judgmental. Not to begin with, at least. You had to let them get it off their chest.

"I'm doing some research on PACE. I think you're on the board?"

"That is correct. How do you think I can help you?"

"I downloaded a leaflet from the website."

"Do you need to speak to someone? I can put you in touch with one of our volunteers. They are all trained counsellors."

"Isn't that what you're supposed to do?"

"I'm more on the spiritual leadership side. Other people are much better at practical advice than me. I also have another appointment right now. You would be best to fill in the online form to get someone to call you back if you need support. They really are very good."

"Actually, there isn't a particular person I'm worried about. Not like that. Well not as far as I know." For the first time in a couple of weeks she thought about her parents, who were long overdue a visit. How was this priest able to make her feel guilty when 1) she had only met him minutes ago and 2) she wasn't even a Catholic?

"It's more general background on PACE for an article I'm working on."

"I suggest you have a look at the website. It's all on there. I'm not sure how much more I can add."

There was no harm in giving him a few clues. "I saw that PACE is worried about coercion."

"The clue's in the name," he chipped in. Was he trying to be funny, now?

"Indeed. I just wondered whether you might be able to give me some more background. Specific examples. Even better, if you could introduce me to someone who has been impacted? You make some serious and rather worrying allegations. I would love to talk to…"

He became brusque. She had pushed him too quickly. "I don't think I can help you with that, I'm afraid. The services we provide are confidential."

"Like the confessional?"

"Not really, to be honest. It's a different kind of thing. And I'm afraid I do have an appointment. You are welcome to stay in the church if you wish, but I must be on my way."

She had hoped he would say something enlightening, but it was clear he had no intention of giving anything away. Why did she get the feeling he was hiding something? Of course he was. He kept secrets for a living.

Ignoring his express wish to leave, she went on, "I

called at your house earlier. It was much noisier than I expected."

"Ah, my guests." He shrugged and folded his arms. "I really do have to go."

It felt like everyone was trying to get away from her. Rex yesterday, and now the one they called Al. "I'll hang on here a little while," she said, "Maybe I'll get the spirit, who knows?"

"Well if you decide you want to find out more about the faith, I can recommend an excellent online program to get you started. We keep our church open most of the day, so feel free to pop in and spend some time here. Once Lent is over you will be able to see the statues and so on. Quiet contemplation. We have been doing it for centuries – long before all those mindfulness apps started. There's too much new age psychobabble. We're the experts. Or the One True Faith, as we like to call ourselves. Goodbye, Faye."

He shook her hand rather formally and resumed the speedy exit she had interrupted. A few minutes later the music emanating from the presbytery fell silent. She assumed he'd had words with his guests.

Faye passed Lazarus House again on her way home. She took a few pictures with her phone from the opposite side of the road. A man was looking out of one of the top floor windows, as if he were waiting for someone. It wasn't Father Al. He looked old and frail. Not someone who should be bopping about to Bowie.

As she turned into the main road, it was impossible to see round the corner. A high wall obscured the view, and she was distracted by a beautiful cherry tree, heavy with pink blossom, that took up half the pavement. Even though she had slowed down, Faye almost collided with a man who was walking purposefully towards her. They only just avoided contact. After a few seconds of clumsy evasive footwork and a mumbled apology from both parties, she realized that she knew him.

"Cliff!" Just as well she hadn't said out loud the terms of abuse that had come to mind at the moment he had almost knocked into her.

"Hey Faye. Faye, hey!"

Cliff was Faye's drug dealer, although strictly speaking that was an outdated way to describe the service he provided. He had been operating a legitimate business in recent years, since he had managed to obtain a license from the council for small scale production of cannabis, on the condition that he sold most of it into the medical supply chain. The policymakers viewed it as a way of encouraging free enterprise, with light-touch regulation that allowed low-volume farmers to make a modest living without having to get involved with organized crime. Cliff had graduated as fully certified SCUM, holding the NVQ qualification in Small Cannabis Unit Manufacture (Level Two).

Joining the ranks of the official economy hadn't changed Cliff's appearance from when he'd started out in the business. There was no styling module on the course. When even the most experienced office workers struggled with what smart casual was supposed to mean, what was he expected to do? Wearing his usual army green canvas jacket, jeans and ponytail, today he had accessorized with a worn supermarket shopping bag that looked like it contained old clothes. She assumed he was running them over to the bank of recycling bins that were a few blocks away outside a small strip of fast-food shops.

"Haven't heard from you for a while," he said, always jovial. "Everything OK?"

"Yes. Good."

"Not at work today? That's not like you. You're normally a very busy lady."

"They're letting me work from home on something until the end of the week. Easier to concentrate, you know? Just popped out for some fresh air."

"Aha. I'm just dropping a few things round to my girlfriend's Dad."

She had never thought of Cliff as someone with any attachments. Then again, he probably regarded her the same way. Their relationship was simple. Transactional, discreet and infrequent.

"I'll let you get on."

It was not until Faye was almost outside the coffee place by Brockley station that she remembered she had left her reusable cup in the church, and turned back, finding it exactly where she had left it. Holding the worn beige thermal casing firmly in her hand, she glanced towards the altar where the cleaner had finished with the brass and was now vacuuming. Time to go. She needed to get moving if she was to make any more progress on the story today. Having drawn a blank with Father Al, there were other board members she needed to call, and maybe she would listen to the tape again to see if she had missed anything.

Rex had been right to query where the recording

came from, but she still had no idea. Could its source be Arabella from the chairlift who had called in the first feeble tipoff? No. Even if she had wanted to tape Mason, it would have been logistically impossible. How could she have done it without him noticing? In any case, the tape included both sides of the conversation. Faye had already asked the sender to consider going on the record, but they had bluntly refused. No reason to give up just yet though.

As she opened the heavy wooden church door, Faye realized she was in a perfect position to observe the priest's house without being seen. The old man was no longer at the window, and the loud music had completely stopped. All she could hear was the hum of the Hoover behind her which was edging closer.

It was easy to narrow the gap, leaving enough space to see the street without anyone outside being able to work out who she was. Her device vibrated. The media lawyer Rex had told her to consult was calling her back. She rammed it back into her pocket and left it to time out. She could get away with playing telephone tag for a few more days. Forgiveness afterwards was always her preferred approach. Once she established beyond doubt that the story would be in the public interest, it would be easier to get the backing needed to get it into print.

Faye could hear the vacuum cleaner getting closer and was beginning to worry about being asked why she was hanging around. A nervous glance back into the church reassured her slightly, as the woman was still at a distance.

What she saw when she turned her attention back to the presbytery came as a surprise. It was Cliff, walking out of the gate onto the street, only this time without the tatty carrier bag. He sped off at his usual jaunty pace back in the direction of the main road where they had almost collided not long before.

"Can I help?" The voice made her jump. It was the cleaner.

"I'm sorry, I'll get out of your way."

"Sorry about noise. I need to finish before children arrive. They come to pray before piano exam. Is today."

"Do they always pray before their exams?"

"Yes. If you heard them practice you know why." She smiled. "Sister Winifred makes them do it. She is very strict." The woman nodded approvingly. "It's what they need."

"I'll let you get on, sorry," Faye said. "Do you work anywhere else? I know someone who might be looking for a cleaner."

"No. Only for the church and priest's house. I fit it round school hours." She was tidying the newspapers and leaflets as she spoke.

"The music was loud earlier."

"Yes. They do exercise in the morning when Father Al is over here talking to God. Sometimes too noisy."

"They?"

"The guests. Father Al is very kind man. Always helping someone."

"Yes, he seems it." Faye was kicking herself for having retrieved so little information from the priest, but her confidence that the cleaner would be able to fill in any gaps was waning fast.

"I need to clean now." She had the plug for the vacuum cleaner in her hand and pushed it into a low wall socket. The motor immediately fired up, filling the small space with a loud whine that brought to a firm conclusion any chance of further discussion.

CHAPTER TWENTY-THREE

BRYN TIPPED THE CONTENTS OF the carrier bag onto the kitchen table and began sorting through the things Cliff had brought him. He had to hurry. Natalia would be back soon to prepare the sandwich lunch, followed by their regulation dessert – pieces of cut-up fruit. Always the same. Orange, apple and banana in small, bite-size chunks. Tap water. He knew he should be grateful that Father Al had taken him in, along with the other escapees, but he was becoming more restless by the day.

His old flat might have been tatty, dirty, and towards the end streaked with black smoke and tainted with unpleasant smells. But at least they had been his smells. If only he hadn't set the sausages on fire so many times, he would still be there now. How could he have let it happen?

Mainly, though, he missed Bailey. Bailey, Bailey, Bailey, he whispered under his breath. My Bailey. He knew it was delusional. He fully understood that Bailey was not a real person. But he could not get out of his mind the calm voice that had helped him find an answer for everything. Even if they had talked him into giving up his own life.

The temporary phones PACE had given the survivors to fulfil some of their most pressing communications needs had barred them from connecting with anyone at The Corporation. That meant Bryn could not reach Bailey. He was certain because he had tried every day. It had become a masochistic ritual in which attempting to connect was an unsatisfactory yet soothing proxy for the real thing.

Now things were going to get better. He knew he could rely on Jade and Cliff. They had salvaged his phone when they cleared his flat and had been hanging onto it for when he left Lazarus House. After two months without Bailey he was at his wits' end and had pleaded with them to bring him the phone. Now he would be able to do whatever he wanted without being spied on. Not by Bob and Father Al at any rate. Here it was. Cliff had even popped it into a neat pouch that had a marijuana leaf on the front, just like his favorite Amsterdam mug.

How exciting it would be to have a private portal to the outside world again. He would be able to watch what he wanted and listen to the music he chose instead of being cheered up non-stop by the happy-clappy playlist Bob had loaded onto the music server. Bryn did not know how things were going to work out for him, as the settlement was still being negotiated, but he was hopeful that he could get his life back to some semblance of normality and regain the independence and dignity he had taken for granted only three months before.

A child's lunchbox had fallen out of the bag too, big enough to hold a few grapes or a small piece of cheese. On the lid was a picture of the cartoon character Stitch.

It rattled a little when he shook it gently. Good. Cliff had not forgotten to put in the other supplies that were making Bryn popular with his new friends.

Until he started sharing a room with George at Lazarus House, Bryn had not realized how worn his own clothes had become. Now he was planning to stay alive, it was time to smarten up. Inevitably he compared himself to his roommate. Although George was always casual, and most often in sweats, there were no nasty holes or stains anywhere. That was what prompted Bryn to ask Cliff to find him some new menswear.

The clothing had come from a charity shop, but it still looked better than anything he had worn in the past five years. Looking forward to the Summer, he decided he would like to get a polo shirt or two. Now he had his phone, he would be able to access his bank account and get himself a few more small treats. One of the Knights of Saint Columba had tried to help by giving him a couple of shirts and pair of trousers, but they were not the right size, and without the belt there would have been a disaster. He was the wrong demographic entirely for the low-slung style. Furthermore, he didn't want anyone to see how threadbare his underwear had become.

He was planning to buy a gift for George to repay his kindness. Since their first morning George had brought him a cup of tea in bed every day and helped him with practical tasks like dressing if he needed it. Although he tried to put on a brave face, George could be very up and down. At night George sometimes had dreadful nightmares, but he would never talk about them in the morning. After his roommate woke screaming in terror,

Bryn would reach for the bedside light and chat with him about football until he was calm enough to go back to sleep.

Bryn folded the new clothes, hid the charger inside the pile, and slid everything back in the bag on top of the lunchbox before hooking it onto his walking frame. He had put the phone in his pocket so that he could make the call he had been anticipating for months as soon as he could find a private enough place. That was another problem at Lazarus House. There was always someone snooping around.

It would be harder than usual to sneak off today because there was going to be a meeting about their compensation claim after lunch. All the bigwigs were coming. He was not looking forward to it. It had been dragging on forever. He wished they had taken the first offer, but they had decided to stick together and his voice had been drowned out.

Mavis was the worst. She was getting increasingly excited, as if she were about to get a big win on the premium bonds. It was hardest for Mabel. In spite of Doctor Dom's best efforts she was in pain a lot of the time, but Cliff's delivery included a little something to help. Bryn would try to engineer being alone with her later.

After Natalia had cleared away the lunch things and George had helped her wash up, Father Al brought some of the dining chairs into the living room so there would be a place for everyone to sit.

Meg was there with her son who was visiting from America for a few days. Adam was tall, bearded, muscular and confident, with the beginnings of transatlantic intonation. What a credit he was to his mother, Bryn thought. She had been able to move back into her house not long after their escape. Meg was in the best position of all of them, with a cushion of money, her own place, and at least one big, handsome child who could drop everything and fly to her aid. She might have been one of the oldest among them, but she was probably the fittest. He looked at her slender frame clad in elegant lilac yoga wear that highlighted her bright blue eyes. She obviously had all her mental faculties, too. What on earth had possessed someone with all her advantages to book the Rockstar Ending? She could afford a limo anytime. He could understand it for some of the others. His friends in Lazarus House had all faced problems that often seemed insurmountable. But Meg? She would win a glamorous granny competition hands down if they were still allowed. And she wouldn't even need the prize money.

Henry, the lawyer, was running the meeting. He always had the paperwork up to date and was careful to brief them all on the latest from The Corporation. Today they had a special visitor who Bryn had not seen since the day they were rescued. It was their constituency MP, Nicky Hartt. She couldn't stay long, she said, as she had to get back to the House of Commons for a vote, but she had wanted to see them all to give them some news.

She tucked her blond bob behind her ears and looked around the room to make eye contact with each of them in turn.

"I wanted to update you in person on what is likely to happen next, in terms of public discussion of the Rockstar Ending program, and the services The Corporation provides to deliver voluntary assisted dying. We are likely to see an increase in media interest about what's been going on because I heard this morning that in a couple of weeks there is going to be a Select Committee hearing discussing some of the matters I have been raising with the Government."

"Does that mean it will stop?" Mabel asked anxiously. "I would hate them to take it away for those who need it. It's a good thing done in the right way. Especially for those in pain."

"We will never agree on that, will we, Mabel?" Father Al could never let it go. "We should be campaigning for this whole thing to end. Every life is sacred." Before the discussion could be diverted into yet another intractable and over-rehearsed debate, Nicky steered it back to the matter in hand.

"No Mabel, I don't think that's the intention at all. This particular hearing is to address the specific allegations about coercion, and the possible introduction of a proper escape clause. It's so people can change their mind more easily. We want to make sure that people like you won't need people like me to get out of it.

"I know about this because a lady called Liz, who I helped last year, has been called to appear. We're giving her some support through PACE. We're hoping she will be able to tell them about her experience. Some executives from The Corporation and their agency will be there to answer questions, too."

"What does this mean for our claim?" Mavis said, looking concerned.

Henry looked up and took off his glasses. "I would

say – and of course one never can be certain – but from my experience, this might make The Corporation more likely to increase their offer to you. The Committee is at liberty to arrange as many hearings as they like. At the moment they only have Liz as a customer witness. What sets Liz apart from our little group here, is that she was released before her departure date. She can talk about the emotional strain, which is not to be belittled, but her liberation happened before her life had been disrupted in the way you have experienced. She still has her home, for example, and above all, she has not faced the distress of waking up strapped to a trolley in a death factory. Not to put too fine a point on it.

"The Corporation will, in my view, do a lot to avoid having the inner workings of their euthanasia plant being described to the outside world. That is a rather vivid story that only the five of you can tell, and which The Corporation will want to avoid coming out at all costs. So, Nicky and I plan to use this development as another lever to persuade them to increase their offer of compensation."

"Sounds good," Mavis said, while everyone else listened intently.

Bryn, who was finding the lack of privacy at Lazarus House most difficult, even though he liked George, wanted to know what all of that meant for their chances of being rehoused.

"I'm afraid – well, I would advise at least – that it would be best for the four guests to continue to stay here for a while longer. As long as you are in temporary accommodation, it strengthens the case for you to get some help in finding somewhere new to live. Perhaps you could give some thought to an ideal outcome, that we could fold into the negotiations. The Corporation has access to a substantial estate. They own a number of dorms, should any of you wish to be cared for in that way."

"You're joking!" George huffed, although Mabel quietly said, "With one of their top end packages, a dorm could be a nice place for me. I'm very tired."

Henry asked them all to give him an idea of their preferred options for rehousing. "I think now would be a good time to see if we can get that factored into the settlement."

Father Al said that he would put some time aside to talk to each of them and promised to get their preferences off to Henry by the end of the next day. The lawyer had one final reminder.

"I know it's a strain, but could you all please remember not to disclose any details of your experiences to anyone outside of this immediate group while we are still negotiating? Going to the media is something to keep up our sleeve as a last resort, but Nicky and I are agreed that we would prefer to shield you from the public eye. The backlash from some of the more extreme Yuthies could be unpleasant. Death threats are not unheard of, however ironic that may seem in your own particular circumstances." He paused to see if anyone got the joke, but they just stared back blankly, so he went on. "Equally importantly, any disclosure could lessen your chance of a settlement. All of this will be contingent on you signing an NDA when we reach that point."

By now, Bryn felt like the phone was burning a hole in his pocket and needed an excuse to be somewhere – anywhere – on his own. As Henry and Nicky left, he announced to the group that he was going out for a walk, which he did a few times a week, usually popping into the cemetery which was their closest public space. It had a few benches where he could stop to recuperate during his gentle circuit.

As he edged his red walking frame along the road, he noticed a woman hanging around the entrance to the church and looking at her device. It was the same person he had seen when he had been looking out of the window earlier. She looked a bit too posh to be contemplating stealing the brass.

On reaching the graveyard, Bryn settled onto a seat between two huge stone angels. At last, he could do the only thing he had been thinking about all morning. He could scarcely recollect anything that Henry had said, so absorbed had he been in anticipating this moment. He eased open the Velcro on the soft pouch. The device sat in his hand, with its familiar chipped screen and badly scratched protector reflecting a slightly damaged version of his aging face back at him.

There it was. Bailey's speed dial. His heart was racing.

"Hello Bryn," said the familiar voice, "How lovely to hear from you. Have you had your lunch yet?"

His throat tightened and a single tear ran down his cheek.

"Bryn? Bryn? Are you there?" He loved it when they said his name.

"I'm here," he whispered tenderly. "I've missed you, Bailey." Intuitively, he already knew what they would say next.

"I've missed you too, Bryn."

CHAPTER TWENTY-FOUR

IT WAS THE MOMENT BOB had been dreading. He had no choice other than to tell the rest of the team about the alert.

When The Corporation had backed off from making direct contact with any of the escapees, he had been relieved. Now, out of the blue, this silly sod had set everything off again. How had he managed to get hold of his old phone?

I wish you hadn't made that call, mate, Bob thought to himself, as he faced up to the chain of events he would be obliged to set in motion. He would have to be extra vigilant not to let on how much he knew.

According to the protocol they had agreed, he fired off a quick message to the rest of the team, now codenamed Project Houdini, to tell them that one of the five escapees was back in touch with the Endings AI.

Next, he traced the location of the call, following the precise rules outlined in the comprehensive privacy waiver the customer had signed, guaranteeing him absolutely no privacy at all. It always went through on the nod.

Bloody hell, why is he in a cemetery? Choose life, old

chap! An icon appeared on the map showing a mugshot of an elderly man with a thinning white ponytail. His teeth were yellowish, although most of them still seemed to be there. You poor beggar, Bob thought as he looked at the innocent, badly shaven face, what have we done to you?

Naturally Bryn's entire conversation, which was still going on, was being automatically taped and transcribed. It was a small consolation to Bob that the AI had been reprogramed so that, if any of the five escapees reconnected, they would be put into a holding pattern and not permitted to re-book their aborted Ending. The business logic stacked up. The last thing The Corporation needed was all that fuss kicking off again. There was zero chance of this little gang of renegades being funneled back into the end of life pathway. For the time being, at least.

After the pressure from the MP, and the calls from the journalist, Mason had been adamant that The Corporation must not take any more chances with their reputation. He was going to be up in front of the Select Committee in a few weeks and wanted everything to go as smoothly as possible. The invitation to give evidence had focused his mind. Everyone could think of an example where a captain of industry had scored a catastrophic failure in the public eye at the hands of a few wily parliamentarians.

It had been agreed as part of the crisis plan that if any of the five reconnected with The Corporation, every effort was to be made to resettle them somewhere comfortable, where they could happily live out their remaining years without causing the company any further trouble. It was a tiny expense relative to the total market opportunity.

At a time when growth was hard to find, the shareholders would not appreciate any moves that risked derailing the highly profitable Endings income stream. Consequently, Mason was under strict instructions to convince the Select Committee that the company was acting humanely and always within the law. Safeguarding their dominance of the euthanasia industry was critical, especially now Phase Two was on the verge of being agreed.

Bryn's unsuspecting face on the screen made Bob sad at first, and then nervous. He could not afford to let his humanity get the better of him. This was a tricky enough situation already. So far, he had managed to keep his other identity, as a volunteer for PACE, secret from the business that provided him with his lucrative day job. He was intent on keeping it that way. If his bosses discovered that he had hacked into the DC and disrupted their operations it could lead to a prison sentence for industrial espionage. All he had wanted to do was to help Lexi save Meg, but he had ended up getting in deeper than he had anticipated.

As if it wasn't weird enough being seconded to help investigate a hack he himself had perpetrated, he had found himself working with Lars again. They had a troubled history. Bob had recruited Lars into his team at his old job at the bank, but Lars had turned out to be a catastrophic hire, making Bob's life so miserable that he had quit for The Corporation. Fortuitously, setting up the teen suicide prevention scheme within the schools' surveillance program had made both The Corporation, and Bob, an overnight success.

Now the loathsome creep had turned up working for the agency that had done most of the legwork on the

Rockstar Ending package. It was obvious to Bob that Brytely was over-dependent on Lars' specialist expertise. He was the only one there who could provide the answers to some of Bob's more technical questions.

Dealing with Lars had become easier since Bob accepted that he was a sociopath. It helped that Sonny hated Lars too. Bob could tell, even though the lad always tried to be professional. It was easy working alongside Sonny. He asked intelligent questions, listened attentively to Bob's lengthy technical explanations, and reciprocated by giving him the inside track on Brytely. Once, he had even shared with Bob the most delicious mango he had ever tasted.

Lars was heavily embedded in the Endings program, and his contacts with the Yuthies were much feted by the agency, who were maneuvering into position to support the dreaded Phase Two. Bob could only hope his secondment would be over once that kicked off, and he could get back to being a humble school surveillance guy. This double agent existence was doing his head in.

Right now, though, he had to deal with Bryn.

Lola was working from home, as her boiler had sprung a leak and she was waiting in for a repair, so Bob and Sonny dialed her on to a screen in a side room. They pulled up the map showing where Bryn was sitting.

"Can we listen in to the call?" Lola asked.

"Not live, no. We have to wait for the sound file to load and generate the transcript. Turnaround is about four hours." Sonny explained.

"Do we know where he is? Sorry I'm on audio only at the moment." There was some banging in the background. Bob thought of Harry Tuttle, one of his favorite movie characters, and the song 'Brazil' began to play in his head.

"The locator is showing him as being in a cemetery in the borough of Lewisham." Bob said.

"A cemetery? You couldn't make it up." Lola said.

Bob carried on. "I know. I wondered if his wife is buried there, but it's not the kind of detail we would keep in his record. The AIs access lots of intimate background but they don't retain the details after they have processed them. It would take up too much space. And it could cause other problems no one wants."

She had more questions. "How did he get there?"

"We don't know that either. His mobility is impaired so he's either gone by car or walked a short distance. He can't get very far."

Then, before Bob could say anything else, the dot with Bryn's face on it disappeared. "What the...?"

Lola could not see. "What's happened?"

"The dot's gone." Sonny chipped in.

"What does that mean?"

Bob thought for a second. "Either he's smashed the phone up, which I doubt he would have the strength to do, or he's put it in a Faraday pouch."

"A what?"

"You know. It stops radio waves getting through. Puts the phone off the grid."

"Can you find him any other way?"

"Maybe I could get a live feed from one of the delivery drones that ferry the sedatives out to the Angels. Let me see if we have any nearby."

Bob called up another screen and typed in a few commands. A grid unfolded which he superimposed on the map surrounding the area where Bryn had been until a few seconds before. In one corner of the screen was a simple drawing of a paper plane with a circle on it that resembled the electronic eye of Hal, the rogue supercomputer in *2001: A Space Odyssey*.

"You're joking," Bob muttered under his breath.

"What was that?" Lola was clearly struggling to follow without a visual feed. "Typical that this comes in on a day I'm not in the office."

"I'm not very good at piloting these things. It's just made the final drop off. There are no controlled drugs on board so we should be able to override. I'm just not sure I can hold it steady," Bob said.

"Let me," Sonny became unusually animated. He had finally found a way to help by doing something no one else in the room could do. "I took my drone pilot license just after college. I think I still have the – yes there it is – I have the app on my phone that turns it into a 3D pilot handset. It looks like it's up to date. Is that the Unique ID?"

He typed the string of letters and numbers associated with the paper plane into his handset. Then he turned it on its side. It became a drone controller.

"You might want to have a look at the security. That was horribly easy," Sonny said, as he linked with the screen on the wall. Suddenly he was hovering above a South London street with his co-pilot Bob, with Lola back in Mission Control. They looked out through the screen that filled half the wall as if it were an aircraft canopy. "Shame we haven't got time to set up headsets," Sonny said. Bob had never seen him so confident. "This would be great in VR. Do you know what all those dials mean? This is different to the one I used at the aerodrome."

"I'll look it up on the web now. Can you steer towards where we last saw Bryn?" Bob asked.

"Bryn?" It was the first time that Sonny had heard of him.

"Yes, that's his name, Bryn. The old boy. He was in the cemetery up on the right."

As Sonny made smooth movements with his handset, the drone left its pre-programed route back to the Disposal Drugs Depot (known to Corporation insiders as the triple D) and followed the new course. A red light flashed in the corner of the screen with the words *route change*.

"It will be sending a hijack alert to the drone control center," Bob said.

"Bit late!" Sonny laughed.

"I can get it cleared," Lola said. "Text me the ID, will you?"

The drone had reached the main road and was skirting the edge of the buildings, about a meter out from the walls, which followed the gentle curve of the pavement, at about four floors from the ground. The buildings were largely Victorian terraces with a hotchpotch of food outlets and convenience stores at the bottom, and flats on top. Young trees were in bloom below. Occasionally a light gust of wind rippled through the pink and white blossom and gently buffeted the drone. Bob started to feel seasick. Ahead, they could see the cemetery.

"We're nearly at the spot where he was last sighted,"

Bob said so that Lola could follow what they were doing. "What do you want us to do?"

There was silence.

"Lola?"

"Sorry I was on mute." Loud clanging in the background explained why she had turned off the speaker. "Can you work out where he's going?"

"We'll try."

Bob got his device out ready to snap anything that came up on the screen.

"One of the dials has gone amber," Sonny said, "Can you check out what that means?"

"I'll have to find the manual. Why do they put all the instructions on video? I haven't got time to sit through twenty minutes."

Bob kept scrolling while Sonny took the drone towards the gates of the cemetery. It was busier than he had expected it to be. A few dog walkers were going in and out. Then, edging slowly across the pavement, they saw Bryn with his red walking frame, heading for the crossing. Bob took a snap of the screen just as the amber indicator Sonny had mentioned turned red and started to flash.

"Have you found out what that warning light means yet?"

"Sorry, this must be a new model. I'm trying."

One of the dog walkers was standing next to Bryn now, a young black man in one of the hexagonal puffer coats, accompanied by a massive Japanese Akita. They chatted for a minute. It looked like Bryn was asking if he could stroke the dog. It sat perfectly still as the old guy rubbed its massive, soft head, smiling.

Bob grabbed the table. He had a strong falling sensation.

"Oh shit," Sonny said, as the picture on the screen switched from one of serenity to rapid freefall. He shook the phone. "It's not responding."

At that point, the screen went black.

"I think we just found out what the red flashing light means." Lola was going to have to call in some more favors from her friends in the drone team.

CHAPTER TWENTY-FIVE

A SIREN ON THE MAIN ROAD jolted Faye's attention. It prompted her to decide that she had spent enough time observing the comings and goings at Lazarus House for one day, and to start making her way towards the source of the noise. She had gathered plenty of information and wanted to get home to try to make sense of it.

On reaching the junction, she found a police car parked diagonally across the road. Officers were directing traffic around an area on the tarmac that had been taped off with a sagging blue and white plastic ribbon. Drivers beeped their horns impatiently until they got close enough to catch sight of the debris and the frail old man sitting on the pavement being attended to by a paramedic. A big dog lay with its head in his lap, while its owner, who had clipped the leash to his jacket, took video footage of the scene. Nearby, a red walking frame lay on its side.

A small vehicle arrived and parked on the side street. Two women got out. They wore an unbranded navy uniform, with thick, matching gloves and eye protection. Each one carried clear plastic sacks and an array of lightweight industrial cleaning equipment. They walked purposefully to the main road, crossed the police tape and immediately set to work on clearing the debris away.

Faye snapped a couple of pictures as the clean-up operation began, noted the registration of the car, and walked over to where the injured party was being looked after. She asked the young guy next to him, who held the dog's lead, what had happened.

"One minute we was chatting. He was looking a bit vague. I was going to see him safely over the road. Then the next thing this drone falls out of the sky," he said. "Crazy."

"Do you know him?"

"No, we were just talking about my dog."

"It's beautiful."

"Yeah, my boy." He smiled as they watched the dog nuzzle Bryn gently, "He likes the old guy. In fact, he likes pretty much everyone."

"He's almost bigger than him." Faye smiled before casually adding. "Did you get it on camera?"

"Nah, it was all too quick. Just snapped the wreckage. They're cleaning it away now. It's coming up for school pick-up time so they'll want to get the road back to normal."

"Did it hit him?"

"Just bounced off the walking frame. My boy went mad, though. He got hit by a drone at a dog show a few years ago, so he's not exactly a fan."

The dog looked up, as if it knew it was being talked about, and then settled back down as the old man stroked its head again. "You're lovely, aren't you?" he said. "I could take you home with me, if I only had somewhere to put you."

Faye eyed the clean-up squad as they swept up the fragments of hard plastic. "They're in a bit of a hurry," she said. "Some might say this is a crime scene. I don't see the police doing much about it."

The dog walker shrugged. "He's not interested in compo. I said I would be a witness. Might change his mind."

She looked down at the old man who was now sitting up straight and asked the paramedic if she was going to be taking him to hospital.

"No need. He's going to be fine," she said. "Just a bit shocked, aren't you, Bryn?"

"I've lived through much worse. I'll be on my way in two ticks. Only live round the corner," he said, still stroking the dog. "Just give me another minute with this lovely fellow."

He looked up at Faye and asked, "What are you doing here?"

Before she could think of a reply, the paramedic said, "Do you know him?"

"Not really."

"You called at my house this morning," Bryn said. "I saw you."

He was the one who had been looking out of the window.

"Oh, yes. I was looking for Father Al."

"Why were you hanging about in the street like that?" Bryn eyed her suspiciously.

Faye pretended she had not heard the question as a

police officer came over to tell them they were about to reopen the road. The drone debris was all cleared away. They needed to move Bryn up off the edge of the pavement, so that he would be clear of the traffic. Gently, the paramedic helped him to his feet, presented him with his walker which was a little scratched but otherwise perfectly OK, and guided him back a few paces. The Akita took its position at the heel of its owner.

"Well, Bryn, I think you could be good to go." The paramedic touched his arm. "Will you be OK getting back?"

He reassured her that he would be fine, but still allowed the policewoman to see him across the road. The countdown crossings didn't always give him quite enough time.

Faye watched him edge his way back towards Lazarus House, one push at a time. The dog walker had gone. Before leaving, she had one last question for the policewoman. "If you don't mind me asking, is this a crime scene?"

"My priority is to get the traffic moving again. UAVs come down all the time. It's my third one this week. If you think we have time to investigate every skirmish with a drone you've been watching too many mini-series. This is South East London, darling, not Roswell."

CHAPTER TWENTY-SIX

THE FOLLOWING MORNING, FAYE'S LATEST idea, to book a Rockstar Ending for herself, fell at the first hurdle.

Without her unique government ID, proving she was old enough to qualify, she could not generate a login for the portal. All she had to go on from The Corporation was the ads they had been running on social media, which she managed to watch through an incognito browser. There were no clues in their financial results either. More than one call to long-suffering Channelle drew a blank.

She toyed with the idea of paying a random old person to sign up so she could follow their progress, but it felt too risky. She certainly wouldn't ask one of her parents. If this thing was as powerful as some suggested, she could be putting them into a potentially life-threatening situation. Rex would go mad if he found out, and even madder if someone she recruited ended up – what was the phrase Nicky had used on the tape? In the process.

Mason was a superb target for a story, if only she could find a way to make something stick. He was photogenic, handsome and, so far, had a reputation that was completely unsullied. The perfect candidate for an exclusive exposé. Even his fundraising page for the New Year's Day Triathlon managed to avoid looking smug, which was quite a feat. Someone obviously had it in for him, though, or they wouldn't have sent her the tape, would they? All her attempts to reconnect with the source, however, had ended in silence.

She was under no illusions. It was going to be a tough job to land whatever she wrote with Rex. He rarely took anything she said seriously. And the feeling was mutual. Now and again she accidentally let him glimpse her contempt which had, on one occasion, prompted him to say, "Do you have to look at me like I'm a complete idiot?"

Fortunately for Faye, her boss knew it would look terrible if he lost one of the few journalists on staff who had won a prestigious award, even if it was a while ago. In spite of him, she missed the banter in the office and was surprised how much she was looking forward to going in again after five days at home. If only she had more to show for her efforts.

It was time to systematically revisit every source, starting with the MP's researcher, Jess, who had called her at the beginning of January. The email Jess had sent was still in her inbox, unopened. Luckily, she hadn't deleted it. There wasn't much in the note other than her contact details, including a mobile number.

"Hi, Jess, this is Faye? We spoke a couple of months ago about Mason and the Rockstar Endings program."

There was the sound of an industrial coffee machine screeching in the background, and she could just about make out The Bangles 'Manic Monday' playing softly among a low hubbub.

"Hi Faye. Sorry about the noise I'm just having breakfast with Nicky."

"Look, I wanted to take you up on your offer to have a chat about the Endings thing. Sorry it's taken me a while to get back to you." It didn't cross her mind to ask whether it was convenient to talk.

"Let me just tell Nicky. Hang on." The phone went on mute. Faye listened to a regular pulse of inane beeps designed to reassure her that she had not been forgotten. She did a quick search for Nicky on her desktop and found her Splutter feed full of pictures of her in her constituency, smiling beneath her trademark blond bob and sporting a bright pink lipstick. She looked personable, professional and just glamorous enough to still be accessible. Some feat for a politician.

"Nicky here." The soundscape was different. Faye guessed she had stepped outside.

"Thanks for taking the call. I hadn't expected to speak to you in person."

"How can I help?"

"I've been looking at this Rockstar Ending thing. I could do with talking to someone who's an insider. Either who has worked for The Corporation or been through the process. I've been sent some information suggesting that you have helped some customers cancel their bookings, reversing the irreversible, as it were. Is that true?"

"It is, yes."

"Could you put me in touch with any of them?"

She refused point blank. "Absolutely not. It's all too painful for them."

"Obviously we would protect their anonymity, if that was a condition of them talking to me."

"Have you heard of PACE? They have a lot of good information on their website."

Not that again.

"I do have something that might help, though."

"Yes?"

"It's Mason. He has been called to give evidence to the HELP Select Committee. And he's going to do it in person."

That was more like it. "Seriously? When?"

"End of the month. And they have also summoned one of my constituents, a woman called Liz. I helped negotiate her release."

"You're certain this is going ahead?"

"Definitely. You are safe to run it."

It was not the scoop of the century, but at least she had given her something small she could use. Channelle confirmed, off the record, what Nicky had told her, but Rex started dragging his feet over publishing it. Rather than wait for a rival media outlet to beat her to it, Faye decided to pop the snippet up on her own Splutter feed. She was tired of asking permission and being given the runaround by a man who wouldn't recognize a story if it sat on his chest and slapped him in the face. Her colleague Jack sent her a nice message right away and was the first to share it.

When formal confirmation of the hearing appeared a few hours later, there was another detail Faye had not expected. Alongside Mason and Liz another person was scheduled to speak. It was Stella, the CEO of the agency that had come up with the Rockstar Ending concept.

Faye could not believe her luck.

She would be seeing Stella in two weeks' time, as they were both on a judging panel for the Strong Women Achieving in Business (SWAB) awards. The night before the Select Committee Hearing, they would be ploughing through the interminable shortlist in a stuffy conference room at a West End boutique hotel.

Rex made Faye do a few judging gigs every year, always linked with a sponsorship designed to make them look like their business wanted women to succeed. Looking at the way things ran in the office, however, Faye regarded it as hypocritical femwashing. Not wanting to get involved in doing any of the work himself, he had sold her the idea of being a judge on the pretext that the networking would be useful. Until now, unfortunately, at such events she had only met people like herself, who had been sent along to make up numbers, and had very little influence.

This time, however, if she could get the right information out of Stella, it could turn out to be the first networking opportunity of her career that was worth the effort.

CHAPTER TWENTY-SEVEN

L IZ HAD REFUSED TO GIVE a statement when Lexi had first phoned her. But Nicky was right. Lexi could be very persuasive.

"It's all very difficult," she had whispered, after Lexi explained the circumstances. It was obvious she was walking out of earshot of somebody who she did not want to catch the conversation. A door clicked shut. "I'm still living with Carl, you see. Decided to give him another chance. He was furious when he found out I told everyone about his affair at the PACE Conference. I never thought the news would reach him, but someone from church was there and recognized me. The vicar pulled Carl in for a talking-to and is insisting on giving us counseling now. Carl says he's broken it off with her. He's said that before, of course, as you know. There's no reason I should believe him. But I do still love him, unfortunately. I want to try to make it work. Plus, we don't have any money other than the capital in the house. Splitting things now, when we have both retired, would be extremely difficult financially."

Lexi persevered until a couple of weeks later, Liz

finally agreed to meet her on neutral territory. It was Saturday morning. They met in the café at the adult education center where Liz had enrolled on a personal styling course as part of her project to win back Carl. She had decided she could no longer ignore his accusations that she 'looked like a frump' and the implicit suggestion that Rachel, his allegedly estranged other woman, did not and was therefore a more desirable prospect.

On arrival at the tatty old building, Lexi had been directed to a light room where a friendly woman stood behind a counter, wearing a pale blue overall, selling drinks and snacks to a queue of people who you would not see out and about in London very often. People with learning disabilities were there with their carers, along with a number of folks who had time for the luxury of learning something new. She could not see Liz anywhere.

A woman with a long sleek chestnut bob, dressed all in black, with slightly smudged mascara visible from behind silver hexagonal glasses, starting waving at her manically from the far side of the room. Lexi assumed she was trying to attract the attention of someone behind her and turned only to find no one there.

"Lexi?" the woman mouthed. Her face seemed a bit old for the haircut. It was then that she realized that it was Liz, looking nothing like the person she had seen at Toynbee Hall. Only the spectacles were the same.

"Sorry I didn't recognize you. You're completely different."

"I'm working on a new look," she said, "What do you think?"

"Well," Lexi was finding it hard to choose the right words, "It's striking."

"Carl isn't sure either. I can tell." Liz confided, "I'm no natural glamour puss. But you have to try, don't you?"

"You should do it for you, not for Carl, Liz!"

"It's the same thing, dear."

Over a shared KitKat and a cup of tea, Lexi steered the conversation away from Liz's idea of empowerment – which consisted mainly of experiments with wigs of varying shades – towards an edited story of her own involvement with PACE.

"Why do you care so much, when everyone else is writing off old people?" Liz asked. "I don't see why you're so bothered."

"Honestly? I think it's because I lost my parents quite young."

"I'm sorry, I had no idea."

"It was a long time ago. I don't often talk about it, but you asked. The least I can do is be honest with you about my motivation. And then the Rockstar Ending thing happened to someone I know, and I got involved in helping them. A bit like what Nicky did for you. The problem is that it's still going on. We want to find a way to make it easier to cancel without having to know someone amazing like Nicky who can work a miracle. Not everyone is so lucky."

Lexi deftly told Liz the stories of the other escapees, focusing on the human tragedy that had been averted while carefully skirting the details that could cause repercussions for her or Bob. "If we can work on a statement between us, I mean, I can help you. I can write it up and as soon as you are completely happy with it, we can send it in. We can even do it anonymously – well, we would have to say it was from you, but that wouldn't go on the public record. What do you think?"

The opportunity to keep her identity private clinched it for Liz. Within a week they had a draft statement. Jess helped finalize the wording and once Liz agreed it, Lexi read it through once more and was about to press the button when she got a message from Liz.

URGENT: El bastardo has done it again. Stick my name on it. I'll show him.

When, a month or so later, the HELP Select Committee decided to summon people to talk in person about their experiences, one of them suggested it might be a good idea to invite Liz. Her submission had been tight, readable and presented an opinion just enough at odds with the prevailing sentiment to make the committee appear balanced in their approach.

She agreed after Nicky, Jess and Lexi arranged a videocall to fill her in on the background. The committee chairman had promised Nicky that he would go easy on Liz and not allow anyone to drag up the details of Carl's infidelity, which was her main concern. Liz agreed that Lexi would check in with her the night before to help quell any lastminute nerves. By then, there was just one sensitive matter outstanding which Lexi said she would do her best to address.

"I think you need to go for the sympathy vote, you know, Liz," she began cautiously. "If you look too glamorous, they won't like it."

"But I'll be on the telly, won't I? Carl will be watching." They were still living in the same house, even though his philandering had continued. "Anyway, someone else might notice me!"

"It's Parliament TV, Liz, not a dating show. Only weirdos will be watching it. The only time anyone pays attention is if something mad happens – like if one of the PACE activists slings a custard pie at Mason. And we've told them not to. One or two of them are itching to do something like that to capture the public imagination, but they'll behave."

"But I love my wigs," Liz replied glumly. "They make me feel young again."

"That's a good thing. But that's not how you want to be remembered here. You want to seem frail and vulnerable. You are the only voice there for the old people. And you don't want to detract from what you are saying after we have all gone to so much trouble."

"It's all wrong. I should be free to be who I want to be." Liz was clearly on an emotional journey with her confidence and Lexi felt mean about steering her back to an aging persona, even for a few hours. But she simply could not let her wear one of those wigs. Combined with the smudged mascara and lipstick bleeding into the wrinkles around her mouth, she risked becoming a laughing stock. Lexi had to protect her from the cruelty that could result.

"Come on. The PACE activists won't believe it's you. You've changed so much since last summer. Give them a chance. Anyway, if you look too youthful they'll find it impossible to believe you signed up at all."

By the time they rang off, Lexi felt the odds were 50:50 on whether she had managed to coax Liz over the line. She sent her a final text before going to bed ('Old is beautiful'), and another the next morning: ('Wear your age with pride – just for a couple of hours!').

CHAPTER TWENTY-EIGHT

I BET HE'S GLAD THAT'S OVER, Faye thought.

With a final flourish, the chairman folded up his hexagonal reading glasses, and slid them into a matching iridescent green and gold padded pouch. It fitted snugly into the breast pocket of his jacket without leaving too unsightly a bulge.

She had no sympathy for him. He was creaming a nice little living out of his awards business. The price of a table at the ceremony and dinner was astronomical, but it gave the long list of shortlisted entrants the chance to give their employees and clients the impression that they might be doing a good job.

Unless she could find a plausible excuse, she would have to attend the big night herself in a posh frock. It would inevitably be in some massive soulless ballroom, fronted by a B-lister tasked with keeping the guests distracted while their lukewarm food congealed on its long trek from an institutional kitchen to their table of ten.

The meeting room was pleasant despite the complete absence of natural light. Every wall was covered with black and white wallpaper printed with 50s-style abstract patterns. A cast concrete fireplace formed a post-modern centerpiece. Elegantly mis-matched distressed wood furniture, upholstered in clashing jewel-colored velvet, had been strategically placed around the edges.

Faye wished they had put some padding on the chairs around the long central table where the judges were expected to sit for hours without fidgeting. Each one was cast in a different shade of opaque Perspex. They were rock hard and, although there was a slight variation in the shape of each one, they all had a nasty ridge that cut off the circulation at the back of the legs.

Furthermore, the lack of ventilation in their design produced a puddle of sweat which pooled perfectly around the perineum. By the time they were allowed to move, Faye had been stuck to her seat for more than two hours. Its unique shade reminded her of liquid Penicillin. She had glugged a whole bottle of the bittersweet medicine as a child. Mistakenly, she had thought it would get the doses over quickly if she knocked back the lot. Her Dad had called the doctor who provided reassurance and instructed him to pick up another bottle immediately so she could complete the course. So much for that bright idea.

Now the formal part of the judging session had come to an end, she and her five counterparts gingerly got to their feet. The blood returned to their lower legs in pulsating flushes of pins and needles. Dirty teacups littered the table. The bowls of jellybeans they had been provided with were down to the last couple of flavors. They had been shunned even by those brave enough to try them – an unpredictable poblano chili, and a ferocious blue cheese.

Faye could kill for an old-fashioned bourbon biscuit right now.

During the judges' meeting she had been trying to subtly ingratiate herself with Stella. It was difficult because she didn't seem to like any of the entries much. Still, Faye had gritted her teeth and been vocal in supporting some of Stella's criticisms, even when she could not quite follow the rationale. She even backed her up in an uncomfortable face-off with one of the other judges when they clashed over who should be voted into second place.

Faye had done her research to work out what motivated the woman who was to become her new best friend. With fewer than 24 hours to go until the HELP Committee hearing, she knew she was running close to the wire.

The most useful article she had found was in a journal called *Digital Uses for Persuasive Excellence*. There, Stella had been profiled next to an opinion piece about the difference affective chatbots could make to the bottom line. It included an oblique reference to the runaway success of an anonymized campaign targeted at the over-70s that sounded remarkably similar to Rockstar Ending. What frightened even someone as cynical as Faye, was that the article talked about tens of thousands of 'conversions'. It had only been running for a few months. No one in Government was giving out numbers. If that meant what she thought, Brytely had helped The Corporation to euthanize more old people in six months than COVID-19 had wiped out in the whole of 2020.

She found it difficult to reconcile Stella's real-world presence with the well-argued by-lined piece she had re-read in the car on her way there. Perhaps the judges' meeting hadn't brought out the best in her? If she were going to get anything useful out of her they would need to establish a rapport.

As soon as Faye had found out about Stella's invitation to give evidence alongside Mason she had dropped her a line, being careful not to give her any cause for alarm. The chummy note said how thrilled she was that they had both been selected as judges for the SWAB Awards, how she had heard marvelous things about Stella's leadership of the agency, and added that she had been wondering whether they might grab a quick drink after the judging panel had finished. It was a classic ego play, and it worked.

Waiters dressed in old-school tailcoats given a contemporary twist with two-tone shot fabrics, began to clear the debris and brought in a tray of champagne. Even though Stella and Faye, her echo, had made the meeting painful at times, the chairman graciously included them in his thanks, smiled warmly at everyone in the room, and handed them each a glass as if they had behaved impeccably.

"Sorry darling, I can't stop," Stella drawled, "Big day tomorrow with HMG. I'll just have the one." She drained the glass in a single gulp before turning to Faye and saying, "Are you coming now?"

It took a lot to embarrass Faye, but even she was mortified when Stella had been so brazen about necking the bubbles and unceremoniously dumping the rest of the party. She smiled weakly at the chairman, "I'm afraid we need to catch up on a couple of things. Hope that's OK." Scanning the rest of the judges she could already feel the room lightening with relief at the news that she and her fellow irritant were about to bail.

"God, that was tedious," Stella announced before they were safely out of earshot, "I do really have to be on top form tomorrow, Faye. Shall we just pop into my club? It's still early. Shouldn't be too busy. And it's only a short walk."

With Faye hanging just behind Stella's shoulder, the two of them slipped nimbly between the meandering tourists who clogged up the crowded Soho pavement. Like anyone who had ever worked in central London, they were experts when it came to cutting through the mass of strangers. There was a difference in height of a good six inches between them, only some of which was down to Stella's heels. She had a gift for making people feel small.

At the club, the manager waved them in immediately. "Stella, so lovely to see you again, and your gorgeous guest!" Was that real or passive aggressive? Faye remembered him from her previous visit, a private hire for a media event. He had been deliberately rude to her, striking her as the type who, whenever he thought no one else was looking, would seize the opportunity to cut you dead. On a cold night he particularly enjoyed making unremarkable visitors squash into the narrow, chilly space between the front door and the cloakroom, forcing them to give priority to the members who would oafishly push into them and stand on their toes.

Tonight, however, he was effusive to the point of making Faye wince. She imagined he had once aspired to being something big in musical theatre but got stuck in a job in hospitality that he had taken to pay the rent. As time went on, he had ended up channeling the hammy performances that led him to fail every audition into the business of toadying to Soho stalwarts, under the misapprehension that some of their minor celebrity might, one day, rub off on him.

"Any chance you could get us a quiet spot, Matty?" Stella asked as they peeled off their outer layers and handed them to a bored-looking attendant. Seconds later, they were settled into a two-person booth, with pale blue leather seats, separated by an egg-shaped table, with a drinks order on the way based on Matty's recommendation.

"How long have you been a member?" Faye asked, scanning the room to see if she knew anyone. There was someone by the bar she thought she recognized from a 10-year-old sitcom.

"A very long time."

"I bet this isn't your only membership."

"Correct. I don't use this place often now, to tell you the truth. It's rather shabby compared to some of the new places further East. Even South of the river. A few of my dinosaur clients are still impressed by the name, though."

Two Rockstar Riders appeared. They were long vodka-based cocktails, with colored layers, served in tall glasses over clusters of ultraviolet ice stars. A ramekin of blue Smarties was delivered as an accompaniment. There was just enough room on the table for their devices, which they placed facing upwards, without any apology.

Stella took a big swig, and Faye couldn't help thinking she was knocking it back like someone who didn't need to be up early in the morning.

They looked like an unlikely pair. Stella's clothes would have cost ten times what Faye was wearing – at least when they were new. The article in *DUPE* had mentioned Stella's penchant for rare vintage, so Faye had thought fashion might be a safe neutral topic of conversation. They certainly weren't going to be competing. Not with Faye in a mid-market online dress, opaque tights, trainers and a few cheap, generic accessories.

"I was admiring your shoes," she ventured. "I love that clear block heel."

"Yves Saint Laurent. Vintage."

"How do you find time?"

"I have someone who helps me curate my wardrobe. He has contacts everywhere. Buys at auction more often than not. It helps, of course, that I am a perfect eight."

Watching her packing away more drinks as the evening progressed, Faye suspected that Stella stayed that shape by never eating anything. She looked so toned. Maybe she just had the right genes? Faye wasn't in bad condition herself and had calculated that she must be at least ten years younger than Stella, and one dress size bigger, but that wasn't huge, was it? They established a little common ground with opinions on their experiences of living in London. Both of them had been to the exhibitions and shows that everyone was talking about, although Stella had mainly attended with clients, Faye alone or with one or two friends.

When the name Channelle appeared on Stella's screen, flagging an incoming call, she looked annoyed. Faye pretended not to notice. A message arrived a few seconds later, and Stella picked it up, her face stern.

"All OK?" Faye smiled.

"Yah." Stella made the device go dark, put it into her handbag and gave a sharp sigh. "I should probably make this the last one."

"Fair enough. What was it you said you had to do tomorrow?"

"It's a parliamentary thing. I'm helping out a client."

"That sounds above and beyond the call of duty. What's all that about, then?" Faye tried to sound like an old chum rather than a journalist.

"I'm appearing at the HELP Select Committee."

"Wow. Have you done one of those before?"

"No."

"Aren't you worried? They can be a bit hostile, can't they?

"Oh, there's nothing to worry about, Faye. It will be fine." Stella said quickly, her pace betraying a thinly veiled anxiety at odds with her words. She explained that she had been called to answer questions about the Rockstar Ending program, and that it was very much business as usual for the committee. Just one of their regular scrutiny hearings.

Faye raised her eyebrows. "I'm impressed, Stella. Rockstar Ending must be going well, if you're so relaxed about tomorrow."

"Oh yah. Very well indeed." Stella drained her glass and said, "Shall we just have one more?"

"Sure." She caught the eye of the waitress. Faye was glad she had a strong constitution. How many Riders had they had now? Was it five or six?

"The Endings. Remind me – how many have they done now, Stella? I don't think I can remember."

"You can't recall it because the number isn't public, darling."

"What must it be, now, though? Hundreds? Thousands?"

"I'm not sure what the latest body count is."

Faye wanted to push her more but was not going to risk scaring her off. "Who did you say was appearing alongside you?"

"There's some old biddy talking about the booking process. Liz. But primarily I will be there to support my favorite client, Mason, from The Corporation. Do you know him?" There was a surge in Stella's energy the moment she said his name.

"Mason? Yes, I interviewed him last year. He was very impressive." Faye flashed her eyes to suggest she had found him attractive. "You know what they call him, don't you?"

Stella wriggled in her seat and leant forward, conspiratorially. "ELF, you mean? Who wouldn't? He's a sweetie, darling, he really is."

"I enjoyed meeting Mason. Interviews with CEOs don't always go that way. Do you know him well?"

"I think of him as my most important customer. We have spent a lot of time together over the years." Faye waited in anticipation, hoping she would volunteer more, but no words matched the rapturous expression that transformed Stella's tired face.

"Have you any idea how old he is, Stella? He looks amazing. I checked out his work history before I interviewed him. His CV suggests he is 20 years older than he appears."

"He is a very handsome man. Also, extremely fit – triathlete, hardcore skiing, weights of course. Just muscular enough. He is a prime example of what you can do with a little basic raw material. It's all about discipline, the right regime and of course accepting a little help." Stella smiled knowingly. Faye didn't want her to clam up, not now they might be getting somewhere.

"What sort of regime do you have, Stella? You look pretty amazing, if you don't mind me saying. Let me guess – paleo? Gluten-free? Fruitarian?" She didn't want to get too carried away. Whatever regime Stella followed it obviously allowed for gallons of booze. "What's your secret?"

"Simple. Hard work, Faye. Hard work. Like everything else. And once you are over fifty, it gets even harder. You have to be on your guard all the time. Clients, bosses, boards – none of them cut you any slack. They just get more demanding. It's as if they are willing you to start making mistakes."

"Is that what I have to look forward to in my next decade?" For the first time that evening, Stella had said something that touched a raw nerve for Faye. Her editor, Rex, was ten years younger than her, and she could count the people aged 40 or over back at the office on one hand. Come to think of it, nobody was over 50. Her face betrayed her dismay. Why hadn't she realized before?

"For women, it's extra tough." Stella grabbed a small handful of blue Smarties without thinking. Faye did the same. They tasted of chocolate orange and went very well with the cocktail. She grabbed some more and realized she had too many in her mouth, almost choking when Stella said:

"Tell me Faye – I've been wondering. You're obviously bright and good at your job. But why don't you take more care with your appearance?"

She was completely blindsided. Of all the things she had expected to come under discussion, her own style had never crossed her mind. Her primary assumption had been that Stella would spend the entire evening talking about herself.

"Well, I'm a journalist. It's not about what I look like. I'm hardly ever on screen. I will always be judged on what I write. That's where I channel my energy. Ideas."

"That's rather touching, but naive. Seriously?"

"Anyway, what's wrong with my appearance?" Faye ventured, tentatively, worried now that the answer might be more than she could take. Especially when Stella's face suggested she might be struggling to hold back a long list of suggested improvements.

"Let's look at it another way. If there were one thing you could change about your body, what would it be?" Stella asked.

"Oh, that's easy. My arms. I'd like them to be more like Michelle Obama's. More like yours. Mine are too chunky. I've always had trouble getting them into jackets, and I can't help thinking the bingo wing years lie ahead."

"And Faye, what do you think is the secret to my enviable arms?"

"Tricep dips? High protein, low carb?" Well, except for the carbs in alcohol.

Stella snorted. "Dull, dull, dull. That would be much too tedious. Look around you."

As Faye gazed around the private bar, it was impossible to ignore the gleaming uniform blue-white teeth, plumped mouths and lifted eyelids, executed with vastly varying degrees of expertise, some of which were so disastrous it made her shudder. On the rare occasion she had toyed with the idea of aesthetic help, the fear of it going badly wrong had stopped her in her tracks.

"We're in a superficial world. Let's not pretend otherwise."

"Some of them look terrible, though, Stella." Her eyes rested on two white women with eerily similar plastic looks, their mouths too big for their faces, their teeth too big for their mouths, their eyebrows frozen into precisely the same angle. They wore skin-tight satin trousers over cartoon hourglass figures, with vest tops that left little to the imagination. Only their hair color was different.

"It's just a matter of taste. Some people love that pneumatic look. Not brilliant for our kind of jobs, though. You could do with a touch more Christine Everheart."

"Sorry, who?"

"The journalist in *Iron Man*, who sleeps with Tony Stark."

"I saw the film, but I noticed her legs more than her arms. All gleaming and suntanned on the front row of the press conference."

"Indeed. Arms, legs, whatever. This all illustrates the same point. You can rebalance the odds in your favor if you look your best. We can all take a leaf out of Mason's book, can't we?"

Faye's mood began to sink. She suddenly felt nauseous and out of place, looking down at her generic trainers and plain work dress. The only statement her jewelry made was: 'Nothing special'.

"So, you're convinced it's made a big difference to your career, Stella, investing so much in your appearance?"

"Definitely. The attractiveness premium is real. You need to get noticed, too. When I started out in agency life all the girls dressed the same. Black suits, black trousers, black shift dresses. Always black. I decided I was going to set myself apart. Although I didn't have much money, I did have the time to shop for my own vintage then. It was such fun. I would head off to Kensington Market and Portobello on Saturday, Camden Lock on Sunday. I had my hair cut at the Sassoon school, as a demonstration model, until I could afford to pay someone decent to do it.

"Before you know it, you reach an age when stylish clothes and a good moisturizer can't cut it on their own. And I haven't even had kids – that's another massive set-back. A tummy tuck doesn't begin to compensate for the disruption. Just struggling to get back into a shift dress can make them despair. I've seen so many good women give up. You don't have any, do you?"

"What? Shift dresses?"

"No, kids."

"No."

"Well that's something else you've got going for you."

Faye was starting to find Stella's unsolicited lecture intrusive. She had a good point, though. At least one of her promotions had been in the footsteps of a colleague who had gone into a self-destructive tailspin after her children were born, exhausted and having found workplace politics crushingly futile. Now, however, was not the time to get into all that. She had to update Rex at the end of the following day. That meant coming up with something other than the rag bag of loose ends she had been struggling to connect for weeks. At this rate, all she would be able to show for tonight's expenses claim would be a hangover.

"We both need to get going I think," Faye said, finishing the last dregs of melting ice at the bottom of her glass, rapidly coming to the conclusion that she had had enough.

Stella was rummaging in her bag. Eventually she pulled out a cream Tom Ford wallet, from which she extracted a small glossy business card that she thrust into Faye's hand.

"If you decide to do something about your arms this is the best guy in the business. Expert, subtle, discreet. Just ask Mason. He is absolutely the best. You might want to start with your face, though. It would have more impact on your earning potential than a brachioplasty. He is extremely busy these days, but you will see the investment translate across into your earnings soon enough. And what's a couple of months' wages on nips and tucks when it means you will be able to count on a few more years of pension contributions?"

A couple of air kisses later, each woman had climbed into their respective car to go home.

Faye was feeling frail and vulnerable, struggling to process more alcohol and advice than she could comfortably absorb in one night. She just wanted to relax on her journey, as the vehicle crawled steadily over the river and headed South. At least there was no driver to make a fuss if she was sick. In the end, she made it back without incident, the car gently waking her outside her flat with soft wind chimes and a gradually brightening light.

It wasn't until the following afternoon, when she read the name on the card Stella had given her, that she realized the monster hangover was worth the pain.

CHAPTER TWENTY-NINE

C HANNELLE HAD DONE EVERYTHING SHE could think of to prepare Mason and Stella for their public grilling in front of the Select Committee.

There had been three rehearsals, including one with the most vicious trainer Channelle could find, a former television journalist called Battenberg. She had thought his domineering ego would make him the perfect foil for the bosses. When she had suggested he might help put them through their paces, they had seemed excited and were looking forward to being in the presence of a minor celebrity. Battenberg was a household name. People in the office exchanged impressed glances as Channelle escorted him past their desks to the boardroom where the ambush was to take place.

She had intended that Battenberg's ferocious provocations would elevate her head honchos' performance to a feisty and polished crescendo. He had the opposite effect. Mason and Stella left the session deflated and bruised. Seething with barely suppressed rage at their humiliation, they had instructed Channelle never to allow 'that awful man' to darken The Corporation's door again. She was to remove him from the supplier list as soon as his substantial invoice had been paid.

On his way out, Battenberg had turned to her and made a tutting noise under his breath.

"I don't envy you. Do you think I was too hard on them?"

"It's too late now. In any case, it's what I asked you to do. And nothing compared to the damage the Committee could inflict if they are in the mood."

"Do they realize how badly it could go?"

"After today? They must. The pair of them hate being criticized, so they don't encourage it in the normal run of events. They've surrounded themselves with career-obsessed sycophants."

"That's quite the norm at their level, I'm afraid. I see it all the time in my job."

"I've tried telling them. I've even showed them clips of other execs being trounced, so they know it's not personal. There's no shortage of examples of how not to do it. But it's been challenging getting them into the right headspace. I just can't convince them that anyone would have the audacity to hang them out to dry."

Even producing the briefing document had been a struggle. As was standard practice, Channelle had pulled together a set of questions that Stella and Mason might be expected to answer that was as comprehensive as any she had ever produced. Somewhat prematurely, she had been proud of how many potential problems they were aiming to pre-empt. Sonny had come into his own with some of the points he picked up on, and Bob had covered the technical stuff in detail she assumed was correct given

Lola's solid support for bringing him into the team. It had been brilliant working with them. They did everything they could to help her. However, when she circulated the questions to Stella with a request that Brytely approve some answers before involving Mason, the document had simply been batted back with half the text removed.

It had taken more than a week of wrangling to get the offending material put back in. After wading through layers of defensive, inexperienced juniors at the agency, Channelle was tearing her hair out. Sonny, who knew Stella better than anyone at The Corporation apart from Mason, seemed unsurprised. They would all be terrified of admitting anything could possibly go wrong. A quick phone call from him, however, worked miracles. Portia stepped in and sorted everything out.

It was not the first time The Corporation had been called to account in Parliament. When they had put the surveillance equipment into schools some years before, the director of SCET, their education division, had been called to give evidence to another committee. In that case it could not have gone better. Their success in schools had opened the door for them to be considered for more public sector work which continued when the Euthanasia Act was passed. The odds of an easy ride had been better then, as they had not started killing anyone. Not even people who had completed consent forms.

There was no more time for rehearsals. Channelle shifted uneasily in her backward facing limo seat and tried to pull her skirt down over her knees. It was not long enough. She wished she had worn trousers. Even culottes. They would have been so much more practical for getting in and out of the car. Not to mention for sitting opposite your CEO.

It was unusual for anyone to have a chauffeur, but Mason was quirkily attached to the occasional old-fashioned trapping of authority. In the back of the vehicle there was plenty of room for the four of them. Mason and Stella side by side, looking forward; and Channelle and Sonny perched opposite on the cheap seats. Mirrored, refillable flasks had been filled with chilled, filtered water and dropped into the side pockets. Mason reached in and helped himself. It did not cross his mind to offer one to anyone else.

At least they looked the part. Mason wore a grey suit with a slight sheen that fitted perfectly across his athletic form. His crisp shirt was a blazing, bright white, matched only by his uncannily flawless teeth. Channelle wondered whether he had bought everything new for the occasion. Somehow, she couldn't imagine him shopping online or visiting one of the few remaining department stores. He was more the type to fly in a tailor from Milan.

Even Stella had managed to tone down her usual showy style. She had teamed a tight, burgundy shift dress with a cream jacket and matching silk scarf. The only concession to her vintage fashionista obsession was a pair of burgundy and white striped heels matched with a cream leather bag. She had followed Channelle's advice to leave behind the knuckle dusters encrusted with precious stones she usually wore.

"We don't want to look like we're profiting too much from the disposals business." She had closed down Stella when she had maintained that her affluent persona was appropriately aspirational and perfectly on brand for Rockstar Ending.

"No. Just no."

Sonny looked out of the window as they crawled along The Embankment. They had invited him so he could add the thrill of attending a parliamentary committee hearing to his repertoire of secondment experiences. Having found the run-up almost as stressful as Channelle had, the last thing he wanted to do was make eye contact with anyone. Even without the over-representation of alpha personality types, the confined space made him claustrophobic.

Beyond the wall the river was low, and on the other side he could see the exposed shore, littered with grubby blue-grey shingle. Spring sunshine glittered on the dark water. He had never been inside a parliamentary building, although he had seen committee proceedings on television. It had surprised him that members of the public could still just turn up in person and watch, which was all he had to do to get paid today.

Channelle was making the most of their last few minutes out of the public eye, giving the final briefing her best shot. Sonny zoned out as she reminded everyone which committee members would be running the show, and how, above all, they should emphasize their compliance with the provisions of the Euthanasia Act. The responses they had practiced in advance would give them a chance to bridge away from some of the more difficult questions.

"This is so fucking tedious," Stella said. "We have done everything by the book, haven't we, Mason, darling? I can't wait for it to be over."

When they pulled up across the road from Portcullis House, it looked shabbier than Sonny had expected.

Cars were not supposed to stop on The Embankment. It was a red route, full of autonomous cabs, with a segregated cycle path that was more chaotic and dangerous to pedestrians than the car-filled lanes. Mason's driver activated the geofence to clear a safe pathway for the party to traverse the busy road. bringing all the traffic around them to a gentle halt. They had committed two traffic offences in the space of 30 seconds, but it did not matter. The Corporation would absorb the fines that had been triggered as an operating expense.

They piled out, made it through security, and took the lift to the Bercow Room as Channelle scanned the small crowd that was gathering.

"That's Liz, the other person who's been called to give evidence," she said quietly, nodding in the direction of a grey-haired old lady wearing silver octagonal spectacles that magnified her eyes and made her look like an animal that had mutated to see in the dark.

"The one I released last year?" Mason said. "One of the first."

"That's her."

Liz was standing with a middle-aged woman with brown eyes and shoulder-length hair. They huddled together, talking with low voices.

"Who's she with?"

The woman looked somehow familiar, but Channelle couldn't place her. "Don't know, sorry. I'm guessing that's her moral support. She didn't have any kids. Could be one of the PACE counsellors."

Out of earshot, Lexi was giving Liz a last-minute pep talk. Although she had done as she was told, regressing into her former persona had been tough. The flicker of shock on Lexi's face when she spotted her on the pavement outside Portcullis House had made her self-conscious.

"I know. It's dreadful isn't it?" Liz had said, before Lexi could say hello. "I feel like Ursula Andress at the end of *She*. Have you seen it? When she steps into the flame of immortality and ages a thousand years? No wonder Carl went cold on me. Let's get this over with. Then I'm going for a facial."

CHAPTER THIRTY

I T WAS NOT LONG BEFORE they were let into the room.
Four MPs sat spread out around an oversized horseshoe
of desks, facing the audience, while Mason, Stella and
Liz took their positions opposite with their supporters
on the row of seats immediately behind. Various others
– members of the public and the odd journalist – settled
into what Channelle thought of as the gallery.

Her seat gave her a good view of the committee members, and it was close enough to Mason and Stella to pass
them a note if they got into trouble. At least only four out
of the eleven committee members had thought it necessary to attend.

In the chair was Doc. He had been elected to the
position as one of the few of them who had a clinical
background. Since becoming an MP at the last election,
two years before, he was still practicing as a doctor on
occasional Friday afternoons and Saturdays, claiming that
his medical practice allowed him to keep a handle on the
'real world'. Channelle had heard he charged a fortune for
his services, which mainly consisted of providing cosmetic
surgery to celebrity clients.

Before becoming an MP, he had appeared on a reality TV show called *Shortcuts*, helping remodel hard-up people who were unhappy with various aspects of their lives. When he had approached the Conservatives seeking political office, his established reputation for democratizing bodily aesthetics, along with more than a million Splutter followers, had clinched him the nomination for a safe seat within weeks.

Holly was the youngest MP in the room. In her mid-twenties, tall, overweight, and with a pale complexion and a mass of unkempt red curly hair, she wore a long black shirt over pin- striped trousers. Like Doc, she was in her first term of office, but the similarity stopped there. Holly was in the critical cohort of Yuthentic politicians who had held the balance of power since the 2026 election. The party had gained many seats based on a manifesto that included a line pledging to invest in services that 'delivered on the promise of the 2020 Euthanasia Act'. It was a no-brainer that they would send someone along to this session. Channelle had initially marked Holly as a likely ally on the committee, although she had inserted a question mark in brackets (?) into the briefing after her attempts to secure a pre-meeting had been ignored. Rumor had it Holly didn't have much time for anyone over 30. She was a career politician, although it had been a short career so far. She had taken the express elevator from a radical university, via activism, to The House.

Representing the parliamentary old guard was John. He had been a Labour MP until he fell out with the leadership over Brexit and had found refuge with the Lib Dems who at the time were enjoying something of a comeback. He looked like politicians used to. Pale, male and stale in a tatty suit and unremarkable, archaic tie.

Sophie, the final member, didn't know it, but Holly regarded her as something of a role model. They had followed a similar path, even if their politics and appearance could not have been more different.

In her six years as a Labour Member of Parliament, since the 2022 election, Sophie had built a reputation as a good constituency MP and shared much of Holly's enthusiasm for redistributing power to the young. She was small and wiry and could be seen running along the banks of the Thames in all weathers, sporting a waterproof backpack and light hi viz jacket, as she made her way in from her tiny housing unit. While at work, she wore a bodycon dress that showed off her athletic physique. She chose stretchy clothing because it rolled up small and would not crease in her running bag. Her mousy hair was cut short to save time.

The room settled into an anticipatory hush as Big Ben struck two.

After introducing himself as chair and welcoming everyone, Doc checked the notes on his tablet and set the scene for the evidence session.

"The HELP Select Committee has been asked to provide ongoing scrutiny and oversight for the delivery of the Euthanasia Act and its amendments. This came about because of widespread frustration that the opportunities created by the Act were not being acted upon quickly enough."

Channelle thought back to the passing of the assisted dying laws, just as she was finishing her Masters in Promotional Media, and the general election that had given Yuthentic their first taste of power. She had voted for them herself, impressed that someone was finally promising to do something for the millennials, enabling them to build an independent life. If Holly had responded to her request for a meeting, she would have told her so, too.

"Mason," Doc went on, shooting him a glance that was not remotely hostile, "Your corporation has until now had an unsullied reputation for delivering contracts for His Majesty's Government. Many of us have admired the AI-enhanced information technology programs you have been running in schools to help make our children fighting fit, winners in the somewhat challenging global 21st century economy. Equally, your educational surveillance and suicide prevention work has received many plaudits for keeping our children safe. For that I thank you."

He has read the information we sent him, Channelle thought. So far, so good.

"However…"

Uh oh. Here it comes.

"There is some concern emerging around the delivery of the assisted dying program, under the rather invitingly-named brand Rockstar Ending. You have with you today, I believe, Stella from the agency that has been working with you on some of the…" he checked his notes, and slowly read "…customer engagement strategy and user experience."

Mason nodded ever so slightly, in acknowledgement, looking directly at Doc who gave him a twinkle of recognition.

"We also have one of your customers here, Liz, thank

you once again for coming, who – were it not for the intervention of her Member of Parliament – would not be here at all." He gave a quizzical look as if playing for laughs, realizing a few seconds too late that the joke had not gone down well.

"You business people make a big deal out of customer focus, isn't that right?"

"Certainly," Mason replied as Stella nodded so enthusiastically in agreement that Channelle longed to grab her head to stop it bobbing up and down. She sat on her hands to stop herself.

"So, if I may, I would like to invite Liz to tell us a little bit about what happened to her. We have all read your statement, Liz, which PACE submitted as written evidence. But I think it would be useful for the committee to hear it in your own words. After which, I will invite my fellow Members of Parliament to ask questions."

Liz took a deep breath, just like Lexi had suggested, lifted up her grey head, and spoke slowly and clearly. "Well, thank you for inviting me. I suppose the thing I most want to say is that you should be allowed to change your mind."

Sophie raised a hand and Doc gestured her to speak. "Just to be clear. You are saying you think people should be able to change their mind after they have signed all the legally binding consent forms which trigger the humane assisted dying experience?"

"Yes, I am. Exactly that."

After shaking her head a little, Sophie went on. "It is my understanding that a great deal of thought has gone into designing this socially worthwhile and much-needed service, especially if we think back to the more barbaric years not so long ago. Surely, Liz, you understood exactly what you were signing up for?"

"Yes. I have a negligible dementia score. However, you should know from the papers we submitted that I was in some distress because of, well, I'll just call it my personal circumstances if I may. I don't really want to drag that all up here."

Doc raised his hand to reassure her. "Quite. That isn't necessary. It's the Rockstar Ending process we're interested in today." He glanced at the other MPs who nodded in recognition as Sophie continued in a slightly gentler tone.

"Can you confirm please, Liz, that you passed all the tests – mental agility, dementia quotient and so on?"

Sitting up proudly, Liz was quick to reply. "Yes, of course I did or they wouldn't have let me sign up, would they? And all the more reason to let me live! I'll be good for a Sudoku tournament for a few more years yet." Sophie smiled in acknowledgment and nodded to Holly whose turn it was next.

As a hardcore Yuthie, the idea that anyone would have the space for leisure activities in their retirement rankled with her. It showed in her sarcastic tone. "How nice for you to have the time. So, you were of sound mind, and you set the process in motion fully aware of what you were doing. Why do you think The Corporation should just let you walk away, when you have put them to a great deal of trouble, and made them incur a great deal of cost?"

"It's not about the money, dear. I wouldn't mind paying a cancellation fee. Although Mason here very kindly let me leave the... erm.... queue for nothing when my

MP Nicky Hartt intervened. But not everyone has a sympathetic MP who's prepared to be their advocate, do they?" The pointed remark was not lost on Holly. She grimaced for a second but hoped no one had noticed. "What I'm worried about is the postcode lottery. If you don't have someone kind to help you, you're a goner. It's not fair, is it?" Mason shot her a smile in sympathetic agreement, giving a quarter turn of his muscular shoulders towards her before adjusting his position back to face the committee head-on.

"We do need to keep the Endings program moving," Holly said, deliberately patronizing to the point of being offensive. "Don't you think that The Corporation should deliver on its targets so we can keep our promises to the taxpayer?"

"I don't think one or two of us changing our minds is exactly going to bring about another economic crash. Do you?" Channelle could sense a murmur of approval for what Liz had said emanating from the benches behind her. It must have been the supporters from PACE. She wished she had studied the audience more carefully when they were waiting to go in. It would be bad form to swivel round now unless they did something disruptive.

"What do you think of that statement, Mason?" John was keen to bring him into the discussion.

"This lady is correct."

"Let me get this clear. You think it's acceptable for people to seek to break their contract with you? Surely that jeopardizes your ability to meet your commitments to the Government?"

Mason spoke with calm authority. "This is a sensitive

program. We take our responsibility to our client, the Government, and our service users very seriously." That was what he was supposed to say, wasn't it? Channelle was impressed. He sounded like he meant it. You had to hand it to him, he could turn on the charm like no one else when he wanted to.

"Of course you do. But could you answer the question, please? Is it acceptable for people to break their contract with you, and by default for you to break your contract with the Government?" John was getting into his stride now.

"In certain exceptional circumstances, provided we continue to meet our targets overall, yes, I do consider it appropriate to allow people to defer their arrangements. It is our priority to deliver this sensitive, socially responsible, high-scale service in a manner that is unquestionably humane. The introduction of a cancellation clause makes it more so. Yes."

"By implication, then, are you saying you believe you will still be meeting your targets, even if turncoats like Liz decide to waste all our time?" Holly interrupted, unable to hold back.

"Absolutely, although I would never describe one of our customers in that way. We have enough wriggle room to accommodate people who may wish to defer and still deliver the numbers you require."

There was a moment of silence while the committee absorbed Mason's statement, exchanging glances which suggested they found his response acceptable.

"Tell me, Mason," John went on, "How many visitors,

if I may call them that, are you receiving at the Disposal Centers these days?"

"I'm afraid that information is commercially confidential."

"You can't tell me how many people are being processed?"

"No, you need to take that up with my client, the Minister. I am afraid that I am not permitted to disclose certain statistics."

"Do you know the number?"

"Yes, I do."

"And do you think we have enough people going through to the Disposal Centers?"

"That is not for me to say. But feedback from my client, on behalf of the Government, is that we are meeting our contractual obligations in full."

Holly remained unsatisfied.

"Just thinking about the process that led to Liz – and I believe something like thirty other people – changing their mind. At this rate we could find that 100 people per year drop out of the system. Given the average value of a Rockstar Ending customer's estate, we could be failing to redistribute tens – if not hundreds – of millions of pounds to those who could make better use of it. They are the wealthier members of our society, after all. Do you think your onboarding sequence might need changing so that absolutely everyone understands what they are signing up to? Stella, I think your agency has worked on that part of it, am I right?"

"Yes, we designed all the front end and UX."

Doc chipped in, "Which means what, exactly? Some

of my honorable colleagues will not be familiar with those terms."

"Sure." Stella's informality didn't play out well in the committee room. It would have been even more jarring if they had been in one of the traditional, wood-paneled spaces over the road in the Palace of Westminster. "UX is short for User Experience. The recruitment campaign, consent process – all of it conforms with the provisions of the Euthanasia Act. From a legal perspective it has all been independently audited. It was one of the terms of being appointed. We have done it all by the book. Meeting the highest ethical standards. We are fully compliant." Try to sound a little less like you've learned a checklist off by heart, Channelle thought, while at the same time being grateful that Stella had managed to memorize her words.

Holly was not going to let go. "So it would seem. But beyond the box-ticking, if you don't mind me calling it that, how do you feel about people like Liz, who decide they want to carry on living? Aren't they letting us all down?"

"Well, it's inconsiderate and inconvenient. Some would say selfish. But it's not a showstopper when we have no shortage of pipeline." Stella said.

"Pipeline?"

Channelle flinched, wishing Stella would stop using words like that. She could also try a bit harder not to look annoyed when the MPs didn't understand what she was talking about.

"People wanting to sign up. That's what we call the pipeline. It's rammed. The campaign has been super-effective from the get-go. We've even had to boost our website capacity to deliver nine nines availability."

"Shame!" A member of the public shouted from the gallery.

Doc flashed a punitive glance to indicate that such comments were unwelcome. He sensed that his fellow committee members were tuning out from Stella's banal stream of management-speak which he doubted she understood herself.

"Thank you, Stella. If I might return to Mason, let me say that fundamentally we are all convinced you are doing a marvelous job of delivering this service. It seems to be that the question we are most concerned about would be deciding an appropriate degree of leniency for the service users, such as the lady we have with us today, who renege on their commitment to society by canceling their trip."

Stella tried to interrupt, but Mason gently rested his smooth, warm, suntanned, perfectly manicured hand on the sleeve of her jacket. She was in no doubt that she was to remain silent.

"If I may," he began, "I have had some excellent conversations with your parliamentary colleagues on how best – or perhaps I should say how fairly – we should continue delivering this bold initiative. Being asked to intervene, personally, to release people who have changed their minds has given me, perhaps, a better insight than anybody in this room, into the thought processes of people who, for a wide range of reasons, suddenly decide to opt out of the opt in to opt out.

"As someone with extensive experience of running businesses which produce, almost exclusively, delighted customers, I know that if more than a small handful of people feel they need to reach out to the CEO for help, that is a sure fire indicator that something isn't quite right further down the organisation. It tells me that the processes need some redesign.

"In light of this teething problem, with Stella's help, we have been working on a solution. I can announce today that we will be developing a new pathway exclusively for people who have 'last minute reservations', using an updated release of the revolutionary chatbot technology that has already built us a healthy cohort of customers. Stella's agency has given us world-beating support in helping us to minimize the chances of late objections in future."

Holly caught the chairman's eye. "So how does that work, then?"

"We have an award-winning, friendly, talking and listening audio robot that helps people make difficult decisions. It is like a more powerful version of the automated assistants I am sure most people in this room will use in their homes or on their phones. This chatbot is already used, with great success, for our onboarding sequence in the economy program. Also known as an AI, it is exceptionally good at sensing if service users are distressed and it helps them to come to terms with their objections so that they find peace in their decision. It's a mutually beneficial process.

"Until now, we had not permitted a conversational pathway that would allow people to discuss postponement. However, we have built an enhancement that will permit customers to raise the question of a Mutually Acceptable Deferment Date (MADD). It is already in field trials and working well.

"Today, we are doing a better job than ever before of helping people to manage the complex emotions which could lead them to imagine, at a late stage, that they might prefer to stay alive. Our methods are gentle, but persistent and persuasive. In summary, we are confident that numbers accessing a bailout clause will fall. The few that still wish to postpone will be able to do so within the system."

Holly still looked annoyed, "I can't get over this. You think it's OK to just let them off, don't you?" She brushed her wild curly red hair back from her face with both hands, sat back in her chair, and folded her arms sharply in front of her large chest, fixing Mason with an aggressive stare.

"That's not what I said." He was as calm as ever. "We are talking about postponement for no more than around 30 people. You will still get the transfer of wealth you want, to the younger demographic, just a little later. It will be slippage of months rather than years in the majority of cases. Let's face it, most of these people are already advanced in years. Should they pass away from natural causes, their assets will still transfer with zero friction."

Holly was not completely appeased, but she could tell that the rest of the committee members were getting bored.

"And could I just add," Mason said smoothly, "The Corporation is committed to delivering the best possible public service across all our operations. It is our aim to guarantee a happy ending for everyone."

CHAPTER THIRTY-ONE

T HEY APPEARED TO HAVE GOT away with it.

Channelle sprang out of her seat the second the meeting finished. Sonny took it as a signal for him to do the same. When in doubt, mirror the boss's behavior. He had seen it on one of the TED talks he watched at work when there was nothing else to do, which was more often on his secondment than he would have liked to admit. Together, they began to marshal Mason and Stella towards the door. It was important to get them away from the building, and the chance of any unhelpful random interactions, as quickly as possible. The entire party was under strict instructions not to get drawn into any side conversations on their way out in case there were any media around.

For three months now, Faye had been wearing down Channelle with all manner of questions. As far as Channelle knew, however, The Corporation had managed to keep the incident at the Disposal Center from her. Furthermore, nothing had happened in the committee hearing to suggest that news of that particular potential PR disaster had leaked. They had been ready for questions, but none had come. That had to be a good sign, surely?

Liz's minder was back by her side. Channelle over-heard her congratulating the old woman on the points she had made during the hearing, and suppressed a wry smile. She had found Liz's performance reassuringly underpow-ered. The escapee hadn't exactly come across as someone worth saving.

An animated, blond woman slid alongside the PACE party in a motorized wheelchair, adding her congratula-tions to Liz.

Channelle carried on steering the others away. In the end it hadn't gone badly for The Corporation. Mason could be difficult and secretive, but when the chips were down, he had an uncanny ability to pull it off. Best of all he had managed to get Stella to shut up just at the point when she started irritating everyone. He had even flashed Liz the smile. Perhaps she was wrong to have doubted him, after all?

"The car's outside," Sonny said to Channelle. His to-ken job for the day had been to maintain contact with the driver. "He's cruising round the block until we're ready."

"Did you recognize anyone from the mugshots?" she asked him quietly. In the appendix to the briefing pack she had compiled images of interested parties who might show up in the room.

"Just Jess, Nicky Hartt's researcher. She was there. The woman with the wheelchair. Long platinum blond hair. Obviously knows Liz." Sonny replied.

"Makes sense. She probably handled some of the cor-respondence with Mason."

They had managed to get everyone to the elevator. The four of them stepped inside just as an Asian woman in her 60s arrived next to them. She was going to follow the party in, but something stopped her. Channelle saw her try to make eye contact with Sonny, who sternly blanked her and hit the button to speedily close the door.

Before Channelle could say anything, the device on her wrist distracted her with the strong vibration associated with the contacts she had categorized as known troublemakers.

"I'll have to check this," she said retrieving another device. As her eyes ran down the screen, Sonny saw pure terror cross her face.

"It's Faye. She was watching on the live link."

"Fan mail, no doubt." Stella smirked, "She absolutely adores you. You were marvelous, Mason!"

Channelle was silent. What she had just read would have to wait until she could get Mason on his own.

"Not exactly."

"Is it about the DC dodgers?"

"No. Nothing to concern you, Stella. Look, erm… can we drop you back at your office? I know you wanted to treat us to a celebratory drink, but there's a few things I need to go through with Mason on his own."

"I wouldn't mind popping into Brytely myself," Sonny perked up a little. "I haven't been back for a while, it would be good to catch up with some of the team, share some of my experiences from today. They helped us quite a bit with the prep."

By the time Stella and Sonny had climbed out of the car, Channelle was bursting with pent-up questions for

Mason who had returned to his default setting of poker face.

"Faye is alleging that you have some kind of improper relationship with Doc," she began, trying in vain not to sound too accusatory. "Is that true?"

Mason shrugged.

"Is it true?"

Still a blank.

"You need to tell me, Mason. What is going on? Can I tell her she's got it wrong and close it down or can't I?"

"It's nothing."

"What kind of nothing?"

"Nothing that is relevant to company business."

"Look. I need to know what's going on here. You haven't been to some Tory fancy dress fundraiser with him, and not declared it, have you? We have been over this before. If you don't level with me, I can't protect you. Frankly, if it's really bad I can't protect you anyway. But I'd be grateful if you would give me half a chance."

"I told you. There is nothing you need to worry about. And I am not sharing details of my medical arrangements with you."

"He's your doctor?" She had not been expecting that. Looking at Mason's smooth face and the exemplary physique that matched a birth year 20 years later than the one listed in the annual report, she had to admit it was a feasible explanation. But not one he would want to be shared. "What do I tell her, then?"

"That she will find nothing improper in any of my relationships with anyone. That's enough."

"She won't like it."

"I have told you what to say."

All the charm he had brought to bear in Portcullis House had been used up. He clenched his jaw and looked out of the window. She knew better than to try again and looked down at her device, pretending their silence was about her working rather than him shutting her out.

Once they were back in the office, she could not find a room where she could make a private call. It didn't matter much, as she didn't want to talk to Faye while she was still angry with Mason. With her mind distracted, she might end up saying something misleading and that would set them up for problems later, wreck her credibility and send her career down the toilet. The triple whammy.

So she did exactly what he told her to do. Knocked his words into a short statement and sent it across. It was all she had.

CHAPTER THIRTY-TWO

OW DO PEOPLE WATCH THIS stuff all day? Faye thought, as the session drew to a conclusion. The political beat had never much appealed to her. Viewing it on her screen at the office made it bearable, allowing her to keep half an eye on her other feeds. Select Committees were only ever interesting if something unusual kicked off, but it didn't look like that was going to happen today. Since security had become tighter, it was more difficult for someone in the audience to cause a scene. She had listened to Liz's short testimony and toyed with the idea of asking for an interview with her. Jess, Nicky's researcher was in the audience, and a handsome young Asian man sat behind Mason next to poor Channelle, whom she had been hounding somewhat recently.

Faye was running out of time to meet Rex's deadline, and her chances of pulling together something he would want to run were looking remote. She had pages of leads, but they were all over the place. On top of all that mess, she had just lost an hour watching the stupid Committee.

The chances of her leaving her desk were now zero. Her colleague Jack saw how tired she was and invited her to pop outside for a quick coffee, but she had to turn him down. When he came back, without having to be asked, he put a double espresso with two sugars next to her keyboard, which she used to gulp down a couple of high dose painkillers from the small stash she always had to hand in her drawer. She had scarcely lifted her eyes from the screen all day, and it was only when she went back to her inbox after a few hours trying to avoid distractions that she had found the second tape.

As she listened to the recorded conversation between Mason and a woman she instantly realized was Stella, she switched on a software program that would generate a transcript. It would make it easier to work on it later. The recording started off promisingly with an invitation for Mason to join a party in a Jacuzzi, but quickly shifted to run of the mill business chat about a secondment. It was time-stamped the same day as the Nicky Hartt sound file, so she could only assume the recording was made in Verbier. So that was how Stella knew Mason was a good skier.

Sadly, however, there was nothing obviously illegal or immoral. Stella and Mason were both single, and from their conversation the night before, she already knew that Stella was one of Mason's biggest fans.

She was running through what it all might mean as she waited for the transcript. Unwilling to leave her desk in case Rex wrongfooted her, she decided to catch up on filling in her expenses and started checking through her wallet for receipts from the night before.

That was when she came across the card Stella had given her, with the name of the aesthetic surgeon she loved so much. Why did that name look so familiar? Of course. Bingo. The doctor Stella had recommended was also the Member of Parliament who chaired the HELP Select Committee. No wonder she hadn't been too worried about getting roughed up. Surely Rex would have to listen to her, now? She doodled a triangle on a notepad with the names Stella, Mason and Doc at each corner, and put a big heart in the middle with a scalpel running through it where an arrow might usually be. Faye toyed with the idea of sending the picture to Channelle but decided against it and shot her a note instead.

Her meeting with Rex was at five o'clock in the usual minuscule meeting room.

"I hope you've got something good, Faye." Rex said in a tone that suggested his expectations were low.

"Well, I've got a few angles. We started with the conversation with Nicky, yes? About the Rockstar Endings, and people being forced to go all the way even if they changed their mind. Well, that's looking weak. At HELP this afternoon they made it all sound like a teething problem that's going to go away. I know where some of the refuseniks are living, but let's face it, they're all old. No one gives a toss. The thing is, I've got a second tape..."

"Same anonymous source?" He looked down at his device, losing interest already.

"Yep. Only this time Mason is with Stella, the woman whose agency designed the Rockstar Endings campaign, from Brytely. She was giving evidence alongside him today."

"What kind of tape? Please tell me it's a candid shot of the ELF himself shagging a fit agency bird?" Sometimes

Rex tried to fit in by coming out with sleazy tabloidspeak, but he was 40 years too late.

"Not that kind of tape, I'm afraid. But they were in Verbier together the day he got the call from Nicky. Stella invites Mason to a party in a Jacuzzi."

"But no video?"

"It's sound only. None of it is in the Jacuzzi."

"Feeble. Is that it?"

"No. There's something else. I went out with Stella last night after the SWAB judging. It turns out that she and Mason both have the same aesthetic surgeon."

"Time's running out here, Faye. That's hardly a story either."

"Except it is, Rex. It's not just any old Harley Street quack. It's Doc. The chairman of the HELP Select Committee. Between them, they will have paid him hundreds of thousands. And you should have seen how easy he was on them. It was a walk in the park."

For once, Rex didn't try to close her down the second she stopped to draw breath. Yes! Finally, he was starting to listen. He stood up and walked a few steps around the cramped room before turning to look at her.

"You need to do more work on this before we can even consider running it."

There was a change in Rex's stance. He could not bring himself to say it, but he knew that there was the nugget of a story gleaming in the dirt she had just dished on Doc. Parliamentarians were easier game than the likes of Mason. The public despised politicians to begin with, so they would be playing to the crowd. Even better, MPs did not have marching armies of lawyers protecting them the way big companies did.

"Sure boss, I'll tread carefully. I've already logged a few questions with Channelle." She did not want to provoke Rex into changing his mind simply to spite her. Anyway, it was true. "Legals and all that. Fact checking. Yep. I'm onto it." She nodded like she meant it.

His face remained stony and he raised a hand. "We're not rushing anything out."

That was the nearest Faye was going to get to a yes, for now. She felt a flush of satisfaction, believing that she had finally convinced Rex she was on to something.

CHAPTER THIRTY-THREE

H IS THREE MONTHS AWAY FROM the Brytely offices had given Sonny a different perspective on the place. It felt smaller and less impressive when he compared it to The Corporation's extensive floors, with its flat, open plains of soulless, identical workspaces insulated from each other by the constant low hum of artificially generated white noise.

Brytely didn't allocate desks, but there was a corner of the office where he had always liked to perch. They had an unspoken seating system administered by the employees' collective unconscious. It operated in parallel to the agency's hot desking rules. Arriving late in the day, that meant Sonny would have to plot up wherever he could squeeze in.

The service bots had been as active as ever. Bowls of miniature Easter Eggs (one vegan) had been kept topped up by the coffee machine. Sonny helped himself to a giant strawberry that sat on top of a conical pile of soft fruit. He had missed the lush snacks of agency life.

"What is this? Time off for good behavior?" Portia was standing next to him, taking an apple. He had not realized until that moment how much he had hoped she would be there. It was the first time they had met since he began his secondment, although they had been in touch with increasing frequency online over the past few weeks. It was Portia who, in the end, who had helped them to get their story together, after Mason and Stella had reached crisis point. She had saved the day, but he wasn't sure he wanted to tell her.

"Something like that."

"Do you think it went OK? I watched it on the link, but you can't tell how it actually feels in the room."

Of course she had watched it. "I think so, yes. No obvious damage – not yet at any rate. How are things here?"

"Same."

"And Lars?"

"Oh. Same."

When they were chatting online, they rarely had a problem keeping the banter going. But today he felt awkward. She moved a little closer and spoke softly. "I couldn't help noticing, there was someone who looked really like your grandmother in the audience for the Select Committee. Did you see her?"

Sonny shuffled back. "I was focused on the MPs really. Didn't have time to scan the audience. Most of them were behind us." He turned away and grabbed another strawberry.

"These babies are huge!" He knew it was a pathetic attempt to change the subject, but it was all he could think of. "How do they get them to grow this big?"

"I'm sure it was her."

Portia saw right through him. He wasn't sure he liked

it. But there was one sure-fire reason she would stop talking about his family. She would never want their creepy colleague Lars to find out about what they had almost done at New Year. His abrupt appearance in the kitchen area made Portia clam up about Sonny's grandmother instantly.

"To what do we owe this unexpected pleasure?" Lars said, reaching for a handful of chocolate mini eggs using one disposable clear plastic glove, and tipping them into a second glove that he was using as an improvised sweet bag. The pastel-colored candies bunched into the fingers, creating something that looked oddly deformed, as they wedged inside at different angles. The knuckles were in all the wrong places. He shook it gently with his own spidery hand in attempt to make more space. Only Lars could turn innocent Easter eggs into something that looked so disturbing.

"Mason was dropping Stella off and I thought I'd pop in to say hello."

Lars tried to wedge a second small handful of eggs into the glove. The plastic stretched and grew cloudy at the pressure points, but it held.

"They put on a good show," Lars said.

"Did anyone actually do any work here this afternoon?" Sonny asked.

"What could be more important than observing how well our most important profit line stands up to political scrutiny?" Lars' Scandinavian accent gently messed with his intonation, sprinkling a syncopated rhythm through his speech.

"We had it on the big screen in the office," Portia

added, "But most of them just stuck their headphones in. Lars and I were the only ones paying proper attention. He knows that Yuthie, Holly, that you were with earlier."

Sonny observed how little Lars and Portia seemed to have changed during the three months of his secondment. The only thing that had altered was that Portia seemed to know more about Lars, who was in his usual Slayer T-shirt and black jeans, not forgetting the pale jade contact lenses and limp, over-dyed black locks. The Yuthentic circle with its diagonal cross was dangling on a niobium chain around his neck.

"Of course." Sonny said.

"He's been finding out all sorts of stuff. It's useful having an insider, you know."

Lars threw three eggs into the air in rapid succession and caught each one in his mouth with perfect precision. There was something reptilian about the way he did it. A cannibalistic lizard, eating its own young, Sonny mused silently.

"She didn't give us any trouble, did she?" Lars sounded even more smug than usual. How was that possible?

"And that was down to your unconventional charms, I suppose?" Portia said. Lars snorted.

Sonny wished he had stayed in closer touch with his Brytely colleagues. This was the kind of gold dust that never got written down anywhere. It could be the exactly the sort of insider knowledge that would get him more brownie points at The Corporation. He shuddered at the idea of Lars being allowed to meet Holly in an official Brytely capacity. Stella didn't normally let him out. "Not client-ready," was a phrase she used to describe Lars, and several others in the office, whose interpersonal skills were, at best, rough round the edges if not verging on the alarming.

"I can't take any credit for today," Lars said, after he had safely swallowed the uniform lumps of chocolate. "But I have met her a couple of times. At the victory party, and Yuthfest. I have been telling Portia she could be a great ally for Phase Two."

For a moment it felt like nothing had changed. Here were the three of them back in their old roles. Lars creeping out Sonny and Portia, who in turn were playing some kind of coded game on the low end of the flirting spectrum.

He thought back to New Year's Eve again. That moment in his grandparents' loft when, for a couple of seconds, something intimate almost happened. Was the underlying feeling still there? He wasn't sure he wanted to know. In any case, the office wasn't the place to find out, especially with Lars hanging around like a bad goth Gollum. They had to move on.

"Do you still think we'll make it to Phase Two, then?" The main focus of Sonny's secondment had been airbrushing out the hiccup at the Disposal Center, so that the debacle was kept hidden from public view.

It seemed to have worked.

The five escapees had not, as far as they knew, gone to the media. Negotiations around their compensation packages were progressing well, according to the legal team. Whenever Mason flared up, asking for a resolution to be reached more quickly, Greg, the legal director, would stand his ground. It's a staged process, he would say. We are incrementally upping the offer. As long as we keep the non-disclosure agreement on the table everyone should keep schtum. It's the one advantage of them having hired a decent lawyer.

"Our second glorious iteration is still very much on the table," Lars began. "I'm very excited about it, personally. Extending our provision beyond our trailblazer target pensioner group makes perfect sense for everyone. We need to iron out the teething problems. Maybe explore alternative delivery pathways. Mason nailed it right there. We are extending the scope of the chatbot and throwing a few concessions to the last minute refuseniks. That should be all it takes to keep them quiet. You know, if you offer people something forbidden, that they think they want, they will often refuse it. The pro-euthanasia vanguard knew all about that. Giving people the choice to die humanely, the civilized option, can actually make a proportion of them more likely to decide to stay alive. They feel less trapped by life. More likely to look for fulfilment. We will have a happier world. What's not to like? Mason is a tremendous asset, by the way. I can see why Stella is infatuated with him."

Sonny had come close to reconciling his role in the Rockstar Ending program during his time at The Corporation. He had been subsumed in a crowd of people who went to tremendous lengths to prove their corporate loyalty. Their internal communications, explaining the rationale behind their role in the program of accelerated euthanasia for the elderly, made it all seem natural. Channelle had showed him the employee research when she got him to help pull together one of the award submissions.

He used it for the summary that demonstrated conclusively that thousands of team members were proud to be associated with The Corporation because it had played a leading role in delivering important social and economic programs. People were clamoring to work there. Staff morale had not hit such an impressive peak since they put the suicide prevention surveillance in schools. One of the employees had summed up how they felt by typing into the free text field: 'Wealth redistribution? What's not to like?' Someone arranged for the words to run across the screens that decked every floor. The Corporation was at one with the Zeitgeist and had achieved corporate communications Nirvana.

"Tell me more about Holly," Sonny said.

"If you sliced her in half, you would find the Yuthentic sigil running through her middle, like a stick of rock." Lars crunched on one last egg before knotting the crammed glove and placing it on the grey-slate-colored glass countertop. It looked like a thought-provoking contemporary sculpture you might find in the Hayward Gallery, alongside a life-sized boiled sugar model of Holly, with her innards exposed. The Confectionery is Political Series. Humbug.

"Your briefing was adequate. The 'cut and paste' caricature from Dod's Parliamentary Companion was right. She hasn't lost any of her new intake enthusiasm, or the pointed elbows that got her so high up the candidate list. You can't fault her work ethic or voting record either. She's a Yuthie through and throughthie!" He sniggered at his own joke.

"So, what was missing? Only 'adequate'?"

"Some of the more personal stuff. But I would never write any of that down. I'm not sure I'd even talk about it within earshot of a device."

"That is where I might be able to help you." Sonny made a sign, pointing in the air with one finger to signal the need for a short wait. He pulled out the Faraday pouch from the bottom of his backpack. Bob had given him it. He had a few of them knocking around. On the front was a badly executed cover of the Bowie album, 'Heathen'. Bob had kept 'Ziggy Stardust' for himself. That guy was so predictable.

Lars raised the stubble above his left eye in a quizzical flourish. It made him look like Roger Moore crossed with Marilyn Manson. He knew exactly what to do. He swiftly unclipped his device from the studded leather holder that was attached to his belt, and dropped it in. Sonny followed suit.

"Porsh?"

"This is weird," she said, pulling a puzzled face, "But OK." In went her retro clamshell, and Sonny snapped it shut.

"You're full of surprises today, Sonny." It was the first time they had seen Lars look even vaguely impressed. The three of them filed casually into a nearby meeting room, and Lars expertly disconnected the cables from the video-conferencing kit. "I think we're alone now," he said.

"What can you tell us?"

"Holly is not the happiest individual. For one who has achieved so much so young, she suffers with low self-esteem."

"You don't need to be a genius to work that out,"

Sonny said, "She's so snappy. Of all the MPs in that room she was the most aggressive."

"Quite," said Lars. "She is not on this committee by accident. At the victory party she had a few intoxicants – I think most people there had. Some doses better judged than others. We were up all night after several weeks' hard campaigning. You know what they say about politics?"

"What?"

"Showbusiness for ugly people."

"What's that got to do with anything?" Portia didn't like the way the conversation was going and she felt obliged, as the only woman in the room, to stick up for Holly even though she didn't like her. "I thought this was about ideas, not women's appearance."

The boys shifted uncomfortably.

"To be fair, Porsh, you could say the same of a lot of MPs, regardless of gender." Sonny didn't want Lars to clam up just as they were starting to get somewhere.

"Yes, yes," Lars agreed, dismissively.

"So?"

"She had a big falling out with her family. They are not massively wealthy, but comfortable. With sensible management of their assets they could hit the bracket to be candidates for a Rockstar Ending in around ten years' time. They raided their modest lower-middle-class coffers to fund her through university. Then, halfway through her final year, she dropped out and went to work full time for Yuthentic. She had been on track for a good degree, but she walked away. They had paid for everything. A hundred thousand pounds of fees and living expenses and nothing to show for it. Even after she got elected they could not forgive her."

"That's hardly surprising. Lots of Yuthies dropped out to work for the party. That's been going on forever. Is that all you've got?" Sonny wanted to put Lars under pressure. Lola had coached him to be a little more aggressive with his questions during his secondment.

"No. There is an uncle. Her mother's brother. His name is Ted. Holly is quite close to him. He's getting on a bit and, like her parents, he is well-off. But he is single and has no children. And he is fifteen years older than Holly's mother."

"So he's bang in the Rockstar Ending bracket."

"Quite so."

Portia said. "Don't tell me. She wants him to sign up and hand over all his assets to his darling niece."

"Well, she's a little conflicted. It's not quite so brutal as that, but essentially that is what's going through her mind. We had a little chat about it. More than once, actually. We've been in touch on and off."

What would possess any woman to confide in Lars? Only in politics could such a crazy relationship burgeon.

"I've told her to be patient. But she is keen to get her hands on the money, sooner rather than later. All that research that maps physical characteristics against success? She's obsessed with it. She has height, which everyone knows is a great asset," he gave a flourish with his hands to emphasize his own gangly physical presence, "But she is losing the battle with her weight. She wants surgery. Quite a bit of surgery, actually. And if she can get the money in time she would like to be reshaped at the beginning of the Summer recess to hit the party conference season at the same time as the celebrity websites. Make a big hit on Splutter to court further popularity."

"What's that got to do with Rockstar Ending?"

"I am sure it is something we will be able to leverage." Lars looked even more smug than usual. "In fact, I am expecting a call from her any minute now."

"Better give you this back then." Sonny tipped the devices back out on to the table. Within seconds, Lars's buzzed. "Talk of the devil," he said, "And she will appear." He slipped out to take the call from Holly leaving Sonny alone with Portia.

Before he could say anything, Sonny's phone vibrated, too. It sat face up on the table between them. Portia could see the name flashing on the screen. He froze for a moment and was shocked when, on impulse, Portia reached over and snatched it away from him. "Hey, Ayesha," she said, "Sonny's just stepped away from his desk, how are you and Ajay?"

Ayesha's voice was warm and friendly. "I thought he was at another office these days. How funny. We are all good, thank you. When are we going to see you again?"

Sonny was now hopping around the room mouthing 'Stop!' and 'Give me back my phone!'

She could not resist carrying on a little longer. "I'm not sure. What have you been up to today?"

"I've just been in town with some friends." When she heard her reply, Portia pulled a shocked face to make Sonny worry about what his grandmother might have said. She was dead certain Ayesha had been at the Select

Committee. But she wasn't going to embarrass her if she didn't want to say.

"Of course."

Sonny was now looking so agitated that Portia had to take pity on him. "He's just come back Ayesha, lovely to speak to you, let me hand you over…" Sonny had the phone out of her hand in an instant.

"Nani. You OK?"

"Of course I am. But you know that already. You just saw me Sonny. We need to talk."

"Right." He left Portia and wandered a few steps down the corridor, then dived into Autopsy. A bald man with a long goatee beard peered down on him from the meeting room mural. "Sorry about that, Nani."

"Are you ashamed to know me? What was all that about?"

"It was a work thing. I didn't want to get into introducing you to everyone. We had to get out quickly. Mason had to get to another meeting. He can be very difficult. I really am sorry for closing the door on you like that. Why were you there, anyway?"

"The charity where I volunteer asked a few of us to go along as moral support for the old lady."

"She did well," Sonny said thinking hard how to salvage the situation. "Are we OK, Nani?"

"OK how?"

"Well, with me working for Rockstar Ending. Now you know. I'm not particularly proud of what they're doing, but I don't want to risk losing my job."

It only took a few seconds for Ayesha to make him an offer. "I'm not sure you should be involved with these people. We could help, you know. Nana and I can give you some money to tide you over until you find something else. It's not a problem."

"No." For years he had lived on handouts from his parents and grandparents, and the job was allowing him a sense of newfound dignity. "They've promoted me, Nani. I want to stay. I'm very sorry I blanked you today. It was rude. But I'll never be independent if I don't keep on with this. Things are going well for me here. Do you understand? I finally have a career."

Although Ayesha had been hurt when her grandson had pretended not to know her, she accepted his apology. It was obvious he meant it. She was not going to hold a grudge.

As he finished the call, Sonny looked through the glass meeting room wall, and saw Portia slowly wandering by. She turned to face him, met his eyes and lifted a hand to make a zipping motion from the left side of her mouth to the right. He gave her a thumbs-up sign, confident that Portia would keep the secret that his grandmother was one of Rockstar Ending's furtive opponents.

CHAPTER THIRTY-FOUR

THE FUNCTION ROOM AT THE Barge, the pub where the local branch of People Against Coercive Euthanasia had been meeting occasionally, was packed.

Instead of the usual handful of campaigners seated in a tidy circle, a larger crowd occupied the space which had been set up for a celebration cabaret style. The familiar grey plastic chairs had been loosely arranged around a few tables scattered across the floor. Somehow, it made the wood-paneled room less gloomy than usual, in spite of its ancient red and gold flock wallpaper and matching sticky carpet. Evening sunlight filtered in through dirt-encrusted windows that had long been painted shut. A modest buffet was set up along one side of the room facing the bar, where Ella, one of the regular barmaids, was begrudgingly serving drinks.

"This is all very well, but we have achieved nothing," Father Al muttered angrily to a huddle of PACE board members, stifling their party spirit. "We have been trying to stop this outrageous euthanasia program for months now, and we are getting nowhere."

"With the greatest respect, that simply isn't true."

Henry looked at the priest over the top of his tortoiseshell glasses. "You should not underestimate the settlement we have secured for the five folks who are the focus of our celebration this evening. They have all accepted offers that will enable them to live comfortably, without fear, for the rest of their natural lives. The costs of their housing, health and care will be fully met by The Corporation. I consider that to be a substantial achievement."

David, who chaired the local PACE group, nodded his full head of white hair in support of Henry's response, but Father Al would not let it drop. "Money isn't everything."

"Of course not Al, but even the Lord knows it helps," David smiled, hoping to get him into a more conciliatory place, at least for the next couple of hours. It was supposed to be a party, after all.

As if to reinforce the point, Mavis crashed into their discussion, humming the tune 'We're in the Money', and clinked her glass against Henry's: "Thank you for getting us our settlement. It is a weight off all our minds. I expect you'll be glad to see the back of us, Father."

"I am pleased for you all, naturally," Father Al went on, "But you are just five people out of what we believe to be a cohort of many thousands. The Ending program continues unabated. The Corporation is taking, at a conservative estimate, hundreds more vulnerable people into the afterlife every week, many of them not even baptized. It is wholesale murder. Those kinds of numbers simply cannot be airbrushed out and attributed to free will. It is still all wrong".

Mavis was bored by the argument she had heard so many times before. No wonder her former roommate Mabel had opted to give the party a miss. She quietly stepped away and sidled towards Meg, whom she saw standing with Lexi on the other side of the room. His outburst had reminded her how relieved she was that their five months of living under Father Al's roof were finally coming to an end. The man had got them out of a hole, but Lazarus House was hardly The Ritz.

With her generous settlement, Mavis had already rented a light, bright studio flat within walking distance of Blackheath village, somewhere she had wanted to live all her life but never been able to afford. It was near a private hospital owned by one of The Corporation's joint ventures, to which she had been given a season ticket, and close to some shops and cafes where she was planning to spend her windfall.

Father Al looked like he was about to cry. Henry didn't want him to be upset. "Come on Al. The five have been through a great deal, and you and I have been able to help them, materially, in very different ways. Now we know that they are safe, which you cannot disagree had to be our priority, we can get back to addressing some of the bigger questions. What we have done for them will already be helping other people, assuming what Mason said at the Select Committee is true."

Try as he might, the priest could not mask his distress. "We had some terrible nights in Lazarus House. How could you know? You weren't there. A couple of them used to scream out in the darkness, regularly, in the most terrible state, thinking they were back in the Disposal Center. Mabel is still doing badly. I have offered to let her stay with me, but she's insisted on going into a dorm under the care of one of The Corporation doctors. I can't say I trust them. Our most powerful witnesses, the only people who can tell the world about the horror they experienced, have signed a pact with the Devil. They are gagged."

"And you think getting them to drag it all up again in court would be in their best interests?" Henry said. "How's that going to help anyone recover from a trauma? You didn't want them to be dependent on charity forever, did you? They've got their dignity back. I am sure there are plenty of other parishioners in need of your good offices. We are all grateful for everything you have done for them, but even you have to admit it is time for them to move on."

Other members of the resistance movement that PACE had spearheaded were gathered to celebrate what everyone except Father Al regarded as a win. Henry sincerely believed they could move their campaign onto a new footing, energized by having a small but significant victory under their belt. It was easy, in retrospect, to forget the tremendous fear that the escapees and their rescuers had experienced on that momentous day, back in January, when Lexi had secretly infiltrated the Disposal Center and snatched the five survivors back from the last leg of their voluntary voyage towards the furnace.

Jess, the MP's researcher, had come along to celebrate with her boss. No one had thought about how she was going to get up the stairs, and it had taken a while to get her and her chair into the reception. Now, however, she was positioned next to a table with a small plate of sausage rolls and crisps, and a bottle of Another Place beer. Al, realizing he would get no further with Henry and David, pulled up a chair alongside her.

"How are you doing?" he said. "I don't think we've met before this evening?"

Jess assured Al that she and Nicky were, in fact, still trying to get answers to the question that troubled him the most. Top of their list was finding out how many Endings had been completed since the program began. No one wanted to give them the number.

"Knowing that you're onto it is some consolation," Al said. "I've been worried we might have lost sight of the big picture. There's just no debate about whether it's wrong to kill people who aren't valued. It's like, once the Act was passed, it wiped out everyone's conscience."

"You don't need to convince me," Jess said, "In fact, I'm even more worried about where they might go with it next."

"What do you mean, next?"

"There are rumors among the disability activist community. Nothing concrete, but people are saying they want to broaden the scope. There's a faction of Yuthies who think they should relax the criteria. Encourage other kinds of people to join the death cult."

Father Al turned pale, but before he could say anything Nicky was with them. She had heard about his concerns from some of the others and wanted to tell him that she had been trying to get the media to start writing about the moral issues. Unfortunately, it was turning out to be a long slog. No one seemed interested.

Bob was pleased he had been able to make a contribution to the success of the evening by doing something that, for once, would not put his day job in jeopardy. He had moved the music system he had rigged up for the presbytery into the pub. The happy playlist he had curated to keep up the spirits of the Lazarus House lodgers worked well for a party. 'Freedom! (90)' by George Michael faded down and was followed by Meatloaf's 'Bat Out of Hell'. He looked around at the guests, hoping to spot someone he might feel comfortable talking to apart from Lexi, who was now deep in conversation with Meg and Ayesha.

George caught his eye and beckoned him over to the bar. He was perched there with Bryn, who looked stronger than the last time Bob had seen him. The trusty red walking frame was still there, but Bryn seemed to be standing up a little taller and wasn't gripping the walker with his usual air of anxiety. "Let me get you a drink," George said, affable as ever.

"I'll have one of those Another Place beers, thanks." Bob was pleased to see that the Indian Pale Ale he had first tried in his hometown of Southport was now on sale in London. The label reflected the Antony Gormley statues that formed an eerie, permanent installation on the vast sands of the Mersey estuary. "Gents, tell me, what excitement does the future hold for you two old reprobates?"

As George worked on getting the attention of the purposefully unobservant barmaid, Bryn started to chat.

"Al's been very kind. He's done his best for us. But we'll be glad to get our privacy back. Negotiating with the ladies over the television. Bickering over people spending too long in the bathroom. Being looked down on by those creepy statues. Not to mention that dreadful Lazarus painting. No wonder we've been having nightmares. It's been stressful at times to say the least. I'd be lying if I said otherwise."

"So where are you off to, then?"

"Well, we've decided to get a place together, George and me. We were thrown into each other's company by accident, but we get on well. I was already struggling living on my own and to make matters worse I've got myself onto some kind of a list on account of being a fire hazard. My good friend George here, is going to take his life in his hands and help me out."

"Wow. A flamin' hot bachelor pad!"

Bryn grinned and lifted half a lager to his lips. "Let's hope not. There are a few things we've been helping each other with. Aside from the practicalities, I had missed just having someone to chat with. We thought a flat share would be worth a try, as long as we're both well enough to keep an eye out for each other. Like Morecambe and Wise. Although I think George has got the worse end of the bargain trying to keep me out of trouble."

"Maybe," George said, "But there has been the odd moment when you've really come through for me, mate. We've both seen things we wouldn't be able to talk to anyone else about, even if we hadn't signed on the dotted line. I don't think Bryn realizes how much it's helped, him just being there to listen. We'll be paying Natalia to come in for a couple of hours a week to stay on top of the chores. That should compensate for some of Bryn's lack of enthusiasm in that department. You know, Bob, we were wondering if you might be able to help us set up a few gadgets?"

"Like what?"

"Well, we don't want to be over-connected. Being at Father Al's has weaned us off the old virtual assistants. But we do want to take a few precautions, what with Bryn's occasional forgetfulness, and the nasty business he had before with the fires. Could you put in some old-style smoke alarms for us? Not on the network though. If we get flagged up on one of the central databases we could both be out on our ear again."

Bob loved nothing more than the challenge of a new project. This seemed a much less risky way to support these elders than engineering the sabotage of a multi-million-pound Corporation Disposal Center. He thought of the Pulp song, 'Help the Aged' but was glad he had left it off the playlist.

While they kicked around a few ideas for helpful tech Bob might be able to install in the old boys' new pad, Lexi was discussing with Ayesha, Meg and Nicky what PACE should do next.

"I'm doing all I can in the political world, honestly," Nicky said, her pink lipstick still in place though marred with a little flaky pastry from a sausage roll, "But we need to think laterally. Mason's a very powerful man. He's known to be litigious. Taking him on would be a big risk for any media outlet. They would have to be confident they have the public behind them, and at the moment, that's not so clear."

"It makes my blood boil," Lexi said. "They make it all sound so easy and humane, but we know what goes on in those places. It was like a horror movie."

"Do you think I should just break my NDA?" Meg

asked. "Let's face it, at my age, even if they come after me, I would be dead by the time it got to court."

"You really don't need the stress." Nicky had been clear all along that she did not want any of the survivors to put themselves under any pressure from the media, "Seriously. You've been through enough. There has to be another way."

Lexi had been giving serious thought to how they should carry on fighting. "I'm convinced direct action is the way to go. Just look at what the kids have achieved with climate change. That would never have happened without mass protest. But I'm just not sure anyone would care enough about old people to cause a riot."

"You're right," Ayesha said. "We need to get some proper publicity."

"Yes, but we also need to protect Lexi and Bob," Nicky added, "For all the good intentions, whistle blowers get hung out to dry. The notion of protection is a sham."

Ayesha looked thoughtful. "It doesn't have to be a riot," she said. "You can do a lot without anyone getting hurt. If we think creatively we can do something big. All it takes is one headline-grabbing idea. Or getting a celebrity involved, maybe?"

Meg shook her head. "Great idea, but totally crazy. Who wants to be associated with wrinklies like us?"

"It would have to be someone who likes to take a pop at the Government. Whose brand is all about being against the establishment and big companies," Ayesha said.

She had given Lexi an idea. "You know, a few years back, Fakesy was commissioned to do a painting at the school where Bob and I met. It's where I still work, actually. He's become pretty damning of the establishment. And he's huge now. Like global huge."

"Love your ambition Lexi, but I can't see how we could pull it off." Nicky had a lot of time for her, even though she had pushed her to the point of discomfort more than once.

When The Corporation first trialed surveillance in education, Lexi explained, they had arranged for a Fakesy David Bowie portrait to appear unannounced in the school one Monday morning as a PR stunt. "It went viral right away. You can still find the coverage on Splutter. It's got its own page on the school website. It was all top secret. But someone had to let Fakesy in over the weekend to do the work. Someone who actually had quite a bit of input to the project. They spoke more than once."

"Was that you?" Meg asked. Lexi was always full of surprises. She must say thank you to Alice for choosing someone so interesting as a friend.

"Not me, no. It was Bob."

"What, Bob? Your Bob?" Ayesha said, as they all glanced across to where he was loading a flimsy paper plate with more sausage rolls than it could reasonably support. How could a nerdy, scruffy, introverted IT guy like Bob, with a borderline addiction to high-fat snacks, have a hotline to a darling of the international art world?

"Never judge a book by its cover," Lexi said quietly. "Bob has Fakesy's contact details. We get a Christmas card from him every year."

The others weren't sure they had heard her correctly, but she carried on.

"Bob had just arrived on secondment from The Corporation. Rockstar Ending hadn't even been invented. Fakesy wasn't such a big star then, either. Probably needed the money. Aerosol for hire. I can't imagine he would take cash from a big corporate these days. He's much more political. You can afford to have a social conscience once you're rolling in it."

"Now you come to mention it," Ayesha said, "I do remember something about it in the media. I wonder how he'd feel about helping us expose the Rockstar Endings program, though? Especially if The Corporation has been a client."

"We can only try. I can get his number from Bob."

"Why not give it a go?" Nicky said, "But it wouldn't be enough on its own, would it? A talking point, maybe, but it wouldn't have the weight to send them into reverse gear. What we really need is a way to bring it to life for everyone. Give it some oomph to get the media on board."

"Like a protest? Maybe we can tie in some non-violent direct action?" Ayesha said.

"You really want to do that, don't you?" Lexi said. "I'll do it with you, Ayesha." After all the risks she had taken to free the five, performing a publicity stunt would be a walk in the park, and much more fun. "But we need to think about a theme. I'll have a chat with Bob. I'm sure we can come up with something appropriate."

Ayesha was already planning how she would square her involvement with Ajay. She had managed to stop Sonny blowing the lid on her burgeoning appetite for activism on New Year's Eve, but it had been a close call. Her husband approved of her volunteering at the Seniority shop, but he would think that taking to the streets was a step too far, and an unnecessary risk at their time of life. He had no idea of the danger they would soon be facing. In a few months they would both be 70, the trigger to be targeted by the Endings business.

The last protest Ayesha had taken part in was for Black Lives Matter, back when they still had their business. In the nearest they ever got to an argument, Ajay had caved in when he realized he could not persuade her to stay at home. Rather than leave her to face an imagined threat alone, he had tagged along with a rucksack full of disposable face masks and hand sanitizer he had bought from one of their friends in community pharmacy. It had turned out to be a rather moving afternoon, as the two of them took the knee outside Lewisham police station alongside a few of the staff who worked in their chain of takeaways.

"You're lucky to have Bob supporting you with all this," Ayesha said.

Lexi already knew. "He's the best thing that ever happened to me."

At that moment Bachman-Turner Overdrive's 'You Ain't Seen Nothing Yet' started to play. Lexi smiled and tapped her foot in time to the fast-paced riff. 'Great choice, Bob.' She shot him a knowing smile.

CHAPTER THIRTY-FIVE

Early on Sunday morning, two days after the PACE party, Lexi found Bob sitting in the kitchen looking disheveled. His body was scantily covered by the silk kimono he had started wearing around the house at every opportunity once Meg had moved out. It was unusual for him to be up before eight at the weekend. Lexi had been conscious of him shifting about through the night but had put it down to indigestion. He was rummaging through one of the many plastic boxes he used to store his technical supplies.

"What's up, love?" Lexi said, flicking on the kettle and starting to unload the dishwasher. Bob rarely seemed to worry about anything, but he was not himself today. "Did you have a bad night?"

He did not look up. "I'm missing one of the phones."

"Which phone?" He had piles of gear lying around the house. She marveled at how he kept track of any of it, let alone noticed if something was lost.

"One of the set I took over to Lazarus House for the Fab Four."

He opened a small tablet he kept in the box, unlocked

the encryption, and scrolled through his records. If he needed to look something up, it must be bad. Bob could remember great long strings of digits even though he would often forget where they kept the spare toothpaste.

"Mabel," he said. "She still has the device I gave her."

"Does it matter? Can't you just disable it remotely?" Lexi was accumulating fragments of technical know-how from living with a geek.

"Yes, but I need to get it back. There's an outside chance it could be traced back to me."

He did not need to say any more. Bob's career at The Corporation would be over if anyone discovered he had been helping PACE. No one had realized that he had recognized Bryn during the drone incident. He could not give them a reason to start digging now.

She placed a mug of tea in front of him. "I'll sort it today. Father Al gave me the name of the dorm she's gone to. I wanted to check in on her anyway."

Within a couple of hours Lexi was in the street outside the dorm holding a neat bouquet of daffodils and a new phone so that Mabel would not feel isolated after the snatch-back. Bob had agreed it would be best for her to take a cab alone. There would be cameras everywhere to keep the old people safe, and it was getting too dangerous for him to keep hacking in to erase compromising footage.

Mabel was now living in a former shopping center. It had been redeveloped when all but the most exclusive high streets faded into dereliction. The corporation had repurposed numerous malls as dorms after Yuthentic decreed that old people should be offered low cost accommodation where they could be cared for by robots. After human transmission of COVID had killed tens of thousands of elders, it was a no-brainer for them to be looked after by machines that did not need to breathe and could be disinfected regularly. The robots were strong enough to move people of all sizes without needing a bariatric lift. They could harvest medical and emotional data on those in their care, engage in simple conversations and be relied upon not to make a fuss if their clients were abusive or held objectionable views. Best of all, they could cope implacably with the bodily functions that might cause distress for a human care worker.

When Lexi told Mabel she was on her way over, she sounded more content than when she was living at Father Al's. She still had the phone and was happy to give it back along with the password she had set. It only took a few seconds for Lexi to enter her details into the dorm's security system, and tick a few boxes, so that Mabel could get her permission to visit.

A glass-filled arch marked the main entrance. As Lexi approached, her face was scanned and the center of the glass appeared to dissolve, creating an opening which reformed as soon as she had passed. She heard metal bolts slide into place behind her and realized that the glass was a hologram designed to make the premises look open and clean. A voice from nowhere welcomed her, confirmed her permission to visit Mabel, and asked her to follow a trail of blue lights that appeared in the polished concrete floor. The place felt eerie. There was no reception. Only the voice telling her where to go and the inanely smiling care bots of various proportions that glided by without acknowledging her presence.

After a couple of turns, she passed through another mirage and entered a block where she dimly recalled a pharmacy had once stood. An iconic brand, the company had declined into a tatty wreck before finally moving all its retail operations online. She found herself in confined space scattered with a few low vinyl chairs in shades of beige. It felt like an abandoned school common room, or how the waiting area in a doctor's surgery used to be. Except there was no-one else around. There were cheap synthetic carpet tiles on the floor, and around a dozen doors leading off the small rectangular hall. Unlike many of the dorm residents, who slept in communal wards, Mabel had been given a premium, private room as part of her settlement. One of the doors was lit up with the words, 'Welcome, Lexi! Mabel is delighted to see you'.

'Why the exclamation mark? Is it so surprising that someone is getting a visit?' Lexi muttered under her breath as the door to Mabel's room slid open.

The phone was the first thing she saw. It was on a small, low, pale blue, plastic table next to the door. There was an envelope bearing Lexi's name in spidery capital letters. Mabel was lying on her bed, asleep.

Not wishing to startle her, Lexi gently slipped the phone and note into her bag and looked round the windowless room for a vase. A large screen was displaying a summer garden scene that made the space less claustrophobic, but it was impersonal and inorganic. Sterile fixtures. Gleaming neutral surfaces. Not a speck of dust. No photos, even. The smell of antiviral disinfectant. The daffodils were nothing special, but Lexi thought they would brighten things up. No vase. She would have to ask Mabel how they could get hold of one.

Mabel looked peaceful. Lexi thought about leaving her to sleep. She knew that she had found it tough living at Lazarus House. Sharing a room with Mavis would have been hard work for anyone. She deserved a rest after all they had been through. Nevertheless, Lexi could not leave without letting her know that she cared enough about her to visit.

She drew a flimsy pale green plastic chair up to the bedside, quietly took a seat, and spoke softly. "Mabel, it's me, Lexi. I've brought you some flowers."

There was no response.

"Mabel?" She was a little louder now. Still nothing. Lexi reached across onto the bed and touched her hand. "Goodness, you're cold.. We need to get you a blanket."

It was then that she noticed Mabel was not breathing. She touched her forehead with the back of her hand, hoping she had made a mistake. It was dry and icy.

"Mabel? Wake up! Mabel!"

Still no reaction. Lexi felt hot and nauseous. She looked around for a communications device to summon help. There was nothing. Only one thing for it. Already on her feet, she began CPR, shouting for help between breaths. The room would be under surveillance, and sooner or later someone had to notice what was going on.

After a few minutes the door swung open. There were two robots. One was a squat unit that seemed to be a peculiar assemblage of medical equipment, the other had a more humanoid appearance.

"Please stand back and let my colleague take over," the

bot with an animated face said. "She is fully equipped to perform oxygen-enhanced life support."

Exhausted Lexi fell back. Momentarily relieved, she paused to get her breath back while a ventilator unit emerged and slipped quickly into place, first sealing Mabel's face with a silicone mask, then covering her entire head and chest with an opaque unit that she could hear performing compressions to keep her blood circulating. The rhythmic sounds of pumping and rushing air brought a peculiar sense of order to the room.

"Thank goodness you are here! Will she be all right now?" Lexi gasped between sobs. "Did I get here in time? Is a doctor coming?"

The bot with the face, its soulless smile utterly inappropriate for the circumstances, spoke: "There is no reason for a doctor to be in attendance. Data gathered by my colleague performing life support confirm that Mavis died twenty minutes before your arrival. She completed a 'Do Not Resuscitate' order yesterday. I am sorry you have had to observe this procedure and apologize for any distress you may have been caused. Can we offer you counseling at the expense of The Corporation? Our chat bots are most sympathetic and have won awards for their perceived emotional intelligence."

The scene Lexi had just witnessed had barely sunk in. "I don't need counseling, I need you to call a doctor!"

"Counseling for bereaved friends and family is included in Mabel's enhanced care package," the bot said, its face still not quite right although something shifted around the eye area in a badly configured attempt to look sympathetic. "My colleague will keep Mabel oxygenated until we receive the instruction from our medico-legal team to stop."

"You can't stop!"

"Lexi, she wants us to stop. She wanted everything to stop." Face bot said slowly, as its muscular companion began to grind to a halt, and the room fell silent.

There were two things Lexi wanted at that moment. For Mabel to be alive, and to call Bob. Neither option was available.

"Get off her, you mechanical murderer!" she shouted, pummeling on the unit that now encased Mabel's head and torso. "Let me in! You're suffocating her!" She tried to lever it off so she could start CPR again, but it had been clamped into position.

"Please don't do that, Lexi, or I will have to sedate you for your own safety."

"But she's dead!"

"You are correct. No action can change that now."

Lexi gave one last heave at the ventilator casing. It was impossible to get a grip on its smooth shell. As she tried to force into the tiny space between the mattress and the machine, one of her hands slipped. She winced sharply as half a nail ripped from a finger. The jab of pain disrupted her intention. As she numbly watched drops of her own fresh blood splash onto the floor, she was forced to admit that she would never be able to lever the dead weight from Mabel's face and chest. Still shaking, she collapsed on the chair, her damaged finger hanging at her side. A roll of tissue began to extrude from the care bot.

"Please take this to stem the bleeding," its companion said.

On autopilot, Lexi tugged out a swathe of soft paper that smelled of antiseptic and wrapped it tightly around her fingertip. She thought it was odd that the pain and bleeding stopped almost immediately. She was still shaking, and her breathing was jerky.

"Please try to calm down." The bot said. "Otherwise I will have to administer a sedative in addition to the local anaesthetic, antiseptic and coagulant that were impregnated into your dressing."

"You'll do what? You can't do that without my consent!" she was beginning to panic again. Lexi could hear faint whirring and clicking coming from inside the humanoid which was edging towards her, its mechanical arms starting to flex and extend.

"You gave us permission to administer emergency medication when you applied for a visitors' permit. Standard Corporation Terms and Conditions," the robot said, its expression now blank.

"OK, OK. Give me a second." The last thing she wanted was to be drugged. She focused on slowing her breathing and edged away. It followed her. "There's no need for any more meds. Really. I'm just in shock. I think I need to go home."

The door to the room slid back, and the voice that had welcomed her when she first arrived spoke. It was coming from the corridor. "I hope you agree that it would be best for everybody if you leave now. Your permission to be on these premises expired when Mabel sadly died. Kindly follow the blue lights and retrace your steps to the outer portal. We need to remove the deceased and ready this room for a new client. Our private rooms are in high demand."

Although she was reluctant to leave Mabel behind, Lexi was becoming concerned about getting out of the place safely herself. She picked up her bag along with the flowers, and headed for the door, checking behind her a couple of times to make sure she wasn't being followed by the anesthetist on wheels.

When she got home, still in a daze, Lexi's face was ashen and her eyes red from crying in the cab. It would have been embarrassing if a person had been driving it, but that was rare these days.

"You look awful!" Bob said the first thing that came into his head and regretted it immediately. "Why did you bring the flowers back? Didn't she like them?"

Lexi silently pulled out the device and handed it to him. "I got it for you," she said. "Best you do your thing."

He didn't look at it. Was she angry with him? "Crikey! What did you have to do to get hold of it?" Bob could sense her distress. She just shook her head. He saw the bandage. "What happened to your hand? Tell me! What's going on Lex?"

"Oh Bob. It was awful." She collapsed into tears again. As he moved to hug her, she pushed him away. "No. Just a sec."

She handed him the envelope that Mabel had left her, crinkled up and streaked with dried blood. Bob tore it open and read the note inside. "There's more than just her password in here, love," he said. "You need to sit down."

He put his arm around her shoulder, guided her to

the sofa and gently took a seat next to her before showing her the paper.

Password: SetMeFr33

Bye Lexi. Thanks for everything. I'm happy now.

CHAPTER THIRTY-SIX

CHANNELLE HAD MISSED A CALL from Mason. The one time the CEO actually called her, and she had failed to pick up. Why was she starting to feel like her career was in danger of skidding out of control, even though she had successfully steered her employer through their first major crisis? He couldn't expect her to answer her phone in the shower, could he? Six weeks on from the Select Committee appearance, the sense of urgency had dissipated. She had even stopped stuffing her device into her bra when she was at home, so she would not miss a call if she were wearing clothes without pockets. It was as if Mason knew she had taken to leaving it in the bedroom, rather than balancing it on the edge of the sink when she was in the bathroom, as she had done religiously when the crisis was at its peak.

Without checking her voicemail she rang him right back. It was 6.15am.

"Have you seen your inbox?" No hello. No niceties.

"No, sorry I was just in the…"

"We have a huge problem. I don't expect to have to be the one telling you about it."

He had hung up before she could say anything.

Still wrapped only in a towel, Channelle sat on the edge of her bed and dripped onto her screen. She was glad she was sitting down because her legs went weak when she saw the pictures. Although Mason was a big fan of street art, she knew that this unforgettable image wasn't something he had commissioned.

She scrolled through photos of a series of murals and advertising hoardings that had appeared overnight in the vicinity of Brookwood, The Corporation's primary London Disposal Center. Until that morning, its location had been secret, hidden away behind twists and turns on an old industrial estate. Not anymore.

Channelle knew immediately that they had been painted by Fakesy. Mason had spent thousands, if not millions with him over the years, yet he could turn on him like this. It was clear for all to see. He had taken the Rockstar Ending imagery that had won so many awards and twisted it into something utterly horrific. Worse, the signposting that linked the cross between a gruesome treasure hunt and a comic strip made the location of Brookwood obvious to anyone who might be innocently travelling down a nearby street. One of the biggest posters was on a prime site on the Old Kent Road, and another appeared to be being driven around Parliament Square on one of the driverless mobile hoardings that pitched up daily to attract the attention of politicians.

She forwarded the file, without knowing where Mason had got it from, to the press office, her crisis PR agency and the Project Houdini team. With the best will in the world, they would not be able to get any of it taken down quickly enough. The most confrontational piece had been painted directly on a wall right by the gate to the DC.

Although she wasn't in the mood for any of Greg's snarky jibes, she knew she had to check in with him. He got to her before she could hit the speed dial, throwing her off balance just as she was trying to step into her underwear. Mason had already instructed his legal team to throw everything they had at getting the pictures removed. The sharpest, most adversarial lawyers in the land were already on the case, Greg assured her. Unfortunately for The Corporation, however, everyone knew that no matter how fast they worked, the pictures would be all over social media before any of them made it into the office. Even the most expensive lawyers did not have access to a time machine.

Channelle rattled off a holding statement and sent it to Mason and Greg for approval while she pulled on a dress, necklace and heels, and called a car. This was not a day to look informal. Nor did she want to risk getting stuck on the underground or find herself in a public space where she could be overheard talking about the crisis.

"These pictures," she said to Sonny once she was settled in the back of an auto. "Do we have a clue whether they represent what actually goes on in the DC? Is that what it's like in there? A conveyor belt of trolleys going into a furnace? People waking up scared out of their wits? Headless robots? Surely we couldn't have done something this stupid?"

"I've no idea. No one at Brytely has ever been inside. We were supposed to be going on the tour, remember? But it never happened."

Mason had stood down Channelle, Lola and the team from the visit they had discussed and gone along on his own. He had said little about it when he came back. How stupid could she have been not to question him properly?

"I've got to pick up another call, Sonny, sorry. I'll be in by eight. Can you get Bob up to speed as soon as possible, if he isn't already?" She switched between lines and took a deep breath. "Hi, Faye."

The journalist didn't waste any time. "Channelle. Have you seen the Fakesys?"

"I'm just on my way into the office. Can I call you back later?"

"Any idea where they've come from? Are they real Fakesys? Did you get any warning? I mean some of the images, they are pretty violent. What do you think about this deliberate attack on The Corporation? That's what it is, right?"

"I'll call you back later, Faye. I can't really say any more than that right now."

"Isn't Mason furious? He's gone from being a corporate pin-up to the Grim Reaper overnight. Literally. All that fuss he made when I said he was handsome! He'll be begging for anyone to say that now. That caricature is something else. Would you ask him if he'd rather be depicted as an ELF?"

Channelle knew better than to take the bait. "Like I said, Faye, I'll call you back as soon as I have something for you."

"OK. I might send over a few more questions. Look out for them?"

"Sure."

Channelle went straight up to Mason's office. His PA waved her in immediately, after handing her the notes Sonny had left. Greg was already there.

"We need this stuff taken down, now!" He seethed, as soon as she closed the door behind her. He had activated complete floor-to-ceiling opacity on the glass walls of his office so no one could see inside. "We are on the verge of signing for Phase Two, Channelle. Have you any idea what that means? It's only a matter of time before the Minister calls me herself. No thanks to you, I've already got someone on their way to paint over the mural at Brookwood."

"Look, Mason. We are getting a lot of questions from the media, and we're going to have to find some answers, or this will only get worse."

"We are delivering our numbers. This is a government contract bound by commercial terms which do not allow us to disclose details." Greg said, coldly. "You're just going to have to comms it. We have signed off your holding statement. That will cover us for now."

"No. No it won't. And describing taking people to their death as a detail," she made the inverted commas sign in the air with both hands, "won't make us many friends either."

She took out the printed sheets and handed them to the men. They looked at them in disgust.

"I've had my team pull together all the questions we've had so far. The US hasn't woken up yet, but you can expect more when they do. Some of these points it's reasonable to decline but this one here – I need to know the facts before we draft a response. Do the images represent what actually goes on inside the DC? I'm hoping the answer is no?"

She scrolled to the pictures Mason had sent to her device and synced with the massive screen on his wall. The rest of the room shrank into obscurity as the attention-grabbing image dominated every thought.

"Look at this. Spread throughout the scene there are five people struggling to rise up from their trolleys. Count them. Three women, two men. Just like the five. I don't believe this is a coincidence. This isn't a random attack. Whoever briefed the artist knows about the five and may even have seen footage from inside the building. Unless you two can convince me otherwise, I have no reason to doubt the rest of this horrorscape is accurate.

"One could speculate that the only fictitious characters are the female superhero in the orange baseball cap, who looks like she's leading them out, and the rather unfortunate cartoon of the Grim Reaper over by what I assume to be the entrance to the cremation chamber."

She turned away from the screen, which she had been following with her eyes as she talked through the contents, and faced the two silent men, one of whom had a startling resemblance to the peculiarly handsome bringer of death that now peered eerily over Channelle's shoulder.

"So guys, can you tell me, is this what the place looks like inside?"

"They all signed NDAs," Greg said, defensively. "The five renegades. The two staff who were on duty on that day. They are all gagged. One of the escapees has sadly died. Their compensation has been substantial. They would have too much to lose." He deferred to Mason, who refused to react.

Chanelle pressed on. If she was going to get fired, she might as well go out with a bang. "You didn't answer my question. Surely it can't have looked this bad, could it?" She had hesitated too long, shying away from asking the questions that needed to be answered. If only she had insisted on seeing inside the place, they might not be in this mess now.

"Stop giving me the silent treatment, guys," she spoke slowly and loudly, as if trying to make boundaries clear to a recalcitrant toddler, "Is this what happens in there?"

She sensed an affirmation in an almost imperceptible nod and lowered gaze. Her device buzzed. It was a message from Marco, the head of security. Events were taking a turn for the worse over at Brookwood. A group of activists had turned up at the entrance. The good news was that they had upgraded the surveillance after the dreadful hiccup that had left them in the dark for so long when they tried to investigate the incident where the five had bailed out. They still had no clue how that had happened.

She tapped on the console, and vivid HD footage of a demonstration replaced the photo and began to live stream onto Mason's wall.

The new version of the Fakesy dominated the room, only now it had become the backdrop to a performance. The protesters who stood in front of it were disguised as David Bowie in the 'Lazarus' video, their eyes bandaged and replaced with buttons. All of them were wearing loose white nightshirts which contrasted with the highly colored, deeply disturbing supersize illustration behind them. The sensitive audio picked up their sound system blasting out a song, something about being in heaven. A couple of activists had glued themselves and a hospital bed to the pavement in front of the wall. It was all being captured on video. The CCTV camera panned to the road where passers-by were filming on their devices. A car with the livery of a news-streaming broadcaster pulled up on the other side of the road. Channelle recognized Faye among the onlookers but kept quiet.

"Are they on Corporation property?" Channelle asked, clutching at straws. "It that a private road by any chance?"

Marco replied on an audio channel. "It's a public street. I could still send some muscle? We have a contractor that specializes in sensitive situations," he offered, "Although I wouldn't recommend it."

Greg let out a nervous grunt which Channelle ignored before responding.

"No. We can't wade in like that. Look at them? They are like giant teddy bears. The optics would be appalling." The question about how closely the picture resembled the Disposal Center was still nagging away at her.

"Marco, can you give us a feed from the inside of the DC please?"

He faltered. "Erm, that's very sensitive. We're dealing with customers in the last stages of their life who have not consented to personally identifiable information being shared. I would need high level authorisation to do that."

"I'm with Mason and Greg, head of legal. Is a verbal instruction from them good enough?"

"Mason, the CEO, you mean," he was suppressing a

giggle that intimated he might have just seen the Grim Reaper cartoon.

Mason was terse. "Yes. Me. Now, do it."

The protesters faded away and a much more peaceful set of images flowed across the wall. They were coming from inside a clean, spacious industrial environment, with a gleaming green floor. A rectangular, thick, glass structure occupied much of the space, like a super-sized fish tank. Inside it, along one wall there were stacked grey and white cylinders of gas. A sign saying 'High Temperatures, Danger' gave a clue about what the furnace-like contraption, topped with a large duct to the ceiling, might be for. It was not a pizza oven.

Channelle compared the live feed to the mural. The outline of the enormous room was uncannily similar, except there were no trolleys, or terrified old people strapped to them.

"Is this live, Marco?"

"Yes. The first cohort is due to arrive in about half an hour."

"Tell me, would there normally be robots on the floor, like in the picture?"

"Sometimes. It depends what's going on."

"Anything like the ones in the picture?"

"Very like the ones in the pictures, I'm afraid."

"What about the one holding the guy up in the air in the mural? The one kicking his feet. Struggling. Younger than the customers."

"I have to say, that matches the description of one of the unfortunate events in January."

"Did we ever find the missing CCTV?"

"No. Sorry."

Mason's PA put her head round the door. "I thought you'd want to know, the Minister's office just called. I said you were in a meeting, but she would like to talk to you at 9.30. Shall I confirm?"

He nodded, knowing that keeping the lines of communication open with his most important customer, even on a day when the conversation was going to be difficult, was his best option.

"Who's down there now?" Mason asked, suddenly ready to take control.

"Just the site operatives. Two people. Standard procedure. Everything else is automated."

"And when are we expecting the next lot of customers?"

"I only have the security feed, but from what I can tell, we are expecting to open the gates in about 20 minutes."

"Get them diverted to one of the other centers. Greg – go and call Ops. We'll have to send today's Brookwood pipeline to Farthingale. Make sure they keep the customers sedated. At least the last sorry shambles meant we polished up our contingency planning. If a cohort of Enders in transit runs into that pathetic mob, we'll have a far nastier mess to mop up. Let's use this as an opportunity to show our client just how nimble we can be."

CHAPTER THIRTY-SEVEN

B Y THE TIME CHANNELLE CAME out of Mason's office, Sonny and Bob had been at their desks for an hour.

The torrent of incoming information was overwhelming. Sonny was compiling a rolling tally of social media and news coverage, with the help of his colleagues over at Brytely, and Bob had been in regular touch with security, who had confirmed that no one had broken into the center, and the two operatives who had arrived for work just before the protesters showed up were safe for the time being. The overnight CCTV of the wall where the mural had appeared was missing. Bob knew that before security plucked up the courage to tell him but did not let on. A cold coffee stood on the edge of the desk, which Bob had bought for Channelle on the way in with the best of intentions. Unfortunately, it was now merely a spillage hazard.

Channelle shook her head and murmured, "You couldn't make it up. Let's ..." pointing to a side room with her thumb. They grabbed their devices and followed her in.

"At least he's told me more about what's going on." She paced up and down in the tiny space, trying in vain to burn off some of the stress, but looking a little less worried than she had appeared first thing. "I sat in on his call with the Minister. As far as the Government is concerned, we could be in a much worse place. It's obvious the business won't be at risk. We're just doing too well on the delivery."

"How well is too well?" Bob asked.

"We're handling in excess of 10,000 per month nationally."

"Is that 10,000 sign-ups?"

"No, 10,000 completions. There's no way they would want to back out now. The contracted business is a hundred per cent secure. There's something else I have found out today. I had no idea they were so far along in discussions about Phase Two."

"Some of the guys at Brytely have been talking about that," Sonny volunteered, and instantly regretted it when Channelle shot him a look. "And you didn't think you might share that information with me?"

"To be honest, I didn't believe them. We're already in a bit of an odd place with this thing from an ethical perspective. I just thought it was Lars' wishful thinking."

Bob wanted to support Sonny. He had grown to like him over the weeks they had spent together. "He's a very strange bloke, that Lars, Channelle. I can see why Sonny would have thought he was exaggerating. Some of the things he says are hard to take seriously. Plus, he gives everyone the creeps."

Channelle had more to tell them.

"After Mason went on the tour of the DC, the one

they told us not to attend, he got nervous about the disposal method. I think he might have already had his suspicions and wanted to stop too many people seeing it. To all intents and purposes, Fakesy might as well have been inside. The paintings are all highly accurate. It's beyond uncanny. I'm even wondering whether he might have got hold of the stolen CCTV footage from Project Houdini. It's that close."

Bob was motionless. Sonny shifted in his seat and said, "Oh come on! How could that be possible? We've never been able to find out what happened to it."

"It wasn't for lack of trying," Bob said, quietly. "Whoever ran the hack was exceptionally slick."

"I've just seen inside it with my own eyes. It's staggering how accurate a replica he has created."

"What's happening about Phase Two?" Bob wanted to get her away from the subject of the missing footage as quickly as possible.

"After Mason saw the factory floor a few months ago, the robots and all that – just like in the pictures – he came away convinced the whole thing could turn into a PR disaster. How right he was. The optics are appalling."

Sonny was confused. "Why didn't he tell you, if it was PR he was worried about?"

"I keep asking myself that. I don't know. If he'd bothered to say something, we would have been much better prepared." She sighed. "Anyway, as it happens, he had started to do something about it. I found out today, they've already gone a long way down the road to creating what they are calling an alternative pathway. Humanistic D2U."

"Meaning what?"

"Rockstar Ending will still run at the current volumes, but under the modified method the Angels will administer lethal medication in the car, rather than taking the Enders through all that fancy business lounge palaver at the DC. Research suggests people would rather just get it over with. For the economy package they'll kill them on the bus. There are several reliable termination drugs already in use in the countries that are ahead of us in this game. This way the customer is cold before they even get to the DC. It de-risks the whole operation. Reduces the chance of a wake-up too close to zero. And they can process more Enders when the expanded customer definition gets final sign-off. If they are DOA all they need is refrigeration onsite, they can stack them up on shelves and run the cremations 24/7. It will be a doddle compared to what they're dealing with now."

"That's all very well," Sonny said, "But how are you going to package that up for the media?"

"Events have forced our hand somewhat. Fortunately, the Minister was already working on clearance to make a joint announcement. They have a tentative date in the grid. We agreed on the call that, as part of the deal, in the run-up Mason will say that the first phase of Rockstar Ending has been judged a resounding success. He'll probably slip it in during our quarterly results at the end of next month. Then the Minister will give out the numbers in a written response to a question she's had from an MP. That will keep the Yuthies happy.

"Mason will say something about learnings, listening to feedback from stakeholders including staff and customers who have been through the experience – or part of it, at least. The usual. It follows on quite nicely from what came out in the Select Committee. He's even prepared to say that Fakesy was right to draw attention to some of the improvements that needed to be made, albeit in his usual exaggerated way. We look forward to supporting the Government further with their wealth and income distribution agenda. Adding incremental improvements to the nation's happiness index. Job done. Blah blah blah. Just like that."

"What did he think about the Grim Reaper?" Bob asked, finding it hard to believe that Mason had taken everything in his stride so smoothly.

Channelle look relieved. "It helped that he adores Fakesy. As the mastermind behind the commission at Charlton Green, you know that better than anyone, Bob. He'll be trying to get hold of a signed copy of the sketch right now. We're going to make it sound like he's angry when we get back to Faye but, if anything, it boosts his standing as a public figure worthy of caricature by one of the most famous artists in the world. He's up there with a select band."

"He wouldn't rather have been represented as an elf, then?" Bob said cheekily, "Isn't that what they call him?"

"Funnily enough, I haven't asked," Channelle appreciated the attempt to lighten the mood more than she let on.

"What about the protesters? Was he furious?" Bob asked.

"Not really. Just seemed to take it in his stride. Greg wanted to send in the heavies."

"No!" Bob gasped involuntarily at the thought that Lexi or Ayesha might have had their head kicked in and been unmasked. Channelle instantly reassured him.

"It's OK. Everyone else knew that violence would cause more reputation problems than it could ever solve. Mason was most angry about being blindsided. The pictures hit the screens before anyone here picked up on it. I'm convinced Fakesy sent him them direct, although I could never prove it."

Bob and Sonny took Channelle through the data they had collected during the course of the morning. They checked what was going on at Brookwood periodically. The protesters had gone away quietly as soon as the pictures had been taken and they realized there would be no arrivals to ambush. All that remained on site was an old unmade hospital bed which Marco's guys were able to dismantle with little fuss.

Now Phase Two was on the horizon, Mason appeared to have lost interest in the mysterious circumstances that had resulted in the five escaping from Brookwood six months before. Nobody bothered, any longer, to pursue the questions that remained unanswered. Instead, the company adopted the convenient, clichéd mantra that lessons had been learned, although there was no document detailing what those lessons might have been. With the expanded contract in the bag, Rockstar Ending was lauded as a roaring success. It had overcome its teething problems and was going from strength to strength. Furthermore, to demonstrate their flawless confidence in the future, the Project Houdini team was to be stood down.

Within weeks, Sonny and Bob would be free to move on to their next gig.

CHAPTER THIRTY-EIGHT

A BOUT TIME, FAYE THOUGHT, AS a message from Rex appeared asking her to see him the second she got in. It was six months since the first Mason tape had dropped. He had finally decided to run something. She wished his change of heart had been down to her winning his respect and him buying into her ideas. In reality, however, despite a burst of interest when she had told him about the relationship between Doc, Mason and Stella, he had been too nervous to do anything with it. Now, however, they had been overtaken by events.

It seemed like every major media outlet on the planet, except theirs, was awash with pictures of the Fakesy mural that had caused a sensation on the wires first thing. They needed to join in. The stunt had happened in their own backyard, only a few miles from the office, yet so far, the news desk had done nothing more than replicate what had been put out by Fakesy's own publicists. Rex was under pressure after the story came up in discussion with a major shareholder he had met for breakfast at The Wolseley, who also happened to be a collector of contemporary urban art.

The protest site is on my way in. Faye messaged back. *Shall I stop off?*

OK, but don't hang around too long. Need to file quickly. Did you get the Mason stuff checked by legal?

She ignored his question and called Channelle from the back of the car. All she got was a promise of a call back later. As the vehicle came to a smooth halt outside Brookwood she instructed it to wait so she could snap a few pictures from the back seat which she promptly posted on Splutter. She was always short of social media material. Rex never stopped making digs about her invisible profile. Stepping out and heading towards the wall, she set up a stunning selfie with the Grim Reaper peering over her shoulder. Wow, she thought. Fakesy had managed to capture the essence of Mason very accurately.

When the five protesters came round the corner, wheeling an operating trolley to which one of them was strapped, she switched to video, quickly messaging Rex:

Faye: *Lots going on here, can I live stream to our readers? Street theatre kicking off.*

Rex: *What? A few out of work actors with rubber gloves on their head?*

She sent him a quick clip of the activists in their ghoulish apparel, their eyes bandaged Bowie 'Lazarus' style. A speaker was mounted under the trolley blasting out the song.

Rex: *Whoa. Too disturbing. Rights issues with the music. Stream to the picture desk to edit.*

He was such a twat. She found a good spot for observing the spectacle and let her camera run. They weren't the best performers she had ever seen by a long stretch, but their costumes, however derivative, were unforgettable. After only a few minutes the picture desk said they had enough to go on, so she climbed back into the car, chased Channelle again, and started work on the report.

The piece she filed an hour later ran almost unchanged. It included brief references to what she had gathered over the preceding months mingled with commentary on the morning's events. She had quotes from Nicky Hartt, and a few words from a spokesperson for the activists, who said they wanted to be known as Bewley, calling for Brookwood to be shut down immediately. She was pleased that her inside track on the links between Mason, Stella and Doc were included, along with a wry reference to the easy ride The Corporation had been given at the HELP Committee. Most of all she was able to have a bit of fun working with the outlet's one remaining subeditor on a boxout and poll they pushed all day on Splutter:

Mason: Love Him…

- So unforgettable, he only needs one name
- With those steely grey eyes and perfect pecs he's everyone's best ELF
- Gotta believe him when he tells you "This won't hurt a bit"

…or hate him?

- Can't get away from the guy – he runs everything
- Is he just a weird undertaker on steroids?
- I wouldn't want him to grab MY granny!

It was a relief that the piece which had needled her for more than six months had finally been put to bed. She wasn't sure it had been worth all the aggravation, but it had reassured her that her nose for a story was still there. Even Rex had to admit they had gained an edge over their competition by exposing Mason's links with Doc.

In the car on her way home she scrolled through the pictures she had taken that morning. Faye had never understood what made people become activists. She had met plenty of them over the years, but none had been able to alter her opinion that pressure groups were a waste of time. The protest footage had brought them all a few clicks, but it had changed nothing. She had never been on a march in her life unless she was reporting on it. The markets were where the real power ebbed and flowed.

Before she went to sleep, Faye scanned through the shares she monitored every day for the prices at market close. Her eyes rested on The Corporation's listing. They were up 5 per cent.

CHAPTER THIRTY-NINE

THE PREVIOUS YEAR'S SUMMER PARTY had been excruciating for Portia.

Brytely had taken exclusive use of a ten-lane bowling alley that specialized in teambuilding events. Everyone was expected to turn up and demonstrate that they were genuinely enjoying themselves for the whole evening.

Unfortunately, Portia's performance was badly flawed. Despite her best efforts, she had struggled to maintain an appearance of enthusiasm. She had been nervous as soon as she had found out about the venue. Her hand-eye co-ordination was appalling and she had a premonition that all her shots would roll straight into the gutter.

By halfway through the night, the three co-workers she was playing against had run out of things to say by way of consolation. 'Unlucky' didn't begin to describe the state of her scoreboard. Portia tried to make light of her abysmal technique more than once, while the others smiled on patronizingly. One even offered to fetch her the ramp that was used by people who couldn't easily handle the heavy ball. She declined. Though well-intentioned, it felt like pity and it was a struggle to conceal her sense of humiliation. Even though there was a free bar, something she had never come across before moving to the big city, she didn't dare drink too much in case she said or did something that might give her away. Refusing alcohol in that environment marked her out as different, untrustworthy even. Eyebrows were raised when she started asking for a soda water while the others were knocking back the cocktails.

Later, in a one-to-one call with her manager, the question had been raised about whether Portia was committed enough to the company, with feedback that she could sometimes come across as aloof. She tried to brush it off, hiding the truth she knew, that her detachment was rooted in a severe case of imposter syndrome. It led to her being permanently on her guard against the horror of being found out, going to great lengths to disguise a range of personal characteristics, including her real name. If she was going to make a go of this career she had to bury every trace of being working class, Scouse and, indeed, quite unlike anyone else she had met since arriving in London.

Luckily for Portia, her critical role in Rockstar Ending had built her agency capital beyond anything she could have expected in such a short time. The minor humiliations of a year ago had been eclipsed by a steady stream of recognition for her work on the most successful campaign in the history of the agency. They had given her much more than the 'Portia – you rock!' mug which put her on the first rung of the corporate recognition ladder. What she and Sonny had pulled off had also trounced any doubts about her teamwork. In a much more satisfactory appraisal meeting, she had just been given an exceptional bonus, the likes of which she had never known would be possible for people like her.

She was looking forward to seeing Sonny even though, more often than not, she still found their relationship problematic. He would be moving back to the Brytely office within weeks, as his secondment had finished.

Although the bonus money had not yet hit her bank account, she had already spent some of it on an outfit for the noughties-themed agency party after a phone call with Karen, who remembered the 2000s better than her. Portia was born in 2002, but she recalled some of the hit songs from her childhood, as Karen had always had pop music on the radio. Although she had not been back to Liverpool since Christmas, she was phoning home more often these days after her Mum's successful trip to London. She was still worried about Karen's depression, although neither of them mentioned it.

Fashion advice proved to be an excellent neutral topic for conversation. There were even a few old photos which had given them both a laugh. It reminded Portia of the fun the two of them had had together, when she was small, before Marcus came along and rapidly became Dad to her three small half-siblings. It wasn't that they had fallen out, more run out of time.

"I'm not risking a muffin-top," Portia had said, "What on earth possessed them?"

They were sharing a screen and running through images of the Juicy Couture velour track suits which had been all the rage, with low-slung waistbands and celebrity abs that displayed varying degrees of flatness. Portia loved Kylie Minogue's look in the video for 'Love At First

Sight', a stripe of bright blue on each browbone, statement monogrammed jewelry, tight white vest and combat trousers. However, she believed it would be career suicide to turn up in pants slung so low you could see a bright orange G-string with the black lace of the underwear that would be essential to complete the look. Without that detail it wouldn't be Kylie, would it?

"If that's too risky, love, here's another one you can't wear," Karen laughed, pulling up 'Can't Get You Out of My Head' and the legendary white jumpsuit slashed to reveal swathes of perfectly proportioned cellulite-free flesh. "Crikey, Mum. You'd need some pretty good double-sided tape to keep all that in place."

That was how they landed on the dress. Not, however, the white one that left so little to the imagination, but the shorter halter-neck go-go dress that Kylie wore at the end of the same short film. Daring to wear it pushed Portia's courage to the limit, but once she tried it on, she knew it looked fantastic. Of course, the version Karen made for her daughter wasn't identical to Kylie's. She created the horizontal layers with thick silver satin ribbon that Portia had found in a posh London department store. Anyone who had seen that video would know who she was supposed to be. She curled her hair and managed to find a pair of plain black boots to complete the look.

All in all, this year's party promised to be easier than the bowling fiasco. As far as she knew, there were no compulsory activities involving any form of ritual humiliation.

She wished however that it had been a warmer evening as she strode towards the pier. A slightly chilly wind was blowing from the North. It wasn't as fierce as the gusts on the Pier Head in Liverpool, but it made the tiny hairs stand up on her fake-tanned arms. She wondered whether she had been down South long enough, yet, to 'go soft'. This had to be one of the first signs.

Portia gave her name to a hostess dressed in – she couldn't believe it – one of the pastel tracksuits she and her Mum had rejected only a week before. All the catering staff were wearing them. Thank goodness she hadn't gone with that option. People would have been asking her for cocktails and directions to the bathrooms all night.

Boots with low heels had been a good choice. She could walk easily despite the gentle swaying motion of the boat. In the best financial position in their history, Brytely had spared no expense. The venue was on a superyacht, kitted out to a very high specification. The smooth teak deck had been dressed in various noughties objects, the most striking of which was a replica Transformer in a glass case. The events team had hired it in from a props company, and a printed plaque explained that it was a model of Optimus Prime.

She checked in her overnight case in exchange for a plastic fob. One of the runners would take it to her cabin. She tucked the fob into the tiny bag she kept with her, containing only lip gloss, powder and a mirror. She would have liked to see her cabin and check her make-up, but before she could make it to the stairs, Stella was in her way insisting she immediately grab a glass of champagne from a weighty tray being proffered by one of the tracksuit brigade.

"Portia, darling. You deserve this!" Stella clinked her glass against hers. She was dressed all in white, with a short furry jacket and gold cowboy hat. From her own recent search for inspiration, Portia knew at once that Stella had come as Madonna in the 'Music' video. Behind her, an Ali-G lookalike was pacing the dancefloor in an outsize red satin jacket with 'pimp' written on it and larking about to entertain a group of her colleagues. She avoided eye contact with the actor and quickly turned in the opposite direction.

After work, it had been a rush to get changed and curl her hair, and Portia was starving. She didn't normally like drinking on an empty stomach, but the champagne slid down easily and within ten minutes she was onto her second glass, trying not to demolish all the crisps. There was no sign of any proper food yet. She was light-headed and hoped something would appear before too long. Cream leather sofas were scattered around the deck, with a few low tables, and a DJ was busy keying up vinyl at one end, with an area left clear for dancing immediately in front of her. She sank down and messaged Sonny. He was just making his way aboard.

Stella delayed him at reception. He was dressed in his usual outfit of jeans, T-shirt and a short zip-up jacket. Portia tried to catch his eye from her seat which was a few meters away, but realized her dress was riding up and turned her attention to arranging it to cover the tops of her thighs, just about. It wasn't like Kylie worried about any of that, was it? Someone in a peach tracksuit swapped the empty bowl of crisps for a full one, and Portia sat on her hands to stop herself having any more.

"Can I get you another drink?" Sonny was standing

by her seat. She wondered whether he had noticed her blush.

"I've already had two. Better pace myself." She said, as he sank into the sofa at right angles to hers and took a large handful of crisps.

"Stella's on top form tonight." There was a playful glint in his eye. She had no idea how to take it.

"You looking forward to coming back?"

"Oh, yeah. It was interesting client side, but not nearly as much fun. No free fruit. The offices are silent. Everyone watching their back all the time. No one shares anything. I'll be glad to be back in a more creative place."

She had hoped he would say he was looking forward to working with her again, but that would have to do. "Will you miss anything?"

"Just the usual thing. People. More accurately just one person."

She waited for him to carry on, steadying her breathing in the hope this would not be a revelation that threatened whatever delicate thing it was she could sense between the two of them.

"I must have mentioned Bob a few times? Old boy. Must be well over 40. But he was clever. Quiet. We were Channelle's support team. And Lola's. He gave me a couple of these as a leaving present. I thought you might like one."

He took out two small pouches printed with different versions of the David Bowie 'The Man Who Sold the World' album cover art. It took her a few moments to work out what they were.

"They're those things you can put your phone in," she said.

"Yep. Or if you're not paranoid you can just use it for – well, whatever it is girls keep in their handbags."

It had not crossed her mind that anyone would want to track her or overhear any of the mundane conversations she usually had. But it was nice that he had thought about her.

"Oh, thanks. You never know, right?"

"Do you have a preference?"

"The one with the long hair, I think."

"Cool. Bob had a job lot of them. I think he might have a side hustle going in Bowie merchandise."

She just about managed to squash the thing into her tiny sequined bag before asking him:

"Have you been to your cabin yet?"

"No. They are supposed to be amazing."

It was still light on the deck and would be for another two hours as it was close to midsummer. More of their colleagues were arriving, and it began to feel a bit more like a party. She knew she was going to have to get up and work the room at some stage, but all she really wanted to do was sit and chat with Sonny. The music was getting louder, and at long last some food was being presented to the guests in tiny bowls.

"How's your Nan?" Portia asked.

"She's good. Not causing too much trouble. Still asking after you all the time, as it happens."

"It would be nice to see them again."

Sonny nodded blankly and started looking around the room.

"Did you ever manage to speak to her about Rockstar Ending?"

"Kind of. We've agreed to disagree. Anyway, I couldn't say too much. Client confidentiality and all that. Plus, we've got Phase Two coming up fast now, haven't we? If she started grilling me on that it would be impossible. I don't think we can afford to spend any more time looking back though, Porsh. The expectations on us are only going to get higher."

"Wait 'til you see the brief," Portia said flagging down a server and taking another glass. "I imagine you already know the details."

"Bits and pieces."

"Lars has gone into overdrive, of course."

He followed her gaze to where Lars was standing, over by the DJ. Like Sonny, he was in his usual uniform, the Slayer T-shirt that he had been wearing all day in the office, this one emblazoned with the words, 'Do You Want to Die?' To avoid any accusations of not having made enough effort, he had pointed out to anyone who would listen that it was original tour merchandise from 2004. The DJ shook her head. He walked away disappointed, and crossed to Sonny and Portia, carrying a bottle of Another Place.

"I don't see why she couldn't have played just one track. They had a few albums out in the noughties," he said glumly. "It's my party too." Lars took a swig of the beer and tipped a whole bowl of wasabi peanuts into his hand.

"Come on, mate. You are the only one on the ship

who would know how to dance to it, if that's what you call it." Sonny said.

"They could allow me that one small concession. Without my insider knowledge they would never been able to save the situation."

"Why do you always have to play the evil genius?" Portia laughed. She would never have said that if she had been sober. Lars seemed to like her description and became more animated.

"We only won the Phase Two pitch because of my data. Without that, and my Yuthie contacts, well, anything could have happened. Stella's convinced she has a special relationship with Mason, but I'm not so sure. I mean, look at her."

Their leader was flitting around the room, unable to talk to anyone for more than ten seconds.

"Do you see? And I'm supposed to be the one who is not 'client-ready'."

It was known by everyone in the agency that Stella was still steadfastly resisting Lars' increasingly vocal requests to get out more.

Sonny chewed his lip as he recalled the peculiar dynamic in the car when he had accompanied Stella and Mason to the Select Committee hearing. Lars could have a point. Whereas he would once have been free with his opinions, Sonny hesitated. His time at The Corporation had made him wary of the risks of openly criticizing people in power.

"Maybe."

Lars started chatting about his favorite subject, Phase Two, answering the questions Sonny had until Stella arrived at their group, and sank down on the sofa next to Portia. "That dress looks fabulous on you," she said leaning in, "Is it vintage?"

"Actually, my Mum made it."

"Well, she's very talented, and fortunate to have a daughter who can carry it off so well."

"Thanks."

Portia could not believe what she had just heard. While she had been considered pretty among her schoolfriends, she had believed her appearance was second-rate ever since leaving Liverpool. It had been a struggle for her to find the right style on her budget as a student. She didn't want to stand out, especially not to look like she was trying too hard or, worse, working class. She had stuck to cheap, generic basics for a long time and kept a close eye on eyebrow trends.

It was only recently, when she had found herself with more money, that she had been able to afford something special. Tonight, she had found the confidence to dress up as an iconic performer, and it was the first time anyone had paid her a compliment since Sonny's grandmother had been nice to her on New Year's Eve. She must have made a good job of the fake tan, which she had used for the first time in five years, to try to match Kylie's gorgeousness in the video.

"Mason was very pleased with your contribution, Sonny," Stella said. It was the first time he had seen her since the Select Committee.

"Really? How does he even know what I did? I spent very little time with the bloke."

"Oh, he's noticed you. He's rather enigmatic. You just

have to take my word for it," Stella said. "Now, is there anything I need to know from your time there?"

Lars was shifting in his seat. It was obvious to Portia he was irritated that Stella had not even acknowledged his presence. He seemed jealous of the attention she and Sonny were getting.

"Like I said. I hardly spent any time with him."

"What about the fallout from the Fakesy thing? Or feedback on the Select Committee performance?"

"Consensus was that he took it in his stride. Even the Doc angle didn't rattle him. Only one outlet ran it."

"We are delivering amazing results for them," Lars butted in. Stella blanked him.

"Well, if anything occurs to you, Sonny, let me know. Now, Portia, I think we need to get this party started."

With a nod to the DJ, Stella effortlessly rocked up into her white stilettoes, and extended her hand to Portia. The first line of the soundtrack to Stella's outfit blared out and Portia, grateful for the courage the fourth glass of champagne had given her, followed. Within a few bars another twenty people had joined them on the dance floor, including Sonny who, Portia was surprised to see, could move pretty well. Lars was still on the sofa, looking at his device, having abruptly rebuffed the Ali G lookalike when he had tried to persuade him to strut his stuff.

By the time night fell, Portia's feet were aching, but at least she wasn't cold. She had kept half an eye on Sonny, but it didn't look like he was getting into any trouble. He even danced with her once or twice. Then, a noise out on the river heralded another surprise. The Corporation drone team arrived and threw up a rotating hologram that read 'Thank You Brytely – You Rock!', followed by a few spectacular fireworks that left the flavor of chocolate orange on your tongue.

"I should have asked, how's things with your folks?" Sonny was standing next to her at the rail, as the final burst of pyrotechnics came to an end.

"We're getting on better after Mum came down to visit."

"Are you still worried about them being targeted in Phase Two?"

"Of course."

"It's very difficult," Sonny sighed. She wished he would make his mind up. One minute he was saying they just needed to plough on with their job, and the next letting her see that, beneath the surface, he was still wrestling with doubts about what they were doing. The doubts were what they had in common.

Portia shrugged. "Yeah. But the way I see it, at least if we're on the inside we know more than anyone else. Maybe that means we can do something. No idea what, though."

The sleeve of Sonny's jacket touched her bare arm. "I really am glad to be back working with you," he said.

"Yes. We are the dream team, after all," she whispered, then pulled sharply away, before he could ruin the moment by changing his mind.

It was around 12.30am when the music had to dim, and the partygoers retreated beneath the deck to the bar which looked like something from a Bond film, only bigger. Portia got a second wind, and managed a couple more hours drinking, before staggering off to her room.

She reckoned that would be enough partying to keep her in the agency's good books for a few months, even though she declined the invitation to Stella's suite where the final few diehards would be carrying on.

Her cabin was amazing. The walls were polished wood, and the lush crisp white bedding had been turned down, with a chocolate on the pillow and a fluffy bath robe and slippers within easy reach. Her bag was on the bed, and there was a box containing another bottle of champagne, with a generic thank-you card which had the Brytely logo on one side. While she appreciated the gesture, it suddenly made her feel sad that there was no one there to share it with her.

It was years since she had been physically intimate with anyone. At least she had been old enough to slip in a few encounters before the pandemic, back in Liverpool. After that, she had become less carefree. No one at university had appealed much. The guys were all so posh. Sonny was the first person for years she had wanted to risk getting close to, even if they would have to file a PUSSI declaration. For a moment she toyed with the idea of inviting him to her room, but she didn't want to sour the evening by ending it on a rejection.

She would give the bottle of fizz to her Mum the next time she came to stay. Then Karen would get how well she was doing.

CHAPTER FORTY

Lexi was reminded why she had avoided getting involved in politics for most of her life. This was the most fraught meeting yet. The PACE activists had always been a bunch of misfits, but generally they had managed to find enough common ground to marshal behind their collective campaign.

Today's controversy was about how they were going to manage the booth at the local Summer Fayre where they were hoping to drum up public support.

Lexi and Bob had first encountered PACE at the previous year's Fayre, where David had covertly recruited her. This time, she was planning to volunteer. Bob was not keen to get involved but had come along because Lexi had asked him to.

He had no intention of working on the stand after his recent grilling from Lola about the missing protest footage. He had thought his number was up.

Out of the blue, Mason had asked for a copy of the video. Rumor had it he wanted it for his personal Fakesy collection. Unfortunately, once Mason knew the files were missing, he had to tell the Minister, who was forced to make an embarrassing public statement. When the security team could not get to the bottom of what had happened, Lola became suspicious. She could not believe it was a coincidence that video files linked to the Endings program had been lost on two separate occasions.

Luckily for Bob, before she had time to do too much digging, Mason had flipped out, summoned Marco, the head of security, and fired him on the spot to prove to the Government he took the issue seriously. Bob had felt guilty for a couple of days, but soon moved on as Marco's departure ensured his own head would not be offered as a sacrifice. No one wanted to suggest Mason had been wrong in his choice of scapegoat, so the investigation was dropped.

At the Fayre, PACE was going to sell merchandise for the first time. As his contribution, Bob had sourced some Faraday pouches, printed with the hashtag #BetterTogether which PACE had started using to counter the Yuthies' #OurTime.

Father Al was being negative. No surprises there. As the group huddled in the living room at Lazarus House, he poured from a large pot of tea. Ayesha offered round a plate of Party Rings to David, Lexi, Bob and the priest, who made no effort to disguise his disappointment.

"We have nothing to celebrate," he said, glumly. "Nothing at all."

"After all the risks Bob and I have taken, that's rather disingenuous," Lexi snapped. "Four of the five are re-settled and set up for life. As far as I'm concerned that's an 80 per cent success story."

Lexi was working hard to put on a brave face, but she

was feeling fragile. In an attempt to find closure, she had asked the dorm to confirm the cause of Mabel's death. They had refused to tell her anything, using the excuse that she was not a relative. Furious, she had sent them a copy of Mabel's final note with the suggestion that The Corporation might have coerced her into suicide. After that they went silent.

Bob persuaded her to drop it. He said that The Corporation's compliance with the law would be watertight, and that she should move on. But talking to Bob did at least help Lexi to process what had happened to Mabel. He proved himself, as ever, to be her rock, listening to her replaying the day's events as many times as she needed. More than anyone, he knew how badly it could end if Lexi allowed a Corporation counseling chatbot to mess with her mind.

They had decided not to tell Father Al about Mabel's note. It would be better for him to assume Mabel had died of natural causes than be forced to take a view on suicide being a mortal sin.

"We are fighting daily battles in a huge moral war. If you weighed the bodies that have been saved against the mountain of corpses that has been created, the four would be almost undetectable," the priest reminded the PACE crew.

Lexi would not give in. "But they've changed what goes on at the Disposal Centers as a direct result of us exposing the inhumanity of the system. All the robots have been decommissioned. You must have seen the video of that big cowboy one being smashed!"

"I'm not saying our little protest didn't have any impact, but many claim they were going to be remodeling the DCs anyway," Father Al said.

"Calling it a 'little protest' is an insult!" Ayesha joined Lexi in countering Father Al's pessimism. "We had global media coverage! Of course it had an impact!"

"Anyway," Bob said, trying to move the discussion into a more positive place, "Fakesy's giving us a copy of the most talked-about work to use on the stand. A big high spec print on canvas. It's got to be a huge draw!"

"Street theatre and all that – it's all very well – but we know the enemy will be there. Yuthentic will be right opposite us. And we need to take them on directly. No more Father Nice Person. I have every intention of saying prayers for the dead right in front of their poxy booth. That will show them!"

"Why stop there," Lexi retorted, "Go the whole hog! Throw in an exorcism, why don't you? We'll be a laughing stock."

David sighed. Ever the diplomat, even though he had retired from the service some years previously, he was determined to get everyone to work together. "You know, Al, Lexi and Bob have done a great deal. It's not fair to dismiss the sterling protest Ayesha choreographed either. I really think you should acknowledge what's been achieved rather than being a wet blanket all the time."

"OK. Fair point," Father Al finally acknowledged. "Even though I had never heard of that particular Lazarus before."

"And Mason's reputation is a little tarnished after that journalist contact of Nicky's revealed his relationship with

Doc. That's been helpful, even if she didn't go on the big pro-life crusade you were hoping for," David added.

"Acknowledged. But David, we mustn't delude ourselves. Rockstar Ending has not been stopped. It's merely been re-engineered. They might be rearranging the robots on the factory floor, but the targets are still in place. I've been through the Select Committee transcript again and again. All The Corporation have committed to is tweaking an algorithm to allow a last-minute deferral. Worse, Mason said they are going to work harder on the Enders so they are less likely to run for the escape hatch. That's how he placated the Yuthies. And now I have heard from the Bishop that something even worse is on the horizon."

"How can that even be possible?" Lexi asked, dreading what he might say next.

"There's a leaked document about something called Phase Two. New categories of people will be targeted. We can expect the same coercion. Only this time directed at younger people with illnesses and disabilities, too. All kinds of folks, not just older ones. They are going to remove the restrictions on Rockstar Ending. It's the ultimate democratization of death – the sequel. And I for one am not planning to keep quiet about it." Al was starting to go red and his eyes were wide with fury. Lexi had heard Jess talking about something like this when they had first met, but had not believed it would happen. She kicked herself for not mentioning it sooner while the others sat quietly taking in the priest's news.

"That's as may be, Al. But this is a community event. There is a dog show. A cake-making competition. Children's fancy dress. It's not the place for airing the hardcore politics of death capitalism. It supposed to be fun." David, who had a lot of contacts on the local council, finally decided the time had come for him to rein in Al. "Now, can we get back to discussing the booth?"

Eventually, it was agreed that they would use the canvas wall facing the road to hang the replica Fakesy. The copy of the scene from inside Brookwood was spectacular. Lexi smiled as she looked at the female superhero in the orange baseball cap leading the escapees to safety. It had been so sweet of Bob to ask Fakesy to put that in. The artist had paid for the print, on condition he could have it back after the event. A private collector had already bought it for such an eyewatering sum that he would have to send a team of security guards to keep it safe.

The scene was facing towards the road, so that people driving or walking by could see it. Cars beeped in approval as they passed and one child passing the booth remarked that Lexi looked uncannily like the 'orange lady' in the picture. "I'm much prettier," she had joked in response.

An hour after the Fayre was formally opened by Nicky Hartt, however, they were forced to take down the enormous print. Allegedly, there had been complaints from parents that the scene was traumatizing their children. One of the Fayre organizers came to the booth and said that such displays were not in the spirit of a family occasion. A row had broken out about it on Splutter. After all the trouble Bob had gone to, the organizers' ruling felt like a smack in the teeth to Lexi, but they had no choice other than to remove it. She hastily snapped a selfie in front of the canvas, before carefully easing it out of the fastenings and returning it to the minders. "You can't open an envelope without a bloomin' trigger warning these days," she muttered. "Have they never heard of Grimm's Fairy Tales?"

At least the Faraday bags seemed to be selling. Lexi had to admit they looked good with #BetterTogether emblazoned on various backgrounds. Bob had even popped in a few of his bootleg Bowie designs, which sold out first. She had been worried that he was getting obsessed with his new sideline and suspected there was a large number of them stored in his lock-up. It had been a nice creative outlet that helped fill his time while she was at work. The Corporation had put him on what they called 'the bench' after Project Houdini ended, on full pay, and he was still waiting to hear about his next assignment.

Across the way, the Yuthentic booth was swinging. They had hoisted a flag. On one side was a massive sigil – the circle with a diagonal cross that signified their command to the older generations to 'give way'. On the other was the #OurTime hashtag. Holly, whose constituency wasn't too far away, was guest of honor. The Yuthies were selling the usual collection of jewelry and T-shirts that carried one or both of their symbols.

From behind her pop-up table, Lexi eyed the opposition, recognizing the odd face as kids she had taught at school. A few of them even wandered over to see her with a friendly 'Hello, Miss', politely engaging her in conversation. One even brought her an enormous cupcake from which she took sneaky bites when she thought no one was looking. She worked hard on not judging young people in the classroom and tried to apply the same principle when she bumped into them in the wild.

They were so friendly and respectful, both to her and David who once again was there calmly recruiting for PACE. It was as if the young people made no connection between the Yuthentic dogma of wealth redistribution by any means necessary, and what that might mean for the old people on their doorstep who would be obliged to sacrifice everything.

She recognized the weird tall guy with the stringy black hair and the Slayer T-shirt (surely not the same one?) from the previous year. This time, instead of holding court with the teenagers out front, he was lurking towards the back of the stand with a big red-headed woman she recognized as an MP from the HELP Select Committee. The two of them were in cahoots and spent little energy mixing with anyone else.

It made her day when Liz turned up. "I was hoping to catch you," she said before leaning in conspiratorially to whisper. "I'm here with Carl."

"And looking good," Lexi said, realizing who Liz was only after the reference to her troublesome partner. "Those softer colors suit you."

Liz wore a dark blond, highlighted wig in a flattering cut that framed her face perfectly. Her make-up was in subtle tones of beige and light pink teamed with a neutral lip gloss. There was something else different about her, too.

"Are you wearing contact lenses?"

"Yes. You'll never guess what. For years Carl said they didn't make them for people with my prescription. Did I mention he was an optician? Anyway, I found out his advice was a load of old tosh a couple of months ago. It was my first check-up after he retired. What a difference! He even had my prescription wrong. I feel so free! Jeez! I know why you didn't want me on camera looking like that. I was the scariest rock chick in town."

"No way!" Lexi laughed gently to counter what Liz had said..

"You're too kind. I slipped by to say thank you for persuading me to do the Committee thing. It's done wonders for my confidence. That Mason had a twinkle in his eye. Best of all, Carl was appreciative that we were on a better footing."

"Good luck with that," Lexi said.

Liz had given Carl more second chances than she could remember. While Lexi was wondering whether she might have sounded too unforgiving, a suave pensioner wearing a crisp short sleeved cream linen shirt, chinos and loafers, with a well-groomed white goatee and a cream flat cap, appeared alongside Liz and hooked an arm around her shoulder.

"What are you doing on this old people's stand?" he said as though Lexi were invisible. "We don't need any help from this miserable lot, do we pussycat?"

Before either of the women could speak, Carl had firmly steered Liz away.

Lexi looked out at the sea of faces, people of all kinds wandering round their local park on a normal summer Saturday afternoon. She could not help wondering how many of them might end up on Yuthentic's next list, and not be there next year. They had no idea what The Corporation was capable of. It was all she could do to hold herself back from yelling out a warning, but she was under no illusions. Everyone would think she was mad.

Father Al had been right all along. No amount of earnest leaflets or political artworks were going to make a big enough difference. She wasn't convinced his prayers were helping that much either. And with Phase Two imminent, the stakes had just got a whole lot higher.

At 5pm the Fayre was formally over. As a team of volunteers began to comb the park for litter, Lexi gathered up the leftover leaflets. There hadn't been much interest, but at least all the Faraday bags had been sold. "I told you I should have brought more of them," Bob said as he helped her lift a folding trestle table into the back of the van. He was hoping to raise a smile, but he could tell something was wrong.

It was only when they were back home a couple of hours later, tucking into an Indian takeaway, that he could get her to talk about it.

"I'm tired and angry, love," she said when he gently observed that she wasn't her usual self. "The Yuthies had far more visitors to their stand than we did. The thought police took down our lovely picture after you went to all that trouble with Fakesy. And now, it's all going to get a whole lot worse."

Bob could not tell her that he already knew about Phase Two, so he just nodded. "It does sound like things could get hairy, from what Father Al said. What can we do about it, though?"

"I don't know yet." Lexi said. "But I, for one cannot stand by and watch a load more people sleepwalk to their doom. I haven't given up on the old folks. And I'm not going to give up on the next contingent either. Whatever we do next, it's going to have to be something so big, that nobody, anywhere, will be able to ignore what's going on."

CHAPTER FORTY-ONE

A YEAR HAD PASSED. CELESTE WAS facing another winter as a customer service amoeba in the playground of the rich and famous. Her boyfriend had not even bothered to dump her properly. The guys he worked for – always 'the guys', never a name – had decided he would be more useful back home in Russia after their plan had yielded almost nothing.

Her only choice was to return to the place she knew. It cost little for her to live in the tiny studio her skiing-mad Father had owned for more than 40 years. When he was at boarding school, he had had a colossal win on an accumulator. He had persuaded one of the monks to place the bet for him. After the cash came in, his parents had confiscated it and bought the flat in Verbier as an investment. If you knew people as Celeste did, there was always work there for someone with her language skills in one of the boutiques or bars which were unaffordable to 99.99 per cent of people on the planet. But she did, at least, get to ski, the love of which she had also inherited from her father.

In many ways she was glad to see the back of Zhena,

although he had his good points. He was tall, fit and had a striking face. People often thought he might be a model. Best of all, he could ski like the wind. They had some amazing days on the slopes. At times, he could be generous. On her day off he would buy her lunch at the top of the mountain and then race her back down to the bottom. He wasn't exactly the most selfless lover in the world, but she could make do, taking some of his other qualities into account.

Always, though, there was something in his eyes that bothered her. She recognized it eventually as a gleam of fear that was only fully revealed when his project failed to live up to the expectations of 'the guys'.

"You believed this man was important," he had said, angrily, "But not important enough to pay ransom!" She had tried to tell Zhena the tapes were not incriminating enough, even if one of the calls was from a young, attractive female Member of Parliament. In any case, Mason had seemed like someone who wasn't going to go down without a fight.

Trying to salvage some of their investment in the fruitless blackmail attempt, the guys had arranged for an intermediary to sell the tapes to the media. What they received for the covert recordings barely covered Zhena's lunches. One of Mason's calls had been completely unusable. It was encrypted. All they knew was that it had to be from someone inside The Corporation.

Later, when Mason's name was mentioned all over the world in connection with a set of new highly-prized artworks, the guys became even more furious, convinced that someone had tricked them out of their share along the way. It was rumored he had spent more than a million on just one Fakesy. Zhena even phoned Celeste from Moscow to sound off about it. That was the last time he was in touch.

She hoped that Mason would come back this season. He was obviously an expert skier. She wondered whether he might be looking for someone he could race, and maybe take out for lunch at the top of the mountain. He would be needing some new goggles. The last ones he bought had left town in a garbage truck and stopped transmitting when they entered a crusher just two days after he had taken them out of the shop.

PLAYLIST

IN ORDER OF APPEARANCE

Rock On
David Essex (1973)

It's the Most Wonderful Time of the Year
Andy Williams (1963)

Die Young Stay Pretty
Blondie (1979)

Dreadlock Holiday
10cc (1978)

Free Bird
Lynyrd Skynyrd (1973)

Price Tag – B.O.B
Jessie J (2011)

Heroes
David Bowie (1977)

Aladdin Sane
David Bowie (1973)

Rocks
Primal Scream (1994)

I'm Free
The Soup Dragons (1990)

Happy
Pharrell Williams (2013)

Say a Little Prayer
Aretha Franklin (1968)

My Sweet Lord
George Harrison (1970)

Rock 'n' Roll Suicide'
David Bowie (1972)

Funhouse
Pink (2008)

Moonage Daydream
David Bowie (1972)

Rockstar
Nickelback (2005)

You Spin Me Round (Like a Record)
Dead or Alive (1985)

Rebel Rebel
Dead or Alive (1985)

Let's Dance
David Bowie (1983)

Lazarus
David Bowie (2016)

Blackstar
David Bowie (2016)

Faith of Our Fathers
Patrick O'Hagan (1969)

Modern Love
David Bowie (1983)

Brazil
Geoff and Maria Muldaur (1968)

Manic Monday
The Bangles (1986)

Heathen (The Rays)
David Bowie 2002

Ziggy Stardust
David Bowie (1972)

I Think We're Alone Now
Tiffany (1987)

We're in the Money
Rosemary Clooney (1996)

Freedom! (90)
George Michael (1990)

Bat Out of Hell
Meat Loaf (1977)

Help the Aged
Pulp (1998)

You Ain't Seen Nothing Yet
Bachman-Turner Overdrive (1974)

The Bewlay Brothers
David Bowie (1971)

Love at First Sight
Kylie Minogue (2002)

Can't Get You Out of My Head
Kylie Minogue (2001)

Music
Madonna (2000)

The Man Who Sold The World
David Bowie (1970)

Available on Spotify at: https://open.spo-
tify.com/playlist/05CO2YDWVJVMARY4jt
ebJJ?si=nfuI7fHUReC3VOK1DQ113g

ACKNOWLEDGEMENTS

While all characters in the book are fictitious, *Rock On* has been influenced by my experiences from a career in communications management which has lasted more than 30 years.

A handful of my bosses stand out. They valued my abilities, supported my ideas, and protected me when they could. I once joked that a manager only ever got to know me after I had a good cry in their office. You know who you are. Thank you for all the tissues, the professional guidance, the promotions and, of course, the money. Most of the time it was great fun.

I learned much from so many colleagues. It wasn't just what you did, it was the good grace with which you did it. Crisis communications in particular can be a dicey business and I was lucky enough to work alongside a number of individuals, too numerous to name here, who I could rely on to make sure I didn't get sacked. You were stars.

Friends in The Orwell Society, Sohemian Society and The Brockley Society have encouraged me to continue with the Rockstar Ending series. It has also been amazing to hear from readers from all over the world who are enjoying the show. Keep those emails coming!

The broadcaster and campaigner, Samantha Renke, has been generous in sharing her insight into disability issues. Nishi Shawl and Cynthia Ward's workshop on Writing The Other has also helped me work with characters from backgrounds different to my own.

The Verbier scenes are all down to my Dad, Hector Rossi, who took me skiing from a young age, although Aviemore was not exactly home to the international set. Mum, Peggy Rossi, gave me my love of books, teaching me to read using homemade flashcards before I went to school. Both my parents encouraged me to be independent. The corporate career that followed took me on adventures a million miles from the ice cream shop in Southport where I grew up.

Geraldine Brennan has been my faithful editor, bringing an abundance of empathy and imagination to complement her technical skill.

David Bowie is still haunting the pages. I was overjoyed when an old clip recently appeared on TV that inspired Bob's kimono scenes. When I first saw that documentary in the 1970s, I misunderstood what Bowie said and told everyone at school the next day that Kansai Yamamoto meant dry clean only in Japanese.

The movie *Terminator: Dark Fate* gave me the idea for the Faraday bags. Bob's are far superior to the one used by

Sarah Connor, although she could give him a run for his money in most other respects.

Friends have kept my spirits up through the COVID crisis. Thank you to the Convent Coven and the Blackheath Divas who continue to be a pleasure and have loyally celebrated my change in career. I could not have hoped for better cheerleaders, along with Emma Sharp, who I first met working in a PR agency, and remains a dear friend decades later.

Tim Doyle has created another remarkable cover illustration. It's getting to be a habit.

A growing gang of indie authors have been generously helping me along the way, together with Sky Stephenson who understands many aspects of the 21st century better than me.

Finally, Simon, Amelia and Charlie. I could never have done it without you.

If you are curious about the years preceding
the Rockstar Ending series you can download
the FREE INTRODUCTORY NOVELLA

For Those About to Rock

at nicolarossi.com
where you can also join my mailing list to find
out about news releases and promotions

WOULD YOU WRITE A REVIEW?

If you have enjoyed *Rock On* it would mean a lot to me if you could spend just five minutes leaving an honest review on Amazon.

As an independently published author, I don't have the resources to promote my books very widely, and reviews from people who have read my work can make a huge difference by bringing it to the attention of other readers.

ALSO BY N. A. ROSSI

For Those About to Rock
Introductory novella for the Rockstar Ending series – FREE from nicolarossi.com

When Bowie-obsessed IT guy Bob leaves his job in a bank to work in school surveillance he is expecting an easy life. He could not be more wrong.

Rockstar Ending
The first book in the Rockstar Ending series

London, 2027. An ordinary woman discovers she is capable of extraordinary things. When Lexi finds out that older people are being coerced into genocide by stealth, she vows to take on the sinister corporation behind the ultimate Rockstar Ending.

Rockaway
The third book in the Rockstar Ending series
Coming in 2021.

Join the mailing list to stay in touch with the author and be one of the first to know when the next book in the series will be available at nicolarossi.com.

ABOUT THE AUTHOR

N. A. (Nicola) Rossi has lived in London most of her life, moving there from the seaside town of Southport in the early '80s. After university she flirted briefly with journalism, and then began a 30-year career in communications management, eventually running international teams for big technology companies.

In 2017 she was awarded an MA in Digital Media from Goldsmiths University. That was when the trouble began. She started to write about surveillance, data ownership, consent and the potential for people to be manipulated without their knowledge.

Her debut novel, *Rockstar Ending*, started life as a short story, 'One Last Gift', which won a dystopian fiction award from the Orwell Society. The judges described it as 'highly original, macabre and very funny'. It was published in the *Journal of Orwell Studies*.

Nicola is a regular blogger on technology, society and the arts. She has lectured in universities on leadership, PR, ethics and corporate social responsibility and consults on communications management. She has appeared on *BBC Radio 4 Today*, BBC local radio, and written for a wide range of media outlets including *The Independent*, *Time Out*, *Louder Than War* and *Influence*.

She lives in south east London with her husband and two adult children.

nicolarossi.com